TIMELESS *Regency* COLLECTION

A *Night* IN GROSVENOR SQUARE

TIMELESS *Regency* COLLECTION

A *Night* IN GROSVENOR SQUARE

Sarah M. Eden

Annette Lyon

Heather B. Moore

Mirror Press

Interior Design by Cora Johnson
Edited by Haley Swan and Lisa Shepherd
Cover design by Rachael Anderson
Cover Photo Credit: Period Images

Published by Mirror Press, LLC

ISBN: 978-1-947152-76-2

TABLE OF CONTENTS

OTHER TIMELESS REGENCY COLLECTIONS

A Match for Princess Pompous

-SARAH M. EDEN-

One

Bath, 1810

IF ADELAIDE NORTHROP had to listen to one more ode praising Charity Goddard's eyes, she was absolutely going to strangle the offending amateur poet with his own overlarge cravat. But when one earned one's living aiding and abetting the marrying off of the daughters of the *ton*, one endured a great many painful things, saccharinely sentimental poetry being chief among them.

Thomas Toppits was not nearly so unbearable as most of the young pups who had followed the young Miss Goddard around Bath the last month, and, all things considered, Adelaide was not displeased with Charity's choice. But neither would she mourn the "opportunity" to hear Mr. Toppits's self-penned verses now that her latest assignment had come to an end.

The arrival of Mrs. Goddard in the sitting room allowed Adelaide to abandon her post as chaperone and slip into the blessed silence of the corridor. Why was it young suitors always resorted to poetry? She had been instrumental in dozens of matches over the past four years, and nearly every one had, in the end, devolved into poetic nonsense.

This seemed a newer development. Her own courtship nineteen years earlier hadn't involved a single line of poetry. Then again, she'd not had a suitor to speak of during the decade and a half of her widowhood. It was entirely possible that the gentlemen in her age group employed verse as often as the younger set. Fortunately for her intellectual endurance, she didn't intend to find out.

She rapped lightly on the door to Mr. Goddard's study. Upon hearing his instruction to enter, she did precisely that.

"Ah, Mrs. Northrop." He rose and offered a respectful bow. "You are leaving us today, aren't you?"

"Your daughter is soon to be married. My services are no longer needed." She was an expert at these farewell meetings.

"Are you certain you won't stay for the wedding?" Mr. Goddard's long jowls flapped with the force of his frown. "It doesn't seem right that you should miss it."

But she held firm. If she meant to attend every wedding she brought about, she would spend so much time in churches that she might as well don clerical robes and become a vicar. "I am due in London. I dare not be late for my next undertaking."

He nodded slowly. "Ah yes. Barrington's daughter. You'll need a miracle with that one."

Adelaide was to finish out the London Season in the company of Lord Barrington's family and in the course of those six weeks do her utmost to bring about a spectacular match for the baron's youngest. The spoiled miss had in the course of the Season thus far earned herself the title of "Princess Pompous."

Six weeks. Princess Pompous. And all of London knew precisely how terrible the girl was.

The prospect set Adelaide's mind humming with anticipation. She enjoyed nothing so much as undertaking the utterly impossible.

"I will see to it, Mr. Goddard, that you receive a copy of the *Times* in which the wedding announcement is printed."

He smiled, the same almost boyish grin she'd seen from him time and again during her stay in Bath. "You are very confident."

She nodded. "I've not failed yet."

"I look forward to reading all about it."

She rose, and he did as well. "The very best to you and your family, sir. I am pleased to have been of help."

He offered a brief bow and she a curtsy.

"A token of our appreciation will be deposited in the appropriate account," he said. "And a bit extra."

She dipped her head in understanding. A lady did not earn a salary; such a thing was far too crass, no matter that money was a necessity. Payment for her efforts was always explained in terms like that: "token of appreciation" or "a gratuity" paid her through a third party. She understood the necessity—her standing as a lady depended on it. Still, she found the charade a bit tiring.

She returned to the room that had been hers for four weeks. Her portmanteau and traveling trunk were ready and waiting. A footman appeared shortly after her arrival to carry the trunk to the waiting Barrington carriage.

Adelaide took her portmanteau in hand and gave the room one final glance. Another departure. Another challenge. Though she always experienced a twinge of regret, the surge of excitement far outweighed it.

"I hope you are ready, Princess Pompous," she whispered. "I am about to overthrow your little kingdom."

London

Odette Armistead knew the name Society had fashioned for her. She had been aiming for the Contemptuous Countess or the Disdainful Duchess, so to have been granted a title as high as Princess Pompous was really quite an achievement. Her parents were far less proud of her moniker than she was, which was a shame. Young ladies were meant to be accomplished, and earning the simultaneous disapproval and rapt interest of the easily distracted *ton* was an accomplishment. She would far rather have gained some friends and fond memories, but, alas, it was not to be.

Papa was at that moment pacing in front of the windows of the drawing room, pausing repeatedly to look down at the street below. Mama sat on her fainting sofa, sighing as she did so often. Odette secretly referred to that particular spot in the room as the "sighing sofa."

"Are we expecting visitors?" she asked her parents. "Today is not an at-home day."

They exchanged looks but not words. Odette could very easily translate; she knew her parents well. They were expecting someone but did not want to tell her whom.

Hooves and wheels sounded below. Papa snapped to attention like a cadet, spinning on his heel to face the window.

Odette was fairly dying of curiosity. Who was the mysterious visitor? If Papa had invited yet another young gentleman to make a clearly coerced and half-hearted attempt at courtship, she would be hard-pressed not to simply beg the poor soul to leave them all in peace.

"She's here," Papa whispered.

She. Not a suitor, then. Her parents both rose and turned

to face the door. An important *she*, apparently. Odette's interest was fully piqued.

She, too, rose and watched the threshold, half expecting Queen Charlotte herself to step inside. The lady who entered, however, bore little resemblance to the current consort. She was far younger, likely only a decade older than Odette. Though this new arrival carried herself with confidence, hers was not the stone-stiff bearing of a monarch.

She swept over the room's occupants with an assessing gaze. First Mama, who received a quick, generic smile. Then Papa, who was offered a nod. At last, the anonymous lady settled her eyes on Odette. This was no cursory glance or momentary burst of vague curiosity. Odette was thoroughly scrutinized, head to toe and most likely inside and out. The perusal ended with a simple, "Hmm."

Odette didn't know what to make of such a dismissive and dissatisfied evaluation. "Princess Pompous" was not universally liked, but people generally found her interesting at the very least.

The lady turned to face Papa once more.

"What is your impression?" he asked her.

"She does not appear shy nor easily intimidated. That will make things easier. She is pretty, which, though in a truly decent world it wouldn't matter in the least, will also prove beneficial. She has a dowry, I assume."

They were discussing *her.* That was decidedly unexpected and more than a little rattling. She had learned these past months how to give the impression of cool confidence. She would simply do so again.

"I have five thousand pounds," Odette said. "My eyes have been described as sparkling and my smile as captivating. I do not generally want for partners at any ball, am greeted whenever I take a ride about Hyde Park, but am granted a blessed degree of solitude during the day, since most potential suitors have decided to look elsewhere. Is there anything else you'd care to know, or would you prefer clinging to what you have surmised with a single glance?"

The lady, who had not in the course of Odette's response turned in her direction, simply said, "And she is rather pert. That could either be an asset or a liability."

"If you can find someone willing to take all that on, we would be greatly obliged," Papa said. "Her older sisters were far easier to marry off."

Take all that on? Marry off? Odette looked from one of them to the other in succession.

"You don't happen to have a miserly older relative in the country somewhere?" The lady posed the suggestion with not quite enough humor to convince Odette that she wasn't at least partially in earnest.

"I am being sent away?" Odette carefully kept the hope from her voice.

"Nonsense," Mama said. "We have six weeks left in this Season. That is time enough to make it a success."

Papa's shoulders drooped. "The gentlemen aren't precisely clamoring to win the regard of Princess Pompous. What else can we do that we haven't already?"

"What else?" Odette asked in frustration. "What I have been suggesting for weeks: we can consider this Season to have been all that it could be and return home. We'll come back next year and begin again."

Mama shook her head firmly. "You cannot leave having made the impression you have. The *ton* will continue whispering, the stories growing at every house party, every Yuletide gathering. By the time we return, you will not merely be an oddity, you will be a pariah. We must undo some of the damage."

"If we can," Papa muttered.

Odette had worked very diligently at creating that "damage." Undoing it was not in her plans at all.

"I believe I would like to speak with Miss Armistead," the stranger said. "Alone, if you will."

Papa and Mama agreed readily and eagerly. Whatever scheme had been hatched clearly had both their support.

As soon as they stepped out and the door closed behind them, the stranger spoke again. "Introductions ought to have been made, but panic often subdues manners."

"Panic?" Odette began to smile at the exaggeration, but stopped at the lady's expression of absolute earnestness.

"It seems your parents have all but lost hope of you making a suitable match." The lady's assessing gaze swept over Odette once more. "I have been called upon to remedy that."

She squared her shoulders. "To remedy *what*, exactly?"

"I am not certain yet. But I will discover it. I always do."

"This is a habit of yours, interfering in families?"

A quick shake of her head. "It is a calling."

"The heavens have sent you here? That seems a little presumptuous."

The still-unnamed arrival was not the least put off by the criticism. "And yet, all the world has not begun calling me 'Princess Pompous.'"

Odette shrugged, hiding both her annoyance and her amusement. "It's a calling."

"Hmm."

With that cryptic response, Odette's back was up once more. "Perhaps before we continue this very enlightening conversation, we ought to know each other's names."

"I am Mrs. Northrop, and I am here to salvage your Season."

An unexpected answer, but then nothing about this

encounter had been the least predictable. "You are a chaper-one? Or a social tutor?"

"I am a matchmaker." She spoke the four words as if she knew perfectly well Odette would object to them and didn't care in the least. "Your parents wish to see you wed."

"The law does not allow me to be forced into a marriage," Odette said firmly. She'd made absolutely certain of that before embarking on her Season.

"I never force anyone into anything," Mrs. Northrop said, calm and unruffled as ever.

"Coerce, then?" Odette had worried a great deal about that possibility. Papa was of a tentative nature. Yet he had been firm in pushing her older sister toward the match he and Mother had preferred. They would likely do so again if Odette wasn't very careful.

"Coercion is for the desperate."

"And you have never been desperate?" Odette asked.

Mrs. Northrop neither nodded nor shook her head. She kept perfectly still, watching. The smile in her eyes proved anything but comforting.

"Well then." Odette assumed her most resolute tone and posture. "Do as you please. I, however, intend to choose my own future, and neither you, nor my parents, nor the spiteful tabbies of the *ton* will pry that privilege from me."

She left the would-be matchmaker in the drawing room, not bothering with the pleasantries usually exchanged in a farewell. One step into the corridor, Mrs. Northrop's voice caught up with her.

"I will see you this evening for the Farrs' ball." She was clearly not to be easily dissuaded.

Odette maintained her calm until she reached her bed-chamber. Heart pounding, she locked the door. She dropped onto the chair at her dressing table, fighting down an overwhelming wave of worry.

She'd worked so hard this Season making absolutely certain all went according to plan. Everything depended upon it. Her future. Her happiness. Every hope and dream she had. Everything.

And this matchmaker was going to ruin it all.

Two

JACK HEWITT STOOD among his group of friends, pretending he wasn't taking desperate note of every guest to arrive at the Farrs' ball. He worked to hide his dread of seeing one particular guest and his eagerness to see another. Maintaining an aura of utter neutrality was crucial.

The Summerfields stepped inside the ballroom in that moment. Jack didn't let his gaze more than flicker in the direction of the doorway. Mother, however, reached his side in the next moment, wide-eyed and anxious.

"Miss Summerfield is here," she whispered earnestly. "Go ask her to stand up with you."

"I can't," Jack said. "I've promised the next set to Miss Garrett and the one after that to Miss Carlton."

Her jaw set. "You knew Miss Summerfield was coming this evening."

He nodded noncommittally. "I assumed she would be. I'm certain I'll find a set open later in the night that she also has open."

"You must make an effort, Jack."

"Do not fear, Mother." He set a hand on her arm and

smiled. "If I find her in want of a partner, I will make certain to find one for her. Her family are our neighbors after all."

The usual frustrated sigh emerged. "You have only a handful of weeks left in the Season."

Thank heavens. "Perhaps when we return home after the Season ends, we might invite the neighborhood for a dinner. The Bartletts, Lord Barrington's family, the Summerfields."

Lumping his parents' choice of daughter-in-law in with other families who lived near them would subtly reinforce his lack of true interest. Eventually his parents would realize, though they hadn't in all the time they'd been pursuing the match on his behalf.

"We should at the very least go offer the Summerfields a good evening," Mother said.

He nodded. "Certainly." Jack turned to his friends. "I'm off to do the pretty with a neighbor family. Don't grow too lively while I'm gone."

"Yes, Mum," Terrance said.

Of all Jack's friends, Terrance could be counted on for a laugh. That'd been the way of things since Cambridge.

Lady Barrington, her daughter Odette, and a lady whom Jack had not seen before entered the ballroom in that very moment. All Jack's friends took note.

"I'll just beg a dance with Princess Pompous while you're away," Terrance said. "That should add a much-needed bit of dramatic tension to the evening."

"Dramatic tension?" Jack shook his head at the absurdity of that.

Terrance nodded. "There will be no predicting whether or not I will survive."

"She is known as 'Princess Pompous,' not 'the Marchioness of Murder.'"

13

Mother, apparently, had run out of patience. She tugged at his arm. "The Summerfields are waiting."

"Waiting? Do they know we mean to offer a neighborly greeting?"

She lowered her voice as they wove through the guests. "You are well aware that our connection to the Summerfields goes beyond mere neighborliness."

"Yes, you and Mrs. Summerfield have always been good friends."

"Jack." She spoke his name through her teeth.

Though it frustrated his parents, utterly refusing to play along with their machinations had proven his only option. They focused so much of their attention on trying to force him to simply acknowledge their efforts that they'd not yet moved on to attempting to convince him to *agree* with their choice.

"I wonder if Terrance will be granted a set with Odette." He glanced back.

"If he is fortunate, he will not," Mother said.

Jack met her eye once more. "She is also one of our neighbors. Have you chosen to dislike her?"

"There is something different in it since she arrived in London." Mother shook her head. "Lord and Lady Barrington are beside themselves. She will quickly ruin all her chances of making a match. The situation is so dire they have needed to employ the services of Mrs. Northrop."

The lady currently standing with Lady Barrington and her daughter, no doubt. "Is she a lady's companion?"

"Mrs. Northrop is a matchmaker."

That declaration stopped Jack in his tracks. "A matchmaker? By design, not as a casual pursuit?"

Mother nodded. "She has made matches for even the most difficult sons and daughters of the *ton*. With a good match and a bit of time, Odette may yet manage to shed the horrid moniker Society has fashioned for her. Though, to be perfectly honest, she has done more than enough to earn the name."

"Perhaps she is the one we ought to be offering a neighborly 'good evening.' I imagine she could use the show of affection and approval."

Mother pulled him along once more. "Having known her since she was a girl, I have full affection for her, but I cannot approve of her behavior this Season."

"I imagine she has her reasons," Jack said. "Odette has never been impulsive."

"Though you have known her all your life, it is not appropriate for you to use her Christian name, at least not in public."

He offered a reassuring smile. "I call her that only when speaking with you or Father. My friends likely think I don't even know her Christian name, despite having grown up in the same neighborhood."

"After the disastrous Season she has had, they likely think you are *choosing* to forget her name, her friendship, her connection to us."

"I hope they know I am not so shallow as that."

Mother pulled him around a gathering of matrons. "Mrs. Northrop will correct her path, I've no doubt," Mother said. "An announcement will appear in the *Times* before the Season is out, mark my words."

"That does not sound like a happy outcome for Od— Miss Armistead, being pushed into a match." He did not like the idea at all.

"Mrs. Northrop has never failed to make a match for anyone she has been assigned. She is the one who brought about the marriage between Miss Pattington and Lord Beaumont's middle son."

A happy match by all accounts. Jack's mind was still not set at ease.

They had, however, arrived directly beside the Summerfields, and he was afforded no opportunity for pondering the potential for Mrs. Northrop to inflict misery.

Mother and Mrs. Summerfield exchanged their usual greetings, each equally eager for the other's company. Miss Summerfield offered a quiet smile in Jack's general direction, though she did not speak. That was common for her, at least from what he had learned in the year since her family had come to live near theirs. She was almost always silent, though not out of arrogance nor dismissiveness. She was simply not of a talkative disposition. He hadn't the first idea whether she was different when at home or among her closest associates.

"The evening promises to be quite a crush," Jack said.

Miss Summerfield nodded. Her mother prodded her with an elbow. "Yes, it does," she added, her voice hardly rising above the volume of a breeze.

Mother nudged Jack, motioning with her head in Miss Summerfield's direction. He did not need the message translated. To Miss Summerfield, he said, "I am engaged for the next few sets, but if your quadrille remains unclaimed, I would be honored if you would grant me that privilege."

She nodded. "Of course."

He offered a bow. She a brief curtsy.

"Now, if you will excuse me," he said to all three ladies, "I am engaged for the next set."

"It will not begin for a few minutes yet," Mother said, an edge to her voice that spoke of both frustration and the blossoming of panic. He was, after all, quitting the field quite prematurely.

"I am not entirely certain where my partner is," he explained. "I would not wish to arrive late to do my duty."

16

He beat a hasty retreat, though careful to appear casual. Miss Summerfield was a fine young lady, but they were not at all well suited. Even if they were, no gentleman of sense or decency would marry when his heart belonged to another.

Jack located his next partner, escorting her to join the other couples in the open area of the ballroom. Terrance had secured a partner as well, the very partner he had declared he would dance with. His grin spoke of amusement and triumph. Odette appeared far less pleased.

The movements of the dance progressed. Jack's partner possessed a fluid grace. She also possessed an incredibly high opinion of herself, as evidenced by the remarks she managed to slip in anytime they were brought near enough each other. The title of "Princess Pompous" had clearly been wrongly assigned. Miss Garrett was far more deserving of it.

He moved past Odette.

"Your friend is being ridiculous," she said quickly.

"That is the only way we are able to recognize him."

The tiniest, briefest of smiles flashed across her face before being tucked firmly away. He managed to keep his own under control.

The steps brought him past Terrance next. "You are not making a good impression, my friend."

Terrance only laughed. He really was a good sort of fellow, simply too inclined for a lark when sobriety was called for.

On and on the dance went. His partner continued listing her own fine qualities, though she wrapped up the boasts in a flag of false humility. Terrance grinned a great deal. Odette kept to the polite neutrality Society preferred. And Jack wished for nothing more than to escape it all.

Fate proved kind. The partner to whom he had promised the next set extended her apologies, as she was obliged to return home early. Jack stepped out onto the back terrace and down into the gardens. A bit of weaving brought him to a quiet corner, surrounded on three and a half sides by tall hedges and boasting a single empty stone bench.

He sat and breathed. Six weeks remained of this torture he could not escape. Six weeks that would no doubt feel like six months. Could he endure that much more? Could *she?*

Long minutes passed. He was not engaged for another dance before the quadrille, and it would not come for some time. He let himself relax and imagine himself home again, back in the neighborhood, where he was happiest. How easily he could picture *her* there.

Small, quick footsteps sounded from the other side of the hedge. He watched the entrance to his little shrubberied alcove, curious.

Odette appeared.

He jumped to his feet as she slipped inside. "What are you doing here?" He glanced at the path leading to the private corner.

The night was too dim for her face to be at all discernible. There was no mistaking her worried tone. "My parents have engaged the services of a matchmaker."

"I know," he said. "My mother told me."

"Mrs. Northrop is determined. I do not know how long I can keep her at bay."

"We will think of something, my dear."

She stepped closer and rested her head against his chest. "What if we can't?"

He wrapped his arms around her. "This was risky, Odette. We cannot take such chances with so much time yet remaining before we can return home."

"Or with Mrs. Northrop ready to convince my parents to marry me off to the first person she can get to agree."

He lightly kissed the top of her head. "I would be the first person to agree, if anyone even cared to ask."

"So long as your parents have their hearts set on Miss Summerfield, mine will never even consider a match between us. They don't dare risk overstepping themselves where your parents are concerned."

"We will find a way, my love. I know we will." How often they had told themselves that, yet they were barely clinging to hope.

She stepped back enough for the tiniest bit of moonlight to dimly illuminate her face. "You continue resisting your parents' efforts. I will do all I can to undermine Mrs. Northrop. If we can manage that, it will all be worth it in the end."

"It will be more than worth it." He took her hands in his and kissed them one at a time. "Now, you had best slip back into that ball—alone—and make the best of things."

She nodded. "Until we are able to see each other again."

He tried to sound reassuring, "Soon, my dearest. Soon."

She slipped away. He remained behind, sitting on the bench and thinking furiously. The chances of their plan proving successful had always been slim. Even if he managed to keep his parents off the scent for a Season while simultaneously avoiding their efforts to match him with Miss Summerfield, preventing Lord and Lady Barrington from strong-arming Odette into a match was tricky.

Her older sister had been coerced into a match not of her choosing. The oldest sister had expressed her love for a gentleman whose family her parents felt would disapprove of the match. The star-crossed couple had been kept apart from that moment on; her sister had married someone else. While neither sister was utterly unhappy, their experiences boded ill for his and Odette's future.

19

Odette was not weak-willed by any means, but fate was not kind to young ladies. They were often pushed into unwanted matches and untenable situations simply for want of a choice.

Despite Odette's family being titled, his family was the dominant one in the neighborhood, having money and standing that far surpassed anyone else nearby. No one naysaid his parents. Not even their son. At least not directly. Certainly not any of the other local families.

Odette could not marry without her father's approval. Her father would never give it if Jack's parents did not bestow theirs. Jack feared his parents would never approve of anyone but Miss Summerfield and the possibility of bringing into the vast Hewitt family holdings a very profitable estate in the north that was included in Miss Summerfield's dowry.

Marrying for love might have been a new and emerging preference, but at times it felt utterly impossible.

From her position not far from the terrace doors, Adelaide watched her latest charge slip inside the ballroom once more. She had noticed Odette expertly maneuver her way behind a group of gossipy ball goers and away from her mother's watchful eye without drawing anyone's attention—except Adelaide's, she having kept careful track of a long list of young ladies over the years.

Odette's movements as she'd left and now as she returned were just furtive enough to speak of a desire to not be seen or noticed. Being alone on the terrace or in the garden beyond could bring about a few whispers, but considering the young lady was already referred to as "Princess Pompous" and had done absolutely everything imaginable during their short time at the ball thus far to make certain that name stuck, her concern over more relatively harmless whispers seemed very unlikely.

Something else lay behind this sneaking about and the worry so clear in Odette's posture.

Adelaide had been in her line of work far too long to not immediately piece together the puzzle. Odette had not been alone.

Princess Pompous had a would-be prince.

A great many people wandered in and out, making identifying Odette's assignation impossible. But Adelaide had not been felled by the impossible yet. She would solve this mystery, and she would enjoy it.

Three

ODETTE WAS NOT a naturally sour person. A Season of pretending to be so was beginning to take its toll. She disliked that people thought so poorly of her, though she was grateful for her success in convincing them. It was the only chance she and Jack had of a happy outcome. Yet, she was lonely. Being an object of fascinated disapproval was not at all the same as being a friend, a confidante, a companion.

They had debated Jack undertaking the same approach but had, in the end, reached the inarguable conclusion that doing so would not help. The Summerfields knew him too well already, having lived in the neighborhood for a year and having interacted with him at any number of assemblies and dinner parties. The ruse would be seen through easily and readily. It was also entirely possible they wouldn't care. Such was the balance of things in Society that a gentleman's disposition played far less of a role in determining the desirability of a match than a lady's did.

Thus, Odette sat in Mrs. Hewitt's drawing room the morning after the Farrs' ball making at-home calls with her mother and Mrs. Northrop, with no one even the least eager to talk with her. Even Mrs. Hewitt, whom she'd known all her life, didn't pay her much mind beyond the occasional curious glance. Odette had not been out before this Season, so she'd really known her neighbors only through the lens of childhood interactions. They believed so readily that she was the horror she pretended to be. Her own parents believed it. That was rather disheartening.

Still, if it meant living her life with the person she loved most, she could endure it.

"Why, Mrs. Summerfield. Miss Summerfield." Mrs. Hewitt greeted the newest arrivals.

Odette maintained her impassive air even as pain seized her heart. Miss Summerfield received the warm welcome Odette never had. Even at home when they had crossed paths in the nearby town or after services on Sundays, Mrs. Hewitt had taken only cursory note of Odette, the kind of offhand acknowledgment adults often offered to children.

The enemy and her mother were offered places of honor directly beside their hostess. None of the other guests could possibly misinterpret the preference Mrs. Hewitt felt for these two. Thank the heavens Jack had gone to such lengths to make certain no one in Society who was paying the least attention would think he felt a similar inclination.

Six weeks. We need survive only another six weeks.

To the Summerfield ladies, Mrs. Hewitt said, "You, of course, remember Lady Barrington and Miss Armistead. They live in our neighborhood."

The wording was not truly dismissive, but something in the way she referenced Odette and her mother and their role among the families in their corner of the kingdom felt the tiniest bit disparaging just the same.

Mother, as always, did not particularly notice. She watched with her usual air of eager hopefulness. Father was in possession of a title, a minor one when compared with the rest of the peerage, but a title just the same. The Hewitts were in possession of great wealth and vast swaths of land. Theirs was also a family of long-standing importance. Mother and Father had always viewed themselves as comparatively inferior; the Hewitts had always agreed.

"Of course we remember." Mrs. Summerfield faced Mother and offered a polite dip of her head. "A very real pleasure to see you again. I am sorry we did not have the opportunity to speak at the ball last night. Was that not the greatest crush you've seen in some time?"

That, of course, set the conversation on the previous night's gathering. Mother was far more comfortable with this topic than with the unspoken discussion of the neighborhood pecking order. She eagerly joined Mrs. Summerfield and Mrs. Hewitt in their delineation of every detail.

Being aloof and "above her company" was part of Odette's disguise, so she kept her peace and focused, instead, on returning home, on meeting Jack on her walk back from town and having those precious moments with him. She thought of the joy it would be to spend the autumn and winter finally being herself again and working with Jack to convince his parents of the wisdom of a match between them.

"You danced with Mr. Lexington last night." Miss Summerfield's observation was so quiet Odette did not at first hear it. She certainly didn't immediately realize the words were spoken to her.

"I did," she said, still a bit shocked that the excruciateingly quiet Miss Summerfield had initiated a conversation. Terrance Lexington was a friend of Jack's. He was a flirt and a bit ridiculous at times, but he was harmless and entertaining.

"Mr. Lexington stood up with me later in the evening," Miss Summerfield said. "He makes me nervous."

Odette's heart went out to her. "Mr. Lexington is a gentleman through and through. You need not be ill at ease in his company."

"Oh, I am not nervous on that account. He is simply so witty." Color touched Miss Summerfield's cheeks. "I very much fear he finds me unbearably boring."

Odette shook her head. "He does not seem to me to be someone who requires endless repartee. He appears perfectly content to be the one doing the entertaining."

Miss Summerfield smiled a little. Her hands, clasped on her lap, untensed a bit. "He is very entertaining."

"As he well knows," Odette added drily, but with enough of a smile to take any true criticism from the words.

"Mr. Hewitt stood up with me during the quadrille," Miss Summerfield said. "I was so very grateful. I am not very confident in the quadrille, but I knew he would not scold me for it."

"He is all that is good and kind." Odette felt she could safely acknowledge that much.

Before Miss Summerfield could offer any kind of response, her mother drew her attention, pulling her into the conversation with Mrs. Hewitt, though Miss Summerfield said nothing. Odette let her gaze wander. The guests were all either talking with one another or listening raptly to the conversation being undertaken by their hostess. All the guests, except Mrs. Northrop, who was, in fact, watching Odette far too closely for comfort.

Wrapping her facade around her once more, Odette raised an eyebrow. "Is something amiss?"

Mrs. Northrop simply *hmm*'d. She did that a lot. It was, in all actuality, rather frustrating. The sound was clearly one of pondering but beyond that was indiscernible. Odette suspected she was constantly being evaluated by the matchmaker, and she did not like it at all. Too much was being kept hidden for such scrutiny to be anything but worrisome.

The butler appeared once more in the drawing room doorway to usher in more arrivals. Terrance Lexington, whom Odette was happy to see, stepped in. On his heels came Jack. How Odette hoped she'd maintained an even expression. Heaven knew she'd had ample practice the last months. Still, the role she played was growing more difficult.

The room was greeted in gentlemanly fashion. The guests expressed universal delight at their arrival. The gentlemen were invited to join the gathering, which they accepted with no hint of displeasure.

Jack chose a seat a bit apart from his mother and her preferred guests, placing himself at a disinterested distance from Miss Summerfield. Mr. Lexington sat a touch closer, wearing his usual expression of enthusiasm.

"We were just discussing what a crush the ball was last evening," Mrs. Hewitt said. "Did you not think it a crush?"

"It certainly was." Jack smiled at them all at once. "I believe I saw every last one of you there."

"Indeed," Mr. Lexington agreed. "And we had the pleasure of dancing with any number of lovely young ladies, including Miss Armistead"—he dipped his head toward her—"and Miss Summerfield." He offered the same acknowledgment to her. "A joy."

Odette doubted that on her part. She had enjoyed his company, but the Pompous Princess was high on no one's list of enjoyable companions, more was the pity.

On and on the conversations went. Jack offered a reply when required but kept mostly quiet. Mr. Lexington was his usual talkative self, even managing a few responses from Miss Summerfield. Odette felt more than a little relieved when Mother arose and announced that they needed to be going.

As curtsies were exchanged between Mother and Mrs. Hewitt, Odette caught Jack's eye. For the briefest of moments, he allowed an expression of fond regret to pass over his features. She offered a fleeting smile of sad understanding. His parents had made their choice, and hers would do nothing to earn even a hint of their disapproval.

The carriage ride back to Barrington House was not a long one, but Adelaide knew how to take advantage of even snippets of time.

"I was impressed with Mr. Lexington," she said to Lady Barrington. "What is his situation?"

"His father is a gentleman," Mother answered. "A good family. Well-heeled. Excellent connections."

"Is he prone to debauchery?"

"Certainly not," Mother answered. "I hear only good things of him."

Adelaide nodded. "Excellent. I believe I shall make certain of that, but he is a promising prospect."

Though Odette's expression remained passive, her eyes told a different story. Too few people realized how readily their eyes betrayed them. Mr. Lexington, it seemed, was not Odette's mystery gentleman. She would let the young lady think she was focused on him, though.

She would watch, and she would solve this mystery.

She always did.

Four

JACK WALKED TOWARD the Summerfields' London home wondering how he'd managed to land himself in such a predicament. Somehow, before the Summerfields had left Mother's at-home the day before, he had been wrangled into taking Miss Summerfield for a drive in Hyde Park. Terrance, who knew perfectly well Jack didn't wish to be strong-armed into that particular match, had saved the day with a bit of quick thinking.

"Do join us," he'd said to Jack with every appearance of enthusiasm. "The young lady I am driving out with tomorrow will, I am certain, appreciate the added opportunity to socialize."

Jack had agreed before any objections could be lodged. A time was chosen. Terrance insisted he would meet them at the Summerfield home, his chosen young lady already fetched, and they would drive out together. He'd managed the entire thing without ever identifying his companion, something he'd admitted, upon quitting the drawing room, had been necessary.

"I suppose I'd best secure myself a driving companion, hadn't I?" It had been entirely fabricated.

"Thank you for that," Jack had said.

Terrance had thumped a hand on his shoulder. "A friend worth his salt will always save another friend from a forced courtship."

"That is the standard definition, is it?"

"It is *my* definition."

Jack turned up the short walk to the Summerfields' home, increasingly grateful for Terrance, yet also feeling increasingly guilty. He hadn't confided in his friend the full situation. He had full confidence in Terrance's willingness to keep mum, but he wouldn't reveal the situation to anyone without first making certain Odette was comfortable with the revelation. She didn't know Terrance as well as he did.

The Summerfields' butler answered Jack's knock and ushered him inside. Jack took his hat in his hands. The butler did not offer to take his hat, which indicated he would not be left waiting long. Mrs. Summerfield stepped into the entry-way.

He bowed and received a curtsy in return.

"Tabitha is delighted at the prospect of your company this afternoon. She has spoken of nothing else."

That was surprisingly easy to believe. Miss Summerfield never spoke, so he struggled to imagine her waxing long about their drive. But, then, if she'd spoken even a single sentence about their afternoon together, it might very well have been the only thing she'd said all day. Still, he was likely supposed to be flattered.

"I am pleased she is joining us. I believe it will be a pleasant excursion."

Miss Summerfield appeared on the landing above and quickly and silently descended the stairs. Her mother had insisted she was "delighted" to be taking an afternoon drive with him, but she looked far closer to terrified.

Another bow and curtsy exchange followed her arrival in the entryway. She offered what was likely a commonplace greeting but in a voice so quiet he could not be certain. If only his parents' choice for his bride had been a brashly confident young lady, he could simply express his disinterest, and she would have dismissed him and saved her effort and attention for someone else. A quiet, uncertain young lady whose parents were as forceful as Miss Summerfield's would be made to suffer from the loss of a suitor.

What a fragile dance they were all enacting.

The butler opened the front door once more. Jack offered Miss Summerfield a quick smile of reassurance and motioned toward the door.

"I believe our companions for the afternoon have arrived."

She looked to her mother, who nodded earnestly and motioned her to go.

Jack knew his role in this exchange. "Your daughter will be returned safely and in good time."

"You have my full confidence, Mr. Hewitt." Her tone was a bit too vehement, too earnest for such an ordinary declaration. So much about his interactions with the Summerfields felt forced.

What were Mr. and Mrs. Summerfield like when they weren't in pursuit? He hadn't been home enough in the brief weeks before this match was settled upon by their parents to truly know.

Terrance was coming up the walk with his partner on his arm. Jack could not, for a moment, move toward them. Terrance had invited Odette. *Odette.* On Terrance's arm. Preparing to take a drive around Hyde Park.

Jack didn't know whether to be grateful or frustrated. An hour or so in her company was an unforeseen boon. But spending that time pretending to be indifferent to her would be torturous. They had so little opportunity to see each other. This felt like a waste.

Terrance grinned at them both. "If I'd known you would be stepping out so quickly, we would have simply sat in the carriage like a couple of sluggards."

Odette rolled her eyes. Anyone who did not know her well would miss the laughter underlying the expression. She really had a wonderful sense of humor. He seldom smiled as much as he did during their walks around the neighborhood at home. He certainly never laughed as much.

The four of them returned directly to the carriage. Jack handed Miss Summerfield up, and she sat forward facing, scooting to the far side of the carriage.

"I far prefer being forward facing." Odette spoke with the self-assured air that had earned her that hateful moniker. "I would like to sit beside Miss Summerfield." She did not wait for an answer but stepped up beside Jack. She held a hand out to him. "If you would be so good, Mr. Hewitt."

"Of course." He took her hand.

The touch, which ought to have been utterly common-place, sent a rush of warmth up his arm directly to his heart. Oh, how he missed her. How he longed for the right to simply hold her hand, to offer her his support for something as ordinary as stepping into a carriage. To be able to talk with her again. Laugh with her.

Her eyes held his for what felt like ages, though it could not have been more than a fraction of a moment. What he saw there broke his heart. She was hurting, deeply, and he could do nothing about it.

"I am sorry," he mouthed silently.

She stepped up into the carriage, pulling her hand free of

his, and sat beside Miss Summerfield. He understood the necessity, but he missed the feel of her hand in his.

Terrance grinned at him as he stepped up into the carriage himself. "Looks like we're to be seatmates. Can't say I'm overly pleased by the trade."

Jack managed to find some amusement in the situation. He felt certain Odette had asked for the change in seats to help him avoid being seen in public sitting beside Miss Summerfield and to make certain she was not connected by the gossips to Terrance.

The coachman set the carriage rolling toward Hyde Park. Odette sat with hands primly folded in her lap, her expression unwaveringly neutral. The disguise of apathy had grown more convincing of late. Was she growing more adept at pretending, or was she every bit as miserable as she appeared?

How much longer could she endure this charade?

Terrance, grinning and enthusiastic as ever, dove into the silence. "I believe ours will be the most popular carriage in the park today. I fully intend to tell everyone who asks that Hewitt, here, is the hanger-on, while the three of us are quite the social set."

"Well, two of us." Odette indicated herself and Miss Summerfield even as she tossed Terrance a look of amused taunting.

Terrance laughed good-naturedly. "A challenge?

"A simple statement of fact."

Terrance turned to Jack. "I believe our reputations are being called into question. We cannot allow the ladies to outshine us."

"I don't think it is avoidable," Jack said.

Miss Summerfield's cheeks reddened, but she appeared pleased. Jack did not wish her to be unhappy, yet he also dared not risk encouraging hopes he had no intention of fulfilling.

Odette leaned toward Miss Summerfield. "Shall we take up their challenge? See whether we receive more compliments during this drive than they do?"

"That is unfair," Terrance said. "One glance around this carriage tells me Jack and I will emerge the losers in that competition."

"Shall we center our competition on something more suited to your particular strengths?" Odette very nearly smiled. How Jack had missed the sight of her smile. "I'm not certain I care to let Society determine who among us smells the worst."

Terrance laughed long and loud. Miss Summerfield even laughed, something Jack didn't think he'd ever heard.

Odette slipped her arm through Miss Summerfield's. "The gentlemen are afraid of us. They know there is no chance of besting us in a 'who is more popular' contest."

"Cowards," Miss Summerfield said.

Again, Terrance laughed. Jack couldn't help joining in.

"We accept your challenge," Jack said.

"We do?" Terrance quickly changed his tone to one of confidence. "We do! We'll count the number of people who express pleasure at seeing you ladies or the two of us. The team with the greatest number by the time we leave the park will be declared the winner."

Miss Summerfield, quite to Jack's shock, spoke again. "What prize do the winners receive?"

"Supper dance with the losers at the Salsteads' ball on Saturday?" Terrance suggested.

Odette managed a look of theatrical disapproval. "Dancing with unpopular gentlemen hardly seems like a prize."

They made their way through a few other suggestions, everything from ices at Gunter's to another ride in the park, but in the end settled upon the supper dance.

"It is only fair, though, that we switch partners," Terrance insisted. "Then each winner will not be required to spend more time with the exact gentleman she bested."

Odette raised an eyebrow. "You expect to lose?"

"Fully," Terrance said.

Odette turned to her teammate. "What do you think? Shall we agree to the proposed switch?"

Miss Summerfield blushed ever deeper but agreed without hesitation.

Odette met Jack's eye. "That would leave us partners for supper on Saturday. Can you endure being partnered with a childhood friend?"

Hope, anticipation, eagerness all swelled inside. "More than endure, Miss Armistead. I will enjoy it immensely."

She shook her head. "You will be the first this Season to do so."

"Nonsense," Terrance immediately answered.

Doubt filled her expression. "Princess Pompous does not exactly inspire odes."

"But you do inspire gentlemen to acts of derring-do."

"Like knights of old?" Odette pressed.

Terrance hesitated. "I would answer in the affirmative, but that would make you the dragon, and I know better than to insult a lady."

"You do not think I am the dragon?"

Jack answered aloud without meaning to. "You are certainly not the dragon."

All eyes were on him. Worrying he'd revealed too much, he quickly added, "If anything, you are the knight, not Lexington here."

"Mr. Lexington is the damsel in distress, then." Odette nodded as if the idea were perfectly logical.

Miss Summerfield grinned broadly. This drive was proving far more diverting than Jack had anticipated.

The carriage slowed as it entered the press of Hyde Park. They greeted and were greeted. Miss Summerfield received any number of expressions of delight. Odette was also acknowledged with pleasantries, but there was something in the tone and expression that spoke far more of curiosity. Jack and Terrance proved far less popular, just as they had all predicted.

At the end of each encounter, Odette updated the score. By the time they'd completed half a circuit of the park, Miss Summerfield was joining in the accounting. Odette was more herself during the drive than Jack had seen in months. She laughed and teased. She smiled. Excitement and enthusiasm touched her words and posture. Her attentions to Miss Summerfield had pulled the timid young lady out of her shell.

Jack had always known this part of Odette's character. Terrance was discovering it for the first time. He looked impressed. Touched.

Intrigued.

Perhaps this arrangement had been a mistake after all.

Adelaide watched Mr. Lexington's carriage roll past among the crush of vehicles in the park. She had placed herself on a bench facing the carriage path with the precise purpose of watching for the young people. What she saw was both encouraging and surprising.

Odette looked genuinely happy, something Adelaide had not yet seen. The smile and sparkling eyes fit her far better than the expression of annoyed ennui she usually wore. But what had inspired it?

Mr. Lexington was a jovial companion, but Adelaide knew he had not captured the young lady's heart. Mr. Hewitt and Miss Summerfield were joining in the apparently entertaining conversation. Perhaps it was simply the combination of companions that brought light back into Odette's eyes. Perhaps it was the effect of fresh air. Or time away from her parents.

It bore thinking on.

Five

ODETTE WAS BOTH excited and terrified. She was standing up for the supper dance with Jack during the Salsteads' ball that night, which meant she would be taking her supper with him. She would have his company, but for too short a time and with far too many people nearby. They would be permitted no tender moments, no words of love or longing. They would be allowed only the vaguely friendly interactions of two lifelong neighbors.

She dressed with extra care. This was to be her one opportunity to pretend as though she and Jack were an ordinary courting couple; she wasn't going to waste it. She chose a gown in a flattering shade of pale blue. She asked her abigail to weave into her hair a ribbon of pastel yellow, one Jack had given her many years earlier. He had, while at Eton, used the last of his spending money before returning home for the summer holidays to purchase a length of ribbon. How well she remembered his nervousness when he'd presented it to her.

"I know you like tying ribbons in your hair," he'd said. "There were a lot of different colors and widths and such. I hope this is a good one. I wanted you to have something from me. I wanted you to have something you'd like."

He had been her favorite person even then, though the romantic affection between them hadn't blossomed until years later, when they were both old enough for such things. It had been such a slow and natural progression that she'd been top over tail in love with him before she'd even recognized the change. The Summerfields moved to the neighborhood shortly thereafter, and Jack's parents quickly made clear their preference for their son's future wife. The timing had been horribly unfair.

"You look a real treat, miss," her abigail, Liza, said. "The yellow ribbon against your dark hair. Lovely."

"Do you really think so?" She was not usually so uncertain, but the evening ahead meant a great deal to her.

"A real treat."

She repeated that declaration in her mind as she stepped from her bedchamber. She looked "a real treat." The ball would be enjoyable. The supper dance and meal would be everything she hoped it would. Again and again she promised herself those things.

By the time she reached the entryway, where Mrs. Northrop and her parents were waiting, she had her confidence firmly intact and her exterior of haughtiness in place. She did not care for the role she was playing, but it had worked thus far. No gentlemen were vying for her hand; she would escape the Season unpromised to anyone.

Mrs. Northrop and Odette's parents were deep in conversation and did not note her arrival.

"This may not be the most important event of the Season," Mother said, "but it is of enough significance that we really ought to be in attendance. Her sisters would have made a disaster of their lives if we had left them to their own devices."

Panic grasped Odette's heart. Were her parents intending to interfere more directly? To push for someone in particular?

"I feel it best for your daughter to first begin addressing her notoriety," Mrs. Northrop said. "I have helped young ladies do precisely that many times. Leaving her in my care will accomplish what you seek far better and far faster than if I am made to juggle the entire family."

Odette relied upon that notoriety. Utilizing the pompous tone she had so perfected, she entered the fray. "Suppose 'their daughter' could not possibly care less about 'addressing her notoriety'?"

Without the slightest hesitation, Mrs. Northrop said, "Then 'their daughter' is rather foolish, something I do not believe for a moment."

"You think you can restore Society's good opinion of her?" Father pressed.

"I am certain of it." Mrs. Northrop shooed them away. "The two of you leave her social calendar in my keeping. All will be put to rights."

Quick as that, Odette's parents abandoned her to the keeping of Mrs. Northrop and her insufferable nosiness.

"Come along, then," Mrs. Northrop said, motioning to the now-open front door. It seemed she had taken control of the household as well as Odette's future.

Had she been less determined to attend that evening's ball, she might have put up more of a fight. But the time she had been promised with Jack was worth being browbeaten for the moment.

They climbed into the carriage. Mrs. Northrop tapped on the ceiling, and they began immediately moving forward.

"Your parents seem particularly intrigued by the possibility of Mr. Lexington choosing to court you," Mrs. Northrop said.

"He has given me no indication that he intends to do so." That was not entirely true. Mr. Lexington always asked her to stand up with him at balls and spoke to her at musicales. He had chosen her to join him on a drive about Hyde Park. She didn't think he was truly *courting* her, but he was showing her attention.

"Young gentlemen seldom make sorting out their intentions as easy as that."

Odette allowed the tiniest of smiles. "I don't think ladies are entirely innocent on that score, either."

Mrs. Northrop shook her head. "Love is a bit of a mess at times, isn't it?"

"Oh, were we speaking of love? I thought the topic was courtship." She did not entirely keep the cynicism from her voice.

"Do you not think the two are one and the same?" her traveling companion asked.

"In my experience, the two are not generally permitted to be connected," Odette said.

"That is unfortunately often the case, and it ought not be."

Odette had not expected this lady, a matchmaker to the *ton*, to harbor any preference, however small, for matches based in tenderness and regard. "Do the matches you engineer take affection into consideration?"

"The matches I *facilitate* are governed by three unbreakable rules." She left the comment there, not elaborating or seeming the least eager to explain.

"What are the three rules?"

Mrs. Northrop's lips turned up ever so slightly. A bit of mischief entered her gaze. "Do you know this is the most interested you have been in having a conversation with me since my arrival? I am sorely tempted to offer only a partial answer, if only to force you to speak with me again."

Despite her determination to be a touch cold with Mrs.

Northrop, especially considering she had come to undo all that had been managed that Season, Odette could not entirely hold back an answering smile of her own. "I am to receive only one rule at a time?"

"Yes." Mrs. Northrop nodded regally. "One at a time, beginning with the first: Neither the gentleman nor the lady can be a truly horrid person."

The rule was an odd one and certainly unexpected. "Has this rule come into play often?"

"More often than it should."

Odette was decidedly intrigued. "What do you do if the person for whom you are charged with securing a match proves to be horrid?"

"I leave," she said baldly.

Odette picked at a stray thread on one of her gloves. "You have not left Barrington House yet."

"No, I have not." There was a gentleness to her response that pulled Odette's gaze to her once more. "I know what people say of you, Odette. In the short time I've been here, I've seen why you are viewed the way you are."

She tried to assume her haughty expression. "'Horrid' is not the same as 'pompous,' though."

Mrs. Northrop arched a brow. "Neither is 'masquerading.'"

Odette's mind simply stopped. Had Mrs. Northrop seen through the act so quickly, so thoroughly? More to the point, what did she mean to do about it?

"Ah, we are here." Mrs. Northrop gave her a rather disconcerting smile. "This should be a very . . . interesting evening."

Time dragged as the night wore on. Mrs. Northrop kept nearby, offering friendly welcomes to the gentlemen who requested a dance with Odette. Gentlemen's mothers were pulled into Mrs. Northrop's conversations at alarming rates. Were they interested because of the matchmaker's connection to Odette in particular or simply hoping to capitalize in the future on their acquaintance with Mrs. Northrop?

When Terrance came to offer his greetings, Mrs. Northrop was particularly welcoming. She asked questions, inquired after his family, made absolutely certain he knew he had met with approval. Though Odette did not know the remaining two rules of Mrs. Northrop's matchmaking service, she could not deny that Terrance Lexington met the first requirement. He was a fine person, but he was not the gentleman she loved.

The supper dance arrived. She watched Jack approach. The joy she had anticipated feeling had been replaced with anxiety. She had to tell Jack what had happened; they needed to determine what to do, how to salvage the quickly deteriorating situation. And their moments together at supper would likely be the only opportunity to do so.

Could fate not give her even one evening of simple tenderness?

He bowed over her hand. Smiled. Pulling her arm through his, he led her toward the dance floor. His pleased expression did not slip as he whispered, "You appear distressed."

"I thought I kept that well hidden."

"I know you very well, Odette." They would soon be too near the other dancers for even whispered words to go unheard.

"Mrs. Northrop is suspicious of Princess Pompous," Odette said, rushing the words. "And she is worryingly interested in Terrance."

"Terrance?" Jack looked and sounded shocked.

"I don't know what to do. She is too clever and too observant to be kept in the dark for five more weeks."

"We will sort it." He likely would have said more, but they'd reached the line of dancers and were obligated to separate.

The musicians struck up the tune, and the dance began. Whenever the movements brought Jack and Odette together, they undertook precisely the inane, empty comments a romantically uninterested couple would. Jack, as always, wore an expression of friendly pleasure. He had insisted upon that. He would hide the depth of his regard, but he had utterly refused to appear displeased with her company.

That decision had been a balm to her oft-wounded heart the past months. It was again now.

By the time they walked in to supper, her worries had calmed, though not entirely disappeared. Mrs. Northrop sat at a bit apart from Jack and Odette, far enough to afford a bit of privacy. Indeed, Jack had chosen seats for the two of them at the very end of one of the many tables set out for guests to take their supper. He sat beside her rather than going directly to the buffet to fetch them both plates of food.

"How set is Mrs. Northrop on a match with Terrance, do you suppose?" he asked in a nearly silent whisper.

"Not entirely, though she does seem keen on it. I'm far more worried that she knows I am feigning my arrogance and disdain and has expressed her intention to repair that perception."

He did not look as displeased with the prospect as she was. "I would so like for you to be known as your true self. You deserve to have friends here, to associate with people, to be happy, and you have not had any of that, aside from our ride in the park."

"That was rather foolish." She had worried over that again and again in the days since. "Anyone looking on was likely struck by how very different I was. We are too close to risk undoing what we have managed thus far."

"What we have managed is your unhappiness."

She shook her head. "We are securing our future. That is of utmost importance."

Beneath the table, hidden by the long linen tablecloth, Jack took her hand in his. "Perhaps we should reconsider the possibility of Scotland."

She could smile a bit at that, though only briefly.

"I do not think there is harm in softening Society's perception of you," he said. "Gradually. Bit by bit. You will still be viewed with wariness, which should keep suitors at bay. But when we return—"

"We," she whispered the word as much to herself as to him.

"*We.* When we return next Season, together, you will have far less ground to make up, and that is a very good thing."

"It is the very best thing if we are together."

"We will be." He spoke with utter confidence. "I swear we will."

She took a cleansing, reassuring breath. "You had best go fetch us plates before people take too much notice."

His hand released hers. She mourned the loss on the instant. When would they ever be permitted such a simple touch again? And what kind of miracle could possibly bring about the seemingly impossible dream they shared?

Now this was an interesting development. Odette and young Mr. Hewitt were quite good at giving the impression of mere acquaintance, friendship at most; Adelaide gave them full credit for that. But she knew people well. She'd learned long ago to see what they attempted to keep hidden.

The truth of the connection between these two showed

in every quick glance, in the easing of tension in their faces and postures when the other was nearby, in the way they sat just a little closer to each other than was necessary. They were in love. Why, then, were they hiding it? Why was Odette pretending to be such a haughty and miserable person? Why was Mr. Hewitt pretending to have no interest in her?

Helping people piece together their futures meant delving into the chaotic corners of their lives. Something stood in the way of these two simply claiming their happiness. In Adelaide's experience, the culprit was usually family, status, or money—sometimes all three.

My dear Princess Pompous, it is time to discover just how much you are hiding.

Six

MOTHER FLEW INTO the informal sitting room with all the excitement of a child who had just learned she was to have her very own pony. Dread settled heavily in Odette's chest.

"It is working," Mother declared, eying Odette and Mrs. Northrop in turn. "I know I should not have doubted, considering your success in the past." This last was directed at the matchmaker. "Yet, how very exciting to see progress is already being made."

"Would you be so good as to elaborate?" Mrs. Northrop's question did not emerge as anything short of a gentle demand.

Mother took a seat nearby, though she did not hold still in the least. "I have been speaking with my dear friend Mrs. Hewitt."

Jack's mother. Odette held her breath.

"She spoke at length of the difference everyone is seeing in Odette these past days, that she is softer and less pompous." Mother turned an apologetic gaze on Odette. "You have given that impression, dear."

"I am well aware." Her dry comment inspired the usual consternation in Mother and utter lack of response from Mrs. Northrop.

Mother pressed onward. "I do not know what has led to this improved opinion, but it is quite real, I assure you. Mrs. Hewitt was beyond pleased that you were more the Odette she has known all these years."

Jack's mother thought well of her, it seemed. That was encouraging. It wasn't enough, but it was encouraging.

"And she could not stop speaking of you and a certain young gentleman we all know and her belief that he has developed a keen interest in you."

Odette hoped she kept her expression adequately unconcerned even as her lungs froze. Had Mrs. Hewitt realized the affection between her and Jack? Had they been unable to fully hide their feelings? At least Mother's recounting didn't indicate the realization was an unwelcome one on Mrs. Hewitt's part.

Mrs. Northrop was as utterly detached from the topic as ever. It was decidedly odd that a lady who spent her life making matches never seemed overly concerned about the subject of her efforts.

"How do you feel about this young gentleman?" Mother asked the marriage broker.

"I would happily offer my opinion if I knew to whom Mrs. Hewitt referred."

Mrs. Northrop, then, had not noticed any particular shows of affection between her and Jack. That set Odette's mind a little at ease.

"Why, young Mr. Lexington, of course."

Odette made a very unladylike sound, something between a snort and a choke.

"He is quite eligible," Mother insisted. "He is near to you in age—you specifically objected early in the Season to gentlemen more than fifteen years your senior."

"A reasonable objection," Mrs. Northrop said. "One of

my rules, in fact." She looked at Odette. "Rule two: Both halves of any potential couple must be fully comfortable with each other's age, life experiences, and character."

Odette knew young ladies who had been married off to gentlemen of an age with their grandfathers and others joined to rakes of such profligate appetites that no hope existed of them being faithful or conscientious husbands.

"Surely," Mother replied, "if the young lady's parents do not object to a suitor's age or habits—"

"The parents do not have to build a life with their daughter's husband. *She* does." Mrs. Northrop met Odette's eye once more. "Her wishes will not be ignored."

To Odette's horror, she felt emotion building in her throat and behind her eyes. Both her sisters' wishes had been so easily brushed aside. To have Mrs. Northrop advocating for *her* was greater reassurance than Odette had felt in months.

Mother seemed to realize the matchmaker would not be easily swayed to support any particular suitor. "Mr. Lexington has a tidy income from his father's estate and will inherit. The two of you get along. He was not put off by the horrid display you've been making this Season." Mother counted off on her fingers the points she was making. "He has asked you to stand up with him at every ball you've both attended these past months. He's taken you for a drive. He has spoken with you at musicales, and he even once visited us in our box at the opera."

Mrs. Northrop *hmm*'d. She assumed an expression of pondering that washed away some of the relief Odette had felt only a moment ago. "I had not realized he was so attentive."

"He really isn't," Odette insisted. "He is a friend of Jack's, is all. He was, no doubt, wrangled into being kind out of pity for his friend's childhood friend."

"Odette." Mother spoke her name through tight teeth. "You were permitted to call him by his Christian name when you were tiny, but you mustn't do so now. It is simply not acceptable."

"It is merely a habit," she lied.

Another of Mrs. Northrop's *hmm*s. This was devolving quickly.

Odette rose, her chin at a proud and defiant angle. "I will leave the two of you to discuss your fondness for Mr. Lexington. I mean to go for a walk around the back garden."

She made her dignified exit, Mother's "I do not know what to make of her any longer" following her into the corridor.

Only upon reaching the quiet, tall-shrubberied garden did Odette let her shoulders sag. She was absolutely certain Terrance had no interest in her. She didn't know if Jack had ever told him of their situation. Whether he had or not, Odette did not detect in him the signs of affection her mother and Jack's seemed determined to see.

Yet, she knew her mother would never contradict Mrs. Hewitt. Father would not, either. They practically worshipped them, idolized them. They coveted the standing Jack's family so easily claimed. If Mrs. Hewitt promoted a match between Odette and Terrance, that match would be pursued with all the tenacity of a terrier hunting a fox, and it would end just as badly for her as it always did for the pitiable prey.

I need to talk with Jack. This is far more tenuous than we realized. But how? Even their long-standing acquaintance was not enough to permit her to visit him or send him a note. There had to be a way.

"This does not appear to be a pleasant walk." Mrs. Northrop really needed to begin making more noise when she walked about.

"Is Princess Pompous not entitled to be in a sour mood?" She hoped her pretentious tone proved enough to send Mrs. Northrop back inside.

It didn't.

"Mr. Lexington is an admirable young gentleman," Mrs. Northrop said.

"He does seem to be." Odette thought that noncommittal enough.

"And your mother appears eager to pursue that possibility."

She could not help a tense sigh of frustration. "She is eager for nothing more or less than precisely what Mrs. Hewitt deems worthy of eagerness. Nothing motivates her as thoroughly as the chance to meet with our neighbor's approval."

"She would go so far as to agree with or disagree with a match simply because Mrs. Hewitt felt one way or the other about it?"

Odette nodded even as the weight on her heart grew. "They are a family of great influence in our corner of the kingdom, and my parents are—" She did not wish to speak truly ill of her parents, but neither could she think of an innocuous way of phrasing the truth. "They find comfort in the reassurance of a seemingly risk-free path."

Mrs. Northrop's gaze narrowed on her. "And bowing to the dictates of the powerful and influential feels less risky than having an opinion of their own?"

"Unfortunately."

"And none of them realizes you and young Mr. Hewitt are in love with each other?"

Shock. There was no other word to describe the visceral reaction she had to Mrs. Northrop's unanticipated question.

The matchmaker actually laughed, not a shoulder-shaking guffaw, but a laugh of pure enjoyment. "You didn't realize I had sorted that out, did you?"

Odette clutched her hands together, nervous, wary. "We thought we hid it very well."

"Oh, you have hidden it exceptionally well. I am simply very, very familiar with the symptoms of love, especially love unacknowledged."

Mrs. Northrop did not appear to disapprove. If Odette could convince her to champion their cause, there might be some hope.

"Jack is a wonderful, upstanding, good-hearted gentleman. I have known him all my life, so I know he is not pretending to be good in order to advance his suit. He would simply have approached my father and made his case if not for his parents' preference for Miss Summerfield and my parents' inability to contradict anything the Hewitts believe or embrace, coupled with their history of forcing their daughters into marriages they felt most likely to meet with the approval of important people."

"Your mother hinted at interfering in your sisters' decisions," Mrs. Northrop said, "but you feel your sisters were forced?"

"Heavily coerced," Odette said. "Jack and I know my parents would do so again. It is a frustratingly impossible situation."

A gentle smile answered. "I have yet to encounter a truly impossible situation. This one will be difficult, though."

Odette hardly dared believe what she thought she was hearing. "You do not mean to object? My parents might be upset."

Mrs. Northrop slipped her arm through Odette's and began walking with her along the garden path. "I did not become a matchmaker in order to make certain that the whims of the parents of the *ton* ruled supreme. I did just tell you of my second rule."

Odette shook her head. "But I cannot object to Mr. Lexington's age or life or character."

"That is not the principle beneath the rule, Odette. Rule number two is my requirement that any match for which I advocate must be one *both* people feel will contribute to their happiness, a match they both choose freely and fully."

"And if I told you that a match with Mr. Lexington would not secure my happiness?"

"I would be so shaken by surprise as to be incapacitated for weeks on end." Mrs. Northrop delivered the declaration with too stony an expression and too dry a tone to be truly serious.

For the first time since coming to London, Odette drew a nearly serene breath. "Jack and I don't know what to do. The closest thing to a plan we could concoct was to do our utmost to avoid a match while in Town and then spend the autumn and winter bringing our parents around to the idea of a connection between us."

"His parents in particular, no doubt." Mrs. Northrop's brow puckered in a look of thoughtfulness devoid of true worry. "But they, you said, have their hearts set on Miss Summerfield."

Odette nodded.

"How does Miss Summerfield feel about this?"

"I cannot say."

They walked a few minutes more. Mrs. Northrop did not speak. Odette embraced the rare moment of companionship. She had been quite alone the past weeks with no one to easily share her burdens. Jack would have, if he'd been permitted. Odette might have had any number of friends to lean upon if she'd not been forced to keep all the world at a distance.

"I have the beginnings of an idea," Mrs. Northrop said, "one I think may just prove ingenious."

The lady did not lack for confidence.

"It will require a few things, however."

Odette could not imagine anything that would not be worth securing the future she and Jack were so desperate to claim.

"I will need to speak with Mr. Hewitt," Mrs. Northrop said. "He, you must understand, has been going about this entirely wrong."

Had they undermined their own chances? "What do you mean to require of him?"

Mrs. Northrop shook her head. "You need not worry about that. You have a couple of tasks of your own."

She waited in silence, knowing Mrs. Northrop would press forward.

"First, you will diligently work at shedding your Princess Pompous moniker. I understand your reason for it now, but Mrs. Hewitt's good opinion is paramount in this endeavor. You will never secure it if you continue as you have been."

That made sense, and yet . . . "If the other mothers of the *ton* or any gentlemen who have not entirely lost interest begin to see me as agreeable—"

"I have full control over the remainder of your Season. You will not be browbeaten into an unwanted match. I swear to you."

She wanted so desperately to believe it. "You said there were multiple things you required of me."

"Only one other." She met Odette's eye with her firm and unwavering gaze. "You are to befriend Miss Summerfield. Not with ulterior motives or insincerity, but truly befriend her."

Befriend the lady who might very well steal away all her hopes? "What would that accomplish?"

Mrs. Northrop patted her hand in a very maternal way. "This is not negotiable, neither is it something I mean to debate with you. Repair Society's perception of you. Honestly befriend Miss Summerfield. Those are my requirements."

Odette hesitated. "You will help Jack and I if I agree to those two things?"

"And if Mr. Hewitt agrees to what I will ask of him."

"What—?"

But Mrs. Northrop shook her head firmly. There would be no questions on that score. Odette was meant to simply trust her.

What choice did she have, really? Her future depended upon this.

"I agree."

"Very good." Mrs. Northrop patted her hand, then slipped her arm free. "I have a great deal of work to do. You set your mind to the best means of accomplishing what has been asked of you. I will do the same."

Adelaide might eventually grow accustomed to the self-defeating stubbornness of the young people she worked with, but somehow she doubted it. They had, generally speaking, seen too little of the world to fully understand it but held too high an opinion of their own ability to navigate the shoals they could not even anticipate.

To Odette and Mr. Hewitt's credit, they had found themselves in a particularly difficult situation. Resigning Odette to the task of keeping everyone at bay in order to avoid suitors had proven effective, but anyone who paid even minimal attention could see the toll that loneliness was taking.

Before she would fully commit to helping make this match, she first needed to discover if young Mr. Hewitt had resigned his lady love to months of misery out of a misguided desperation or out of indifference to her suffering. The former could be rectified. The latter would not be tolerated.

$\mathcal{S}$even

JACK WALKED DOWN the corridor of his family's London home, Terrance at his side, laughing as they recounted a particularly ridiculous wager two gentlemen had made at the club that morning.

"Barton is a dunderhead," Terrance said. "He'll be handing over a pony by week's end."

"Never should have bet against Jones. I've seen that man in a prizefight. A monster." They stepped inside the book room.

The conversation died on the instant. The room was not empty. A lady, whom Jack couldn't immediately place, sat in a high-backed chair, facing the doorway.

"Good afternoon, Mr. Hewitt." She spoke with utter calm, as if the situation was not in the least unusual or uncomfortable. "Mr. Lexington."

Terrance shot Jack a look of confusion. Jack shrugged.

"I can find my mother," Jack offered.

She shook her head. "I am not here to speak with your mother."

"My father?" That seemed unlikely.

"I am here to see you, Mr. Hewitt. Mr. Lexington's presence is simply a fortunate happenstance."

This was growing more odd by the moment. "I will confess myself confused."

"What are your intentions toward Miss Armistead?"

Panic seized him, but he kept his expression simply curious. "Which of us are you asking?" He slipped in a laugh to show he wasn't unduly concerned.

"Both."

Terrance sauntered the rest of the way into the room. "I remember you now. You're Mrs. Northrop, the matchmaker."

"Very observant, but you still did not answer the question."

Terrance grabbed a chair from near the desk and moved it to where Mrs. Northrop sat, placing it perpendicular to hers and sitting quite casually. "Miss Armistead is amusing, and I enjoy her company, but I've no interest beyond friendly acquaintance."

Mrs. Northrop nodded, quite as if she had fully expected that answer. Both she and Terrance turned their expectant gazes on Jack.

"She is a neighbor," he said. "And a friend of long standing. There is nothing beyond that."

Neither appeared the least convinced.

"Truly. She is like a sister." How untrue that was. The words actually felt bitter sliding off his tongue.

Mrs. Northrop nodded. "An ill-mannered sister one wishes he could pretend not to know."

Jack bit back a retort, though it required a tremendous amount of effort.

"Or could banish somewhere out of sight and out of hearing," Terrance added.

He had never heard his friend speak ill of Odette. He did not like this change in the least.

"Believe me," Mrs. Northrop said, "I have suggested banishment. I am not certain Lord Barrington has money enough to bribe someone to take that insolent girl off his hands."

"Perhaps they might consider shipping her to America," Terrance said. "They have enough intolerable people there that she would find herself immediately accepted."

"Do not talk about her that way," Jack snapped. "She is not ill-mannered or insolent. She is not any of the things Society says about her. I will not stand here and—"

The grins spreading over their faces cut his words off. *Knowing* grins. All too knowing.

He turned and closed the book room door. "This was an ambush, was it?"

But Terrance shook his head. "I've never even spoken with Mrs. Northrop until now. I'm simply not as bacon-brained as you think I am. I've suspected your feelings for Miss Armistead for months. The carriage ride confirmed it."

Jack looked to Mrs. Northrop.

"The Salsteads' ball," she said.

"We merely danced and went in to supper together," Jack said. They had been so careful.

"It was not your behavior that gave you away," Mrs. Northrop said, "but the manner in which you looked at each other."

Terrance laughed lightly. "Smitten, the both of them."

There was some relief in knowing Terrance was aware of the situation. Mrs. Northrop's knowledge of it was less reassuring.

"And what do you mean to do now that you have sorted this out?" he asked.

"Sort you out." She rose and motioned for him to take her chair. "Do not insist upon standing simply because I now am. I mean to interrogate you and prefer to do so while moving about."

He could tell by her tone and the snapping of her gaze that she would brook no arguments on this score. He took the chair and braced himself. She paced away.

"How did you get in here?" he asked.

"You seem to misunderstand the word *interrogate*. It does not involve *me* answering *your* questions."

Terrance could not have looked more amused if they had been watching a Christmas pantomime.

"Whose idea was Miss Armistead's 'performance' this Season?" Mrs. Northrop asked.

Jack swallowed against a lump of apprehension. "I don't know what you mean."

"Cut line, Jack," Terrance said. "*I* sorted out Miss Armistead's true character, and I see her only at Society functions. Mrs. Northrop lives at the gel's house."

His interrogator had ceased her pacing and now stood watching him, calm and serene but with an edge of challenge to her posture.

Whose idea had the ruse been? "We formulated the plan together," he said. "Her sisters were more or less forced into matches not of their liking. If we could prevent anyone from even pursuing a match, she would not have to endure that."

"Instead she has endured months of loneliness and rejection while you, Mr. Hewitt, have carried no such burden."

"I know." Lud, he'd hated the way this had played out. "I've doubted the idea almost from the moment we conceived it. She does not deserve to be viewed or treated the way she has been. But we didn't know what else to do."

Mrs. Northrop took a step closer to him, her gaze never wavering. "And if you could have thought of a different strategy, perhaps one that sent you into isolation rather than her?"

"I'd have taken it up in a heartbeat. But what good would that have done? A gentleman being disagreeable is seldom reason for rejection if he is in anticipation of a fine income and can claim some standing. Only ladies are judged and rejected so quickly and harshly."

Mrs. Northrop didn't confirm his evaluation, but neither did she contradict it. "What if I were to tell you that this scheme of yours is making her utterly miserable?"

Pain clutched at his heart. "Is she truly so unhappy? I know she has not enjoyed the arrangement, and I am certain she will rejoice when the Season is over, but—"

"She hasn't any friends, Mr. Hewitt. No one to take ices with. No one to walk about a room with in congenial conversation. She is eyed with dismissal and disapproving amusement. She is a caricature in the eyes of those who might have been her associates."

This was worse than he had imagined. "We must do something, then. We must address this. She cannot be required to live this way."

"You would risk your future together?" Mrs. Northrop pressed.

Though he recoiled at the possibility of losing her, he could not simply dismiss the fact that she was suffering. "We could think of something different, something that won't cause her sorrow. Surely we could. We have to."

The first hints of a smile touched Mrs. Northrop's stern expression. "Congratulations, Mr. Hewitt. You, it seems, are not a cad."

"Thank you?" He couldn't help making the answer a question.

"Now, to the business at hand."

"Was interrogating me not the business at hand?"

She arched an eyebrow, but the look was not truly one of

reprimand. Indeed, he felt certain she was thoroughly enjoying herself. "I have begun working on the task of rectifying the mess the two of you have made of Miss Armistead's position among those who would otherwise be her friends and companions."

He actually sighed, something he'd not been anticipating. The impact of this plan on Odette's happiness had weighed on him the past months.

"While that damage is being addressed," Mrs. Northrop said, "you and I will begin seeing to your future in a way that is not absurdly foolish and, therefore, will actually work."

He was both hopeful and insulted.

"First"—she turned to Terrance—"our efforts would be greatly helped if you would put it about that Odette is something of a sister to you or a pleasant but ultimately neutral companion."

Terrance paled a bit. "Has my name been coming up in connection with hers?"

Had it? Jack shot him a look of warning.

Terrance shook his head with tremendous emphasis. "Not intentional, Jack. I've been kind to her, and few people have paid any real heed to Princess Pompous."

"Do not call her that," Jack growled.

"You did it on purpose," Terrance insisted. "That nickname is what has kept the suitors at bay."

"And everyone else," Mrs. Northrop added.

Jack slumped in his chair. "It really was a bad strategy, wasn't it?"

"Horrendous," Mrs. Northrop said.

"I'll put the idea of a sibling-like connection in a few select heads," Terrance said. "That will help squelch any rumors."

Mrs. Northrop eyed Jack. "And you need to put 'the idea'

of Terrance's indifference into your mother's head, since she is the source of many of these whispers."

That was a sticky complication. "I'll do what I can."

"And while you are at it," Mrs. Northrop continued, "mention, casually, what a difficult Season Odette has had but that she seems to finally be finding her footing. Remind your mother that she once liked her young neighbor, but do so subtly."

Jack nodded. "What do we do about Miss Summerfield? My parents and hers are set upon a match between us."

"You leave that to me."

"A matchmaker *undermining* matches?" Terrance clicked his tongue. "That cannot be good for your reputation."

"My reputation, Mr. Lexington, is as one who makes good matches. Quality is far more important than quantity."

For the first time in ages, Jack felt some hope over his and Odette's situation. "You really are going to help us?"

"I am going to help you help yourselves." With that declaration, she left the room. No farewell. No curtsy.

Jack wasn't sure if he liked Mrs. Northrop or was simply terrified of her. He suspected she was the sort of person one underestimated at his own peril.

"If she can't sort out the mess you've made, I don't think anyone can," Terrance said.

"Lud, I hope so."

"For your sake, as well as Miss Armistead's, I hope so as well."

"Which brings me to a grievance." He turned in his seat enough to look at Terrance. "You knew, and you never said anything."

Terrance was not the least quelled by the accusation. "You never said anything to me. You should have. I wouldn't have jabbered. I might have even helped."

Jack dropped his head into his upturned hands. "We've made such a mess of this."

"It'll get sorted now, you'll see."

But what if it didn't? What if Mrs. Northrop, despite her confident bearing and unwavering declarations, couldn't salvage the situation?

He might lose Odette. He couldn't bear the thought.

Young people could be endlessly frustrating. Jack and Odette meant well, but they had made this far harder on themselves than it needed to be. His parents had set their sights on a match, but they had made no announcements to the world. Mrs. Hewitt and Lady Barrington still spoke regularly and were clearly friends. Mrs. Hewitt spoke of Odette in fond and caring terms, despite the fiasco of the past Season.

Bringing his parents around to the idea of a match between their son, who they seemed to love despite not understanding him well, and the daughter of their friends and neighbors, would not be difficult.

Miss Summerfield had shown no particular fondness for Jack, and her parents seemed to be in no great hurry to see her settled.

Odette had suffered the past months needlessly.

Why was that so often the case? A couple took the longest, most difficult route to love they possibly could, not seeing the easier path directly in front of them. Heavens, she'd redirected a lot of people over the years. And, in doing so, she'd saved them from disaster.

Eight

PERHAPS ICES WITH Miss Summerfield had been too bold a first step to take toward forming their required friendship. Odette had panicked when she'd come face-to-face with the young lady. She'd proposed a very public, very impersonal activity. She hadn't reckoned with the necessity of driving in the same carriage, sitting at a small table, and conversing with her secret rival while half of London looked on.

Mrs. Northrop wasn't particularly helpful. She had come along but sat in silence all the way to Gunter's. Odette had done her best to keep up a conversation. Miss Summerfield, however, was far quieter than she'd been during their drive in Hyde Park. Mrs. Northrop could be a little intimidating.

As they sat in Gunter's, the silence between the three of them became increasingly uncomfortable.

"It is a shame you have not been able to spend more time at Hazelfield," Odette said, naming the estate the Summerfields had purchased in the neighborhood. "Ours is a lovely little corner of the world."

"It does seem to be," Miss Summerfield said. "My parents prefer to divide their time between multiple places. I never seem to be granted time enough to come to know any one home or group of families."

Odette could not truly relate. "Coming to London this Season is only the third time I have ever left the immediate vicinity of the home where I grew up."

"That sounds nice." Miss Summerfield sighed.

"As does the opportunity to travel." She offered a smile to her tentative friend. "Perhaps we should attempt to switch places. You could remain in Somerset, and I could wander the country."

"Our parents might notice." Miss Summerfield made the observation with the same subtle dryness she'd used a few times during their Hyde Park ride.

"Does your family mean to return to Hazelfield after the Season?" Odette didn't know what she hoped the answer was.

"I believe we are, though not for very long." Loneliness touched the explanation.

Odette understood the ache of being isolated. She'd spent so much of her time in London feeling precisely that way. She had enjoyed Miss Summerfield's company during their previous ride, which had been surprising enough. Her heart ached for her neighbor now.

"Perhaps," she heard herself saying, "your parents would allow you to stay with us when they grow anxious to begin traveling again. You could come to know the neighborhood."

"Your parents might not appreciate taking on a house-guest so soon after returning to the country. Most people prefer a bit of peace and quiet after the madness of the Season." Yet a hopefulness hung under the words.

"Having a friend nearby is a joyful thing, though. That is its own kind of peace."

Miss Summerfield didn't speak for a moment. She watched Odette, searching her face. "Do you consider me a friend?"

"I would like to." Her own words rang with a truth she had not been expecting.

"I would like that as well."

Mrs. Northrop had remained entirely quiet. She simply sat, serenely sipping at her tea. Nothing ever ruffled Mrs. Northrop. When she had first arrived, her unshakableness had bothered Odette. Now she found it reassuring. This lady meant to help her undo the mess that her life had become. Being firm and confident was an asset in times of uncertainty.

"Has your family visited Burnham, Miss Summerfield?" Odette asked.

"Please, call me Tabitha." The request was made with palpable uncertainty, as if she expected a rejection. Did that unfortunate anticipation come from her own timidity, or had it grown out of Odette's reputation as Princess Pompous?

"And I am Odette."

Surprise was quickly replaced by excitement. "We have been to Burnham. It is a lovely little town, and I do enjoy the sea."

Mrs. Northrop quite suddenly entered the conversation. "Does your family visit any particular places more often than others?"

"Our homes, of course," she said. "Those are our only regular destinations."

"You must have a wide circle of friends," Mrs. Northrop said.

Tabitha's gaze dropped to the tabletop. "We do not stay in any one place long enough for me to gain many true friends. We've been in London longer than most anywhere else, yet, other than Odette"—she looked briefly up, smiling—"I have not made any friends."

"I haven't, either," Odette confessed. "I hadn't anticipated how much having a friend would mean during the Season. All we are ever told to concentrate on is suitors."

"Indeed." Tabitha looked to her fully once more. "But you do seem to have something of a friendship with Mr. Lexington. And, of course, you grew up with Mr. Hewitt."

"You know Mr. Hewitt as well." Odette managed the observation without sounding bitter. To her even greater surprise, she didn't truly feel bitter.

"Yes," Tabitha said, "but he goes to great lengths not to spend any time with me if he can help it. I cannot blame him. It is difficult for gentlemen and ladies to spend time with each other when Society is so eager to create rumors whenever possible."

Mrs. Northrop set her teacup down and folded her hands in front of her on the table. "You wish to avoid rumors connecting your name with Mr. Hewitt's?"

Odette's eyes pulled wide. This was hitting a bit too close to the mark.

"No one wishes to force a gentleman's hand," Tabitha answered.

Not quite the answer she would have preferred. Something more along the lines of "I have so little romantic interest in Mr. Hewitt that I cannot countenance the idea of even a whispered connection between us" would have been far better.

"Mr. Lexington appeared to enjoy your company at the Salsteads' ball," Mrs. Northrop said. "And Mr. Hewitt rode out with you in Hyde Park. Odette happily invited you on today's excursion. I believe you have forged more connections than you realize."

Color touched Tabitha's cheeks. "I hope you are correct."

They had finished their small selection of pastries and ices. They would be leaving soon. Odette found she regretted the necessity.

"We are attending the opera tonight," she said. "If you do not have unchangeable plans, would you join us in our box?"

"I would dearly love that."

They returned Tabitha to her home. Odette repeated her offer, hoping it would be taken up.

On the ride back to Barrington House, when only the two of them were in the carriage, Mrs. Northrop said, "You seem to have enjoyed Miss Summerfield's company."

"I did, indeed. I hope they will stay in the neighborhood for a time after the Season."

Mrs. Northrop tipped her head to one side, watching her. "Even though her parents and the Hewitts intend to pursue a match?"

That reality had very nearly pushed itself from her mind. "She did not seem overeager to pursue that herself, did she?"

"Not at all," Mrs. Northrop said. "Though, if I am not mistaken, she does have an interest in someone."

Odette had not received that impression at all. "Whom?"

"The same young gentleman Mrs. Hewitt insists has an interest in you."

"Mr. Lexington?" She practically spat the name, so great was her shock.

Mrs. Northrop tapped her fingertips together, eyes squinted in thought.

"I saw no indication Tabitha had feelings for him," Odette said. "She hardly mentioned him."

"Precisely." Mrs. Northrop's eyes wandered to the window, but she did not appear to actually be looking at anything. "When I spoke of the attention she had received from Mr. Hewitt and the time she'd spent with you, she discussed it. But my mention of Mr. Lexington was soundly ignored."

It had been, now that Odette thought back on it. "And she did blush rather immediately afterward."

Mrs. Northrop nodded. "I watched the two of them at the ball. Tabitha looked at Mr. Lexington in much the same way you look at young Mr. Hewitt, though her gaze is far less hopeful."

Someone who had *less* hope in her future than Odette did? Her heart ached for her new friend. "What can we do?"

Mrs. Northrop looked at her once more. "Concern for others is not precisely a Princess Pompous trait."

"I am not really—" Her irritation dissipated at the twinkle in Mrs. Northrop's eye. "You are the one who told me to shed my haughty persona."

"And I am so pleased that you are doing so. I like the Odette I have been coming to know these past days."

The compliment was humble and small, yet it filled her heart with warmth. Someone liked her. That had become a rare thing these past months. She'd begun to doubt if it was even possible anymore.

"It has been nice being more myself," she said. "Are you certain, though, your plan will work? What if—?" She cut off her own question. She was trying to have confidence in Mrs. Northrop's expertise.

"Be true to the person you are. Build your friendship with Tabitha. I will sort out the gentlemen."

She would believe it. She had to.

Adelaide wrote out a very specific set of instructions, which she had delivered to young Mr. Hewitt. He and his friend would join Lord and Lady Barrington, their daughter, and her friend in their opera box that night. Adelaide would watch and ascertain a few key things. If all went well, she would begin arranging an intricate dance. She had managed to maneuver far more complicated connections, yet she still figuratively held her breath.

She was not unaware of the fact that people's futures were determined by her success or failure. She did not take that responsibility lightly.

Eight

"DO YOU HAVE any idea why I was included in this little scheme?" Terrance didn't seem truly upset, but there was no denying the nervous tension in his posture.

"Mrs. Northrop didn't offer an explanation, but she was very specific and firm." Indeed, he'd rather felt like a schoolboy again, called to an accounting by the headmaster. "As she is mine and Odette's only hope for happiness, I am choosing to do whatever she asks of me."

"And whatever she asks of *me*," Terrance added with a quick laugh.

"Perhaps she will find a match for you as well."

If anything, Terrance grew more uncomfortable. "Lud," he muttered.

They'd reached the Barringtons' box. The show had not yet begun, but they had been instructed to present themselves before the opening curtain.

The expected bows and curtsies were exchanged. Both he and Terrance were warmly welcomed. Miss Summerfield stood beside Odette; Jack hadn't been expecting to see her. He looked to Mrs. Northrop, unsure what the matchmaker intended with this arrangement.

She simply motioned them to be seated.

Terrance moved a bit faster than Jack. He requested of Miss Summerfield the seat beside hers and was granted it. Terrance's sacrifice meant Jack would be granted the open seat beside Odette. He took it quickly, before anyone could move positions.

"Good evening, Miss Armistead," he said. "A delight to see you."

She looked up at him, affection clear in her expression. For more than a year, ever since they'd realized their sentiments went beyond mere friendship, they had both been very careful to hide their tender feelings. To see her love on display in public caught him utterly unaware.

"Has something happened?" he asked quietly, careful not to lift his voice above a whisper.

"I'm simply happy to see you."

He quickly eyed her parents before returning his gaze to her once more. "And you aren't worried your parents will realize . . . will be upset that . . ."

"Mrs. Northrop is on our side."

"I know."

She took a breath, one clearly underwritten by relief. "She told me not to be afraid to be my actual self and to allow my affections to show, within reason."

"Did she?" He very much liked that idea. "Am I permitted to do the same, do you suppose?"

She nodded. "Though Mrs. Northrop was careful to emphasize that subtlety is important."

"I cannot simply pull you into my arms right here and kiss you thoroughly?"

He had never before seen Odette blush, yet she did in that moment. She also smiled broadly. "If all goes to plan, there will be time and plenty for that."

"I am looking forward to it."

She bit her lips closed and turned her gaze to the stage, though the opera had not yet begun. Jack didn't bother hiding his grin. He had never before been permitted to flirt with Odette. He was rather enjoying it.

Miss Summerfield's light laugh floated over from Odette's other side. "That is not what I said, Mr. Lexington."

"Truly?" Terrance was clearly teasing. "I am almost certain I heard you say you intend to race at Ascot this year."

"I did not." Miss Summerfield laughed through her response.

Jack leaned a little closer to Odette, though not so much as to draw undue attention. "Are you intending to race at Ascot as well?"

She sighed dramatically. "I thought I would give someone else a chance this year."

It was his turn to laugh. Their ride in Hyde Park had been this way. Terrance had managed to pull Miss Summerfield from her usual bashfulness. Jack had been granted the rare opportunity to talk with Odette free of the subterfuge they'd been forced into.

Behind them, Mrs. Northrop spoke to Odette's parents. "These four make a lovely group of friends, do they not?"

"Indeed," Lady Barrington said. "We are very close acquaintances of the Hewitts. Neighbors, you realize."

"Young Mr. Hewitt is an exemplary gentleman," Mrs. Northrop said. "You must be pleased he is so fond of your daughter."

Calling upon every ounce of willpower he possessed, Jack managed not to turn around and insist Mrs. Northrop stop. She was taking an enormous risk.

"They are old friends," Lady Barrington said. "Well, *young* friends, but friends of long standing."

"How wonderful for both of them."

"I suppose it is." Lady Barrington made the observation as if it was the first time she'd ever given any thought to the benefits of his and Odette's association.

"What if this doesn't work?" Real worry had entered Odette's whisper.

"We will go to Scotland if need be."

She turned worried eyes on him once more. "Even if we were willing to destroy our own lives, sacrificing our standing, our reputations, our futures, we cannot do that to our children, or theirs. The scandal of an elopement would haunt us for generations."

He knew it well enough. He'd meant his suggestion of Scotland as an attempt to lighten her heart. She was too worried to be teased into any degree of relief.

"We will find a way," he vowed. "And we have Mrs. Northrop on our side."

He heard her next breath shake from her. "Do you think anyone would notice if you held my hand?"

"Unfortunately, yes."

On the stage below, the opera began. Their conversation ended. He remained at her side the rest of the evening, but they spoke very little. He did not know how much longer he could bear this.

If Mrs. Northrop couldn't manage the seemingly impossible, they might grow desperate indeed.

Jack never would have imagined when the Season began that he would be spending its final weeks answering the summons of a matchmaking matron. Yet, here he was, arriving, as instructed, in the Barrington House book room, ready to do whatever she deemed necessary. Were she not the only hope he and Odette had, he might have objected.

He stepped inside and saw not Mrs. Northrop, but Odette. She offered her hands in welcome. He took them both, raising one to his lips.

The door closed behind him. Without releasing Odette's hands, he looked back. Mrs. Northrop gave him a nod and a smile, then crossed to a chair not far from the door and sat. She took up a book, opened it, and began to read.

"She thought we would appreciate some time together," Odette said.

He returned his gaze to her beloved face. "Truly?"

She nodded. "We cannot be entirely alone. Were we to be caught out in utter privacy, it would ruin us both."

"But might solve our problem."

She smiled and laughed a bit. "A slightly better option than Scotland, but not by much."

He released one of her hands, freeing his to brush gently along her cheek. "If only we were home in Somerset. There were far more opportunities to see each other."

She leaned into his touch and closed her eyes.

He slipped his other arm around her waist and pulled her close. She rested her head against his chest.

"I do love you, Odette," he whispered.

"And I love you. I have for ever so long."

He kissed the top of her head, his arms wrapped around her. How long it had been since he'd last held her. Long minutes passed as they stood in each other's embrace. If fate had chosen to be kind, this would not have been such a rare occurrence.

"How was your day, darling?" he asked.

"Lovely." She made no move to pull away. "Today was the Summerfields' at-home. Tabitha and I were able to speak for over an hour. The more I come to know her, the more I like her."

"I believe Terrance could say the same thing."

She tucked herself more snugly against him. "Mrs. Northrop believes Tabitha is fond of Terrance as well."

"Truly?" He looked over at Mrs. Northrop.

For a lady who could not possibly have helped overhearing their conversation, she was doing an admirable job of paying them no heed.

Jack lightly kissed Odette's forehead, something he'd taken to doing in the weeks before she'd left for the Season. He'd not been permitted to do so even once the past months.

"Let's sit, darling," he said. "We've time enough."

They walked hand in hand to the sofa. She sat near enough to lean against him. He set his arm about her shoulders.

"Did your parents ever agree to bring your harp to London?" he asked.

"No. Their plans for this Season did not include me being happy."

He tugged her a little closer. "Our scheme to render you unlikeable didn't make things any better."

"I would have liked to have had my harp here," she said wistfully.

"Someday, Odette, when we have a home of our own, I will see to it you have a harp at home and one here in Town. Then you need never be separated from your music."

"Or from you," she added.

"That will be the very best part."

Adelaide had arranged this innocent interlude for reasons beyond the enjoyment of the young couple. She wanted to see for herself how they interacted and whether or not they were as good for each other as she hoped they were. She was not in the habit of making unhappy or unhealthy matches.

Listening to Jack and Odette from her spot near the door, she had her answer. He was kind and gentle, careful of the young lady's feelings, attentive. Odette spoke to him with an openness she offered no one else. She was happier in his company, more content.

They were good for each other.

Too many people were not fortunate enough to be blessed with a happy marriage. Adelaide had made it her personal mission to change that one blissful couple at a time. Here was an opportunity to manage two happy matches at once.

In two evenings' time, all four young people and their parents would be at the social event of the Season: a ball at the Grosvenor Square home of the Duke and Duchess of Wickford. Adelaide meant to have all the pieces in place for a very impressive bit of matrimonial chess.

Nine

"I UNDERSTAND YOUNG Mr. Hewitt will be at the ball this evening," Mrs. Northrop said to Mother as they stepped from the carriage outside the duke and duchess's Town home. "You must be very pleased about that."

Mother looked confused for only a fraction of a moment before assuming an expression of delight. "We are always pleased with his company."

"As well you should be." Mrs. Northrop addressed the comment to both of Odette's parents. "An exemplary young gentleman. His connection to your family is quite a boon."

"I suppose it is." Father's lips pressed outward in a frown, as they always did when he was pondering something.

"Come, then," Mrs. Northrop instructed. "We oughtn't delay."

She moved forward, directly toward the front door. Odette hurriedly caught up with her, leaving her parents to do the same.

They stepped inside and were divested of their shawls and Father of his outer coat. They followed the din of voices to the wide corridor directly adjacent to the ballroom where their host and hostess were welcoming their guests one family at a time. The first guests Mrs. Northrop came upon were none other than the Hewitts.

Mrs. Hewitt, in particular, appeared happy to see them. "A pleasure, Mrs. Northrop."

"Thank you again for the lovely visit this morning," she answered. *This morning?* Mrs. Northrop had called on Mrs. Hewitt? "Having been in Bath for most of this Season, I do appreciate getting reacquainted with the details of the *ton.*"

Mrs. Hewitt waved that off. "You knew things I hadn't heard yet. I am in awe of how many very significant people you are very closely acquainted with."

Mrs. Northrop appeared neither flattered nor embarrassed by the praise. "I am pleased to have added you and your family to that circle of acquaintances, as well as Lord and Lady Barrington's family."

That brought Mrs. Hewitt's attention to Odette. "A joy to see you again." While Mrs. Hewitt had never been unkind or cold, this was a warmer greeting than Odette was accustomed to receiving, especially since coming to London.

"And I you," she answered most sincerely. She had always liked Jack's mother. "This promises to be a lovely evening."

"Indeed. Anyone who is anyone is on Grosvenor Square tonight."

Odette caught Jack's eye. He smiled warmly, a gesture she returned. He crossed to where she stood and offered a bow. "Miss Armistead." Did everyone else hear the tenderness in his voice as he spoke her name?

"Mr. Hewitt." She answered the same way.

"Is it too much to hope that you might have saved a set for me?"

She dipped her head regally. "I believe I might be able to find one."

Mrs. Northrop inserted herself once more. "Her Grace wished specifically for you to dance with her cousin as well as Lord Keslington, a close friend of the duke's. And I mean to introduce you this evening to the Earl of Manningford."

Why was Mrs. Northrop arranging for her to dance with these gentlemen when she knew full well where Odette's affection lay?

Mrs. Hewitt's attention was now fixed not on Mrs. Northrop, but on Odette. She watched her with interest. "You are beginning to catch the notice of some very well-connected gentlemen."

"It would seem so," Odette said, attempting to sound at least not displeased by the turn of events.

"She began the Season with a little difficulty," Mrs. Northrop said. "Now that she has found a more sure footing, I am certain she will be a rousing success."

Mrs. Hewitt made a sound of pondering.

Mrs. Northrop indicated with a slight wave of her hand that the Hewitts' turn to greet the duke and duchess had arrived. Jack left Odette's side to join his parents as they offered their bows and curtsies.

Odette whispered to Mrs. Northrop, "Have you truly arranged for me to dance with those gentlemen you mentioned?"

"Certainly."

Frustration expanded in her chest, causing an uncomfortable tightness around her lungs. "I thought you were going to help mine and Jack's cause, not pursue . . . general matchmaking."

Mrs. Northrop arched a single raven eyebrow. "I am not one to rescind my promises, Miss Armistead. You, however, are welcome to doubt me."

There was nothing truly critical in the comment, yet

Odette felt a little chastised. Did she trust Mrs. Northrop? Did she have any choice but to trust her?

The Hewitts had finished their greetings to the host and hostess. Mother and Father stepped forward to begin theirs. Odette stood beside them, waiting to be acknowledged as was customary.

"Miss Armistead," the duchess said after a moment. "A pleasure."

"Your Grace." She gave the expected curtsy.

"I hope you will come call during my next at-home," the duchess said. "I have not had the opportunity to come to know you this Season."

"I would very much enjoy that." How she managed the sentence whole despite her shock, she didn't know. Princess Pompous had not exactly been a highly sought-after companion. To be issued a personal invitation to call upon a duchess was not an insignificant thing.

"Mrs. Northrop." The duchess held out her hands in greeting to the matchmaker, a very personal greeting for such a formal occasion. Were the two ladies more closely acquainted than Odette had realized? "My sister is still singing your praises. I would not be surprised if her first grandchild is named for you."

Mrs. Northrop gave a single nod. "For the little one's sake, let us hope her grandchild is a girl. Adelaide would be a difficult name to bear all his life."

The duchess laughed. "I could not be happier to see you here. If we are unable to spend time together this evening, do call upon me. I have hardly seen you this Season."

"Of course." Mrs. Northrop's smile spoke of friendship. With a duchess. One who wished for her particular company.

Their host and hostess turned to the next guests in line, freeing Odette and her family to move into the ballroom. Jack had remained behind after his parents had moved along. He offered Odette his arm.

She looked to Mrs. Northrop, but the matchmaker was speaking with a matron Odette had seen at nearly every social gathering of significance this Season.

"I do believe we are permitted to walk in together," Jack said, his arm still forward in anticipation.

Odette accepted it with a flip of her heart. "I cannot remember the last time we walked this way."

He smiled at her. "You walked on my arm to the supper dance at the Salsteads' ball a few days ago."

"That was different," she said. "You were required to, so no one would think twice about seeing it."

"Hmm." He apparently hadn't pondered it in quite that way. "Then I am even more determined to walk into the ballroom with you."

They walked through the doors of the ballroom and into the glittering whirl of the Season's grandest social event. Odette received many of the same looks she had the past few months: blatant curiosity, hints of superiority, subtle dismissal. But she also saw something new sprinkled about the room: smiles of welcome, happiness at her arrival, a hint of approval.

"Walking in with you seems to have helped my standing," Odette said to Jack.

"It's not me," Jack insisted. "I have been hearing very positive things about you at nearly every at-home and casual conversation in the park. I would wager Mrs. Northrop has been doing a great deal of talking."

"I am beginning to suspect that she knows absolutely everyone." Odette shook her head. "I had never heard of her until she arrived on our doorstep. Yet, she apparently has more connections than Prinny."

"And she is utilizing those connections to make certain you'll dance with every eligible gentleman of importance in Town." He clearly liked that no more than Odette did. "I am doing my utmost to trust her methods."

"But it is not easy," Odette added.

"Not in the least." He took a breath as they approached his parents and hers, standing to the side of the ballroom, speaking with the Summerfields. "Yet, she is our best chance. We'll simply have to choose to believe she knows what she is about."

She offered a quick dip of her head to a group of matrons they passed. Voice still lowered, she spoke to Jack once more. "I don't know how much longer my heart can bear this."

"Then tell yourself you need bear it only this one night," he said. "Tell yourself all our dreams will come true if we can simply endure for this one night."

This one night. She squared her shoulders. She could do that. She would. She had to.

Jack waited impatiently for the supper dance. He was struggling to keep his own advice. Trusting Mrs. Northrop's methods when she was actively making Odette the belle of this particular ball was difficult to say the least. He kept to the edges of the room, avoiding the necessity of asking any other ladies to stand up with him, while keenly aware that doing so would likely mean being the subject of a great many whispers of disapproval in the days to come.

He happened past the Summerfields just as Miss Summerfield was returned to their side by her most recent dance partner. They saw him, not allowing him the luxury of slipping away unnoticed.

"Mr. Hewitt." Mrs. Summerfield waved him over. "We have not seen much of you yet this evening." She turned to her daughter. "You have a dance remaining, do you not? An unclaimed set?"

"Mother," she whispered miserably, heat filling her cheeks.

Despite his preference for dancing only with Odette, he did not wish for Miss Summerfield to be embarrassed or made unhappy. "I would be happy to stand up with you," he said. "Honored."

Mrs. Summerfield beamed. *Miss* Summerfield looked only more miserable. Jack might have been offended if he didn't see in her eyes a desperation to simply be granted a moment's respite from the demands of the social whirl. She was quiet, precisely the sort of person who, if the exact opposite wasn't absolutely required of her, would have kept home, interacting with only the smallest number of her closest associates. How did her family not see that? Perhaps they simply didn't care.

"This is the supper dance, Mother," she said. "It has been claimed."

The supper dance. He had engaged Odette for the supper dance. How could he politely extricate himself from his current company so he could find her?

"Who has claimed it?" Mrs. Summerfield asked. "No one appears to be approaching."

Both ladies glanced about, confusion and concern on their faces. He could not simply walk away, no matter his commitment to Odette. He could be a moment late, though he could not, *would* not relinquish entirely the opportunity to stand up with her and spend the length of supper at her side.

"Mr. Tolmer was meant to stand up with me for this set," Miss Summerfield said. "Where do you suppose he is?"

Jack knew Tolmer. He was not one to fail in his duties. Jack looked around as well. "I saw him not thirty minutes ago." Odd.

"You don't suppose he has run out on his promise?" Miss Summerfield sounded somehow both hopeful and despondent. She'd likely enjoy a respite for the length of a set, yet abandonment did no young lady's reputation nor happiness any good.

Where was Tolmer? People nearby were beginning to take note of the situation.

"Mr. Hewitt, please will you stand up with her? This humiliation is too much for her delicate feelings."

"I am engaged for this set," he said. "I would not wish to do Miss Armistead such a disservice."

Miss Summerfield, in an admirable show of strength, turned an empathetic gaze on him, but one undermined by the sheen of tears in her eyes. "You must go claim your set. Odette will be quite counting on it."

"I could spare a moment more to look for Tolmer," he offered.

Odette arrived unheralded at his side. "Mr. Hewitt. Here you are."

An overloud whisper from somewhere nearby cut into the brief moment of silence that followed. "The Princess Pompous will order him beheaded."

Jack pushed down a sharp retort and instead smiled at Odette. "Forgive the delay. Miss Summerfield has been engaged for this dance, yet her partner has not yet arrived. I did not wish to abandon her while she waited."

Odette turned to Miss Summerfield. "With whom were you meant to be dancing?"

"Mr. Tolmer." Poor Miss Summerfield was utterly wilting under the attention of the crowd.

"I did hear it whispered that he spilt a glass of claret all down his front," Odette said. "Utterly ruined his clothing."

"He left?" Mrs. Summerfield was clearly shocked.

"What choice did he have?" Odette pressed. "Still, he ought to have sent word to you."

Miss Summerfield eyed the crowd, which was watching her with unmistakable pity.

Odette's brow pulled in worry. She turned to Jack. "Do stand up with her." She spoke quietly, but he could see that she had been overheard by those nearest them.

"Then you will be left without a partner."

She tipped her head, a twinkle of amusement in her eyes. "No one will wonder that Princess Pompous has been abandoned. But they will whisper about Tabitha. Please do not allow her to suffer."

Miss Summerfield looked a breath from tears.

Jack held Odette's gaze for one long moment, hoping she understood both his admiration for her thoughtfulness and his mourning for their lost moments together.

"Miss Summerfield—" He got no further than that.

Terrance arrived on the scene, anxious, focused, determined. Jack had grown suspicious over the past few days that his friend had developed a fondness for Miss Summerfield.

"I saw Mr. Tolmer leave," Terrance said, watching Miss Summerfield with concern. "I know he was to be your partner for the supper dance."

"Everyone is whispering." Her voice broke on the words.

"Please," Terrance said, "allow me to stand up with you for this set."

Miss Summerfield's expression fell. "You have already been my partner once this evening. Two sets will draw attention. People will speculate."

Terrance almost never wore a serious expression, but he

did in that moment. "I have no objections if you don't." He turned toward Mrs. Summerfield. "And if *you* don't."

Odette watched them, wide-eyed. Half the ballroom watched them. Openly requesting a second set was tantamount to declaring his intention to court her. Jack held his breath. Should Mrs. Summerfield grant Terrance a second set with her daughter, speculation about Jack's connection to her would be put to rest. His own parents would have to accept that, as all of Society would be aware of the events of the last few moments before the night was even over. And if his parents did not have their sights set on that particular match, Odette's parents would at last be willing to consider one between her and him.

Please, Mrs. Summerfield. Say yes.

The young lady's eyes pleaded with her mother. Terrance held himself confidently, but Jack knew him too well not to see the nervous determination there. They were both not only willing to begin a very publicly acknowledged courtship but apparently anxious.

Mrs. Summerfield set her hand on her daughter's arm, but her gaze remained on Terrance. "Of course you may stand up with her. Of course."

Miss Summerfield's smile bloomed beyond any Jack had seen her wear. She turned to Terrance, absolute delight written on every inch of her face. She slipped her arm through his and, together, they walked onto the dance floor. Nearly every eye watched them.

"A handsome couple," Mrs. Summerfield observed.

"And both very fortunate," Odette added. "There are not two better people in all the world."

Mrs. Summerfield looked away from her daughter and to Odette and Jack. "I thank the both of you for coming so swiftly to her aid."

"It was our pleasure," Odette said.

"You are partners for this set and for supper, I believe," Mrs. Summerfield said. "Do not let me keep you."

As they turned to walk away, they came face-to-face with Her Grace. She did not speak but offered a smile and nod of approval. The same thing repeated itself several times, always offered to the two of them together. The set was well underway; joining the other couples could have been managed but would have been a bit difficult. Instead, they simply made a slow circuit of the room, made increasingly slow by the many people who stopped to comment upon the evening and their handsomeness as a couple.

They had nearly completed their circuit when they came upon Mrs. Northrop.

"I hear a great many things of you," she said. "Your parents are hearing the same."

"And what is their reaction?" Odette asked anxiously.

"Approval of your chivalrous and kind behavior and, it seemed to me, beginning to consider a connection they had not before."

Odette took in a sharp, audible breath. "Oh, Jack."

He hesitated. "How deeply are they considering it?" he pressed.

"Deeply enough." Mrs. Northrop's calm serenity gave him confidence. "Continue on as you have been tonight, and by Season's end, I will fully expect an announcement in the *Times*."

Odette sighed deeply. Jack did the same. Months of worry were finally easing.

"I know this will sound awful," Odette said, "but I am so grateful Mr. Tolmer accidentally spilled his claret."

Mrs. Northrop nodded slowly. "Yes. *Accidentally*." She offered a dip of her head and turned and walked away.

For just a moment, the reality of what the matchmaker had nearly admitted did not penetrate his mind. Odette, however, grinned.

"I am grateful she is on our side," Jack said.

"As am I." Odette turned a happy, joyous gaze to him. "As am I."

Adelaide spent the remainder of the supper dance and much of the meal that followed inserting subtly into conversations the occasional comment about the tender scene that had played out between Miss Summerfield and Mr. Lexington as well as mentions of Odette and young Mr. Hewitt's kindness during that ordeal. She did not mean to draw attention to her efforts, simply to guide the impression the guests would leave with that night. The two couples would be thought of fondly. More to the point, they would be thought of *as couples.*

Maneuvering all that needed to happen that night had not been easy. Making certain Mr. Lexington engaged her for the supper dance so she could insist he abandon her for the role of rescuing knight. Getting enough people to stop and speak with Mr. Hewitt so that he would be near Miss Summerfield when her disappointment was first realized. Motioning Odette in that direction as the supper dance began. Literally bumping into Mr. Tolmer at the most opportune moment. She likely ought to find a means of compensating him for his ruined cravat and waistcoat. There was no means of secretly doing so monetarily.

He was quiet and unlikely to draw the notice of the young ladies of the *ton.* Yet, he was precisely the sort of goodhearted and devoted young gentleman who ought to be highly sought after. That might be the key to paying the debt he did not realize she owed him. She would, during her various assignments, watch for an opportunity to help him secure his future. Perhaps she might even find someone perfectly suited to the unassuming young gentleman.

Her efforts never truly ended. Every time she accepted a new post, she met new people struggling to find what they sought, struggling to secure a happy future rather than the one too often forced upon them by a Society far more concerned with wealth and power than the well-being of its sons and daughters.

So long as that held true, she would continue her work.

Ten

THE SEASON WOUND to its inevitable close. Most of the important families had or would soon abandon Town for house parties throughout the countryside before returning to their homes. Odette's family was no exception. Her belongings were packed and ready for placing in the traveling carriage. Mother was frantically directing the servants' efforts.

Odette stood outside Father's library, waiting. Mrs. Northrop was leaving London that day as well, but not with them. She had another assignment, this time in the country. While Odette suspected she would see Mrs. Northrop in Town in the Seasons to come, she would miss having her nearby. She had come to value the lady's straightforward, serene, calm approach to difficulties. She had also discovered a kindness beneath her originally implacable demeanor.

After a time, the door opened. Mrs. Northrop stepped out. She seemed only slightly surprised to find Odette there waiting. "Good morning, Odette."

"You are leaving." She hadn't intended to make such an abrupt declaration, but her mind had simply pushed the words out without softening them.

"It is time." Mrs. Northrop never was one for senti-mentality. "I did read the announcement in the *Times* last week. There is nothing left here for me to do."

Odette kept pace with her as she walked along the corridor. "You needn't remain as a matchmaker. You could simply visit as a friend."

"As much as I would enjoy that—and I genuinely would—there is a young lady in Dorset who is in need of my help."

Odette understood, but she was still disappointed. Perhaps she could yet convince her. "Dorset is not so very far from Somerset. You might at least make part of the journey with us, then visit for a time."

Mrs. Northrop shook her head. "When it is time for me to leave, I must do so. I have found it best."

"Is that your third rule?" Odette asked with a smile.

"It is."

She had not been expecting that.

"My third and final rule: arrive when I am needed and leave when it is time."

They had reached the landing of the grand staircase, affording a view of the entryway beneath.

Mrs. Northrop motioned to the space below. "Your sweetheart is here, no doubt to bid you farewell until he, too, returns home."

Odette hesitated. "You mean to leave immediately, don't you?"

"I do."

She gave in to the impulse and gave the often-prickly matchmaker a hug of sincere gratitude. "Thank you for everything, Mrs. Northrop. Please come see us in Somerset."

The embrace was returned gently and kindly. "You are most welcome, Odette. Now, off with you. If you wish to offer your dear one a kiss, now is your best opportunity. No one will be watching."

Odette slipped down the stairs to where Jack waited. Encouraged by Mrs. Northrop's light teasing, she threw her arms about him and buried herself in his arms. He held her tenderly but firmly.

He kept his arms around her as Mrs. Northrop passed. "Thank you, again," he said to the matchmaker. "We would have had no hope of this happy ending without you."

Mrs. Northrop tipped her chin upward the tiniest fraction. "This, Mr. Hewitt, is not an 'ending' at all. This is a beginning. What comes next depends entirely on the two of you."

Odette rested her head against Jack's chest. "I intend to be very happy."

"As do I," Jack said.

Mrs. Northrop nodded decisively. "Very good. See to it that you each decide to be happy and to do all you can to contribute to the other's happiness. I do not want to hear any different."

Jack pressed a kiss to the top of Odette's head. "'Take all my loves, my love, yea, take them all.'"

"Poetry, Mr. Hewitt?" Mrs. Northrop shook her head. "You very nearly managed this entire thing without a single stanza." She sighed. "I am sorely disappointed."

Jack laughed lightly. "I cannot help myself."

"It seems the young gentlemen never can." Mrs. Northrop turned and stepped through the open front door. Odette would miss her deeply. And she would forever think of the dear woman with deep, abiding gratitude.

"I love you, Jack." She knew how very fortunate she was to finally be allowed to acknowledge her love openly.

"And I love you, my dearest Odette."

Adelaide made herself as comfortable as possible in the traveling coach provided by the Brockton family for her journey to Dorset. She set on her lap the portable writing desk that had made these journeys with her the past five years. Inside its hinged compartment were the details of her next assignment.

She did not open it immediately but took a moment to watch the sights and listen to the sounds of London disappearing behind her. She had managed to help secure the futures of four people these past weeks, a fact she hoped Mr. Goddard noticed when he read the announcements in the copy of the *Times* she had sent him in Bath. She had renewed friendly associations. She had even met a few people who might very well benefit from her assistance in the years to come.

By all standards, this assignment had proven an unmitigated success. She looked forward to hearing how Odette and Jack, and Mr. Lexington and Miss Summerfield were getting on in life. Her correspondence was extensive and frequent. She loved it. She absolutely loved it.

It was time once again for her to take up the mantle of matchmaker and do what she could to guide a young lady toward a happier future than she currently anticipated. As always, she was tremendously excited.

She opened her portable desk and pulled out the sheets of paper topmost on the pile inside. Snapping the lid shut once more, she set the parchment atop it. She straightened the papers and tipped the desk a bit toward the light spilling in through the carriage window.

"Miss Brockton," she said, eying the list of information, "let us see what kind of challenge you have for me."

Sarah M. Eden is the author of multiple historical romances, including the two-time Whitney Award Winner *Longing for Home* and Whitney Award finalists *Seeking Persephone* and *Courting Miss Lancaster*. Combining her obsession with history and affinity for tender love stories, Sarah loves crafting witty characters and heartfelt romances. She has thrice served as the Master of Ceremonies for the LDStorymakers Writers Conference and acted as the Writer in Residence at the Northwest Writers Retreat. Sarah is represented by Pam Victorio at D4EO Literary Agency.

Visit Sarah online:
Twitter: SarahMEden
Facebook: Author Sarah M. Eden
Website: SarahMEden.com

Confections and Pretense

-ANNETTE LYON-

One

IN THE BACK of Gunter's Tea Shop, Anne eased the back of a mold into a basin of tepid water, then slowly counted to ten before pulling it out again, just long enough to release the ice cream from the metal. With a practiced hand, she flipped the mold over so it landed perfectly centered on the waiting platter. Now came the tricky part: removing the ice cream without destroying the design. These desserts were a big reason wealthy Londoners and tourists stopped by the shop, which had a reputation to maintain. She gently lifted the mold, relieved when she saw the unmarred halves of a pear. She never breathed easy until she knew the ice cream had released properly.

The treat was an expensive luxury for many reasons, not the least of which was the ice required during months ice didn't naturally exist, making it a resource nearly as precious as gold. Ice harvesting happened months prior, and the ice was irreplaceable until next winter. Every bit that melted without making salable ice cream was money lost. But she hadn't ruined this batch; all she had to do to the pear halves now was put them together to make a seamless-looking piece of ice cream fruit and top them with sugar.

Anne rarely ruined molded ices anymore, but she remembered the disappointment of both Mr. and Mrs. Argus, the couple who ran the shop, when she was first learning the trade. She was immensely grateful that she'd never received punishments extending beyond the garnishing of her wages to pay for the lost supplies, or the occasional criticism yelled at her. After years of living in a boardinghouse, she'd heard plenty of horrible stories to well know that she had an enviable job. She had the opportunity to work in a safe, fashionable neighborhood, where the most powerful—and richest—Londoners spent their time. When she'd first come to Gunter's ten years ago, Mrs. Gunter had likely taken pity on her after learning that Anne had no family.

The shop relied on her during the warmer months because she'd become adept at making ice cream and working the molds. With summer upon the city, locals and tourists alike swarmed the area: Belgravia, Mayfair, and Hyde Park. Stopping by Gunter's Tea Shop for an ice had become the fashionable thing to do for both tourists and members of old families alike, so much so that young Freddie and the other serving boy, Conrad, practically ran back and forth between the tea shop and Berkeley Square, the park directly across the street, to deliver orders to the carriages carrying lords and ladies and who knew who else.

The flow of customers had ebbed over the last hour, which meant that closing time was approaching. Anne's feet and back ached, and her hips hurt something awful, yet she had a long walk to the boardinghouse ahead of her. She dreaded that journey as well as what waited for her on the other side. She would ready herself for bed, alone. Tomorrow, she would wake, alone. One after the other, her days looked remarkably similar, each one a drearier link on a never-ending chain that fettered her to her station.

Yet she often reminded herself that she had a much easier life than many old maids in similar situations, without family, connections, or money. She had a roof over her head, modest food to eat, and worn but serviceable clothing. She'd need to buy herself new boots soon, though. Her current pair was worn far past the point of scuffs and thin soles; they had multiple holes that required careful navigation, or she'd end up stepping into puddles and soaking her feet. She'd squirreled away coins here and there but was loath to spend any of her hard-earned money unless absolutely necessary; each penny taken from the jar under her bed represented a delay in fulfilling her dreams.

Anne's savings had begun as a way to forever avoid debtor's prison or, worse, living on the streets. But as the amount had grown, the seed of a dream sprouted, and over the years, it had grown into an expansive vision of opening her own sweets shop one day. She'd worked in Gunter's for so many years that she knew plenty about the process of creating sweets and cakes. She'd learned much about bookkeeping—something made possible by having had some education as a child. She knew how to read and write and do basic arithmetic. Most working-class women did not possess such skills. But then, she hadn't been born into the working class. She'd simply landed there.

What she lacked to realize her dream were the physical resources—the equipment, the ingredients, and a location to rent. The whole concept was little better than a flight of fantasy, of course. But that daydream, however remote, kept her warm in particularly dark, cold times, whether that meant winter nights under too-thin blankets or during dark times of the soul.

In preparation for closing, young Conrad was already sweeping the front-end floor and wiping down the dusty shelves, which held jar upon jar of colorful sweets. Many were arranged so as to be visible from the street. The result was that the flavored drops, marshmallows, and other treats wooed passersby inside with their siren calls.

The front door opened suddenly, making the bell on its ribbon jangle in protest. Ten-year-old Freddie raced inside and kept going until he reached the kitchen and finally stopped opposite Anne across the counter. Assuming he'd come for the latest order, Anne dusted sugar on top and then handed over the dish with the iced pear. "Here you go."

She'd assumed that the pear was the final order for the day, but Freddie's red cheeks and heavy panting told her otherwise, as did the fact that he didn't take the proffered dish. He didn't so much as acknowledge it.

"One more . . . order," Freddie said between pants. "For a man . . . and woman."

She could have guessed as much; treats for courting couples to share during a carriage ride tended to be the most common orders. Anne set the dish with the completed pear in front of Freddie. "Don't let that melt before you get it out to the Cavannagh sisters."

His eyes darted downward and then back up, as if he'd only then remembered the previous order. Anne tried again. "What is the new order?"

"Orange-blossom."

Now they were getting somewhere.

"My favorite." She turned to the ice chest to pull out that particular tub of ice cream, which was yet half-full while other flavors had run out hours ago. She'd never understand why some people chose ice cream flavored with roses, violets, or jasmine when they could partake of orange-blossom, a taste at once both invigorating and delicious, equally tart and sweet. Worse were the savory flavors, which Anne had tried, and failed, to convince Mr. and Mrs. Argus to abandon—flavors like coriander, artichoke, and Parmesan cheese. So long as patrons requested grated Parmesan cheese in their ice cream, she was told, they'd get it.

She set the container of orange-blossom ice cream on the counter. "Which mold?"

Freddie leaned farther over the counter and whispered, "They're *American*." His tone suggested that he'd have been in just as much awe had he come across a pair of chimpanzees in the carriage instead.

"Are they asking for something treasonous?" Anne asked with mock fear.

"I don't know." Freddie's mouth drew down into a pout as he pondered her question.

She doubted whether the ten-year-old had any fear of Americans because of the War of 1812. He was young enough to not remember it at all. Perhaps he was in awe of Americans who spoke a different flavor of English. His parents might have instilled a fear or a hatred of Americans.

For her part, Anne had never viewed America as her enemy. Rather, she yearned to live there. Not because of any war or other political reason, but because in America, she might be able to take her hidden dream out of its home in a tiny corner of her heart. In America, she could dust it off, bring it into the open, and make it a reality. Societal rules and laws in England bound her to the station in which she'd found herself after her family members' deaths.

She'd long spent her days thinking of the many if-onlys that would have kept her from this life. If only one of her three brothers hadn't perished in the Napoleonic wars, she wouldn't need employment to survive. If only her parents hadn't died of consumption, she would yet have a monthly allowance. If only she had a living brother to have inherited the family estate, she would still live in the townhouse she'd grown up in—which, though not ostentatious or high class, had been comfortable, familiar, and warm. Now it belonged to some far-flung uncle she hadn't known existed. The boardinghouse would never be home, no matter how many years she lived there.

Oh, please don't let me die a gray-haired woman there, Anne thought.

Freddie slapped both hands onto the counter. "Hurry!"

She blinked and returned to the moment. "Whatever they're asking for, I'll make their dessert perfectly," she assured him.

"Will *you* bring it out to them?" Hope, and a hint of fear, laced each word.

"Why?" Anne almost laughed, but his serious expression kept it in check.

"I'm afraid I'd drop it right there on the street and look a fool."

Despite herself, the corner of Anne's mouth went up a little. "The Americans are intimidating, are they?"

"I'd *like* to bring the ice to them, but I just know I'd trip over my feet doing it." He cupped his mouth with both hands. "Conrad would never let me hear the end of it."

Anne couldn't look into his young, hopeful eyes and deny him, so, despite her aching feet, she agreed. "Very well. I'll do it for you. Just this once."

"Oh, thank you, Miss Preston."

Holding back a smile, she reached for a paddle to scoop the ice cream. "Which mold?"

"Er . . ."

Her head came up. "What?"

"It's . . . the basket."

"Oh, goodness." Another reason Freddie was concerned—they'd ordered the most complicated ice. Tripping and spilling a pear or apple would be one thing, but ruining an intricate design like the fruit basket would definitely be another thing altogether. The detail at the bottom looked like a real woven basket. The rim had yet a different texture, like a twisting vine, and the whole was topped with a pile of various fruits. Even the texture-rich pineapple mold was easier to work with than the basket.

Now *she* was the one who felt uneasy. "Go help Conrad with cleaning up front," she told Freddie so she wouldn't have the boy looking over her shoulder and making her even more nervous about ruining the order.

"Yes, miss," Freddie said cheerfully, as she'd lifted a great weight from his shoulders.

She turned to making the ice cream basket, filling the mold with orange-blossom ice cream. The smell always made her smile. When it was time to release the mold, she held her breath and lifted it—oh so slowly. She'd created a nearly perfect basket half. By some miracle, the other half released just as easily. In one spot, the woven pattern lacked the ideal crisp edges, but she hid the imperfection by pressing a few sweet drops into the ice cream, making them look like an intentional garnish. Mrs. Argus might not approve of serving an imperfect item, but Anne had learned that if customers didn't know what something was supposed to look like, they rarely had any idea that the one served to them wasn't precisely correct.

With the basket assembled, she carried it to the front of the shop, suddenly glad that the boys weren't delivering this dessert. If the Americans were indeed influential and important, this delivery needed to be worthy of their station.

She knew a sight more than they did about such things, and she'd seen both boys making mistakes as they rushed about like puppies with feet too big for their bodies.

While waiting for a carriage to pass, Anne searched the other side of the street. As suspected, the area had largely cleared for the day. Instead of carriages dotting the place and young women eating their treats while their gentlemen friends casually leaned against the carriages, Berkeley Square Park held only one carriage, though several small groups milled about the paths. She headed straight for the lone, shiny carriage. As expected, the door was open, revealing a young woman in a fine lavender gown. A tall man leaned back against the carriage, one knee up, with the flat of his boot on the side, arms folded. His top hat was tilted forward, covering his eyes as if he slept. This man wasn't the driver, who yet sat on his perch.

While Society frowned upon a young woman being seen alone with a man in almost any public place, if that location happened to be Berkeley Square, particularly across from Gunter's Tea Shop, the situation was usually deemed respectable—fashionable, even. Was that because most such occurrences took place with dozens of others as witnesses? If so, would this situation count against the young lady? Surely not. They'd come to Gunter's Tea Shop, a most distinguished and proper business.

Does that mean there is something inherently moral about ices and sugar drops? She smiled and shook her head slightly. *If I live to a hundred, I'll never understand the rules of Society.*

She could make out the woman inside the carriage, who peered through the opening. Anne had never seen a couple in such an arrangement. Usually men and women came during the afternoon heat when they could use a bit of cooling off, and definitely when the park thronged with others doing the same. Most often, such customers were courting. She'd often seen couples talking animatedly, often coyly on the lady's part, as the gentleman preened like a peacock. More often than not, they walked together near their carriage, the lady's arm through his, as they waited for their dessert. Anne had no recollection of ever seeing a woman quietly fanning herself while the gentleman dozed some distance apart.

When Anne reached the carriage, she stopped before the man and held out the tray, but he didn't stir. The woman inside the carriage closed her fan, reached out, and playfully swatted his arm.

"Wake up, Davis. Surely the day hasn't been such a bore that you must recover from it already." Indeed, as Freddie had said, she sounded American. Not that Anne had heard so many Americans speak, but this woman's accent was assuredly foreign.

Anne's eyes widened. She'd never heard a woman speak to a suitor in such a familiar tone. She waited for the man to react with shock or annoyance, but he remained so motionless that she wondered idly if anyone would notice a difference were he to stop breathing altogether. How would anyone know?

Unsure what to do next, Anne ground her boots into the sandy path a bit, hoping the sound would rouse him. When that failed, she looked at the woman, suddenly unsure who expected to be spoken to and who would pay for the ices. *Not a woman, even an outspoken one. Of course not.*

In jovial exasperation, the woman shook her head, then swatted his arm with her fan a second time. "Shall I eat the entire ice cream by myself? I'm quite capable, but I suspect you'd regret the decision."

The man finally responded, lifting his chin enough to

look at Anne through the slit under his hat through barely open lids. "Mmm?"

"Your ice cream?" Anne said, offering it.

"Yes, of course." He'd spoken but a few words, but he, too, had the same accent. With one knuckle, he nudged his hat back into place and tugged off one of his gloves as he stepped away from the carriage. He reached into a vest pocket and withdrew several coins but didn't count them. "I'm afraid I haven't quite figured out your money system—it's far more complicated than American cents and dollars."

A tiny thrill went up her spine at the confirmation of them being from America rather than some other country. She wanted to pepper the couple with questions about where they lived and about what life was like there.

He held out his bare hand, palm up. "Take what you need—the cost of the ice cream, plus a little something for your trouble." At the last, he smiled at her, and she suddenly felt like a besotted maid of fifteen rather than the old maid of twice as many years that she actually was.

"I'm sincere." Holding his hand out a bit closer, he added, "If you were an unscrupulous woman, I'd never know it anyway." He chuckled at that, a comfortable sound that made Anne want to wrap herself in his laugh like a warm blanket on a winter night.

She considered the pile of shiny coins, which to her represented so much more than shillings and pence and pounds. She was so used to thinking in terms of months of rent and days of food that at first her mind went there. He held nearly a year's worth of rent in his palm. But that thought was quickly displaced by another: she could rent out a shop for that amount, at least for a few months, and possibly equip it, besides. Suddenly, images of supplies fluttered through her mind like so many birds passing by—copper funnels, pewter freezing pots, large wooden tubs, design tools, molds of all shapes and sizes . . .

What would it be like to have so much money that you wouldn't mind being vastly overcharged on your luxury dessert?

She raised a hand and counted out the correct amount for the ice cream, plus a standard tip of thruppence. She could have taken three half crowns, and he wouldn't have been the wiser, but her conscience would never have allowed that. With the removal of each coin, she felt sharply aware of her work-worn fingertips touching the warm, soft skin of his hand.

His was not the skin of a servant. She'd known as much upon first seeing him, of course, aside from the obvious fact that servants did not have the resources to buy ices. But something about being close and seeing the truth herself made his position in life a reality. Hands could not lie, and this man's showed quite clearly that he did not work with them for a living.

With the coins tucked into her apron pocket, she looked up at the American and took in his features clearly for the first time. He had a strong nose and jaw that could have been intimidating were it not for his genuine smile. She couldn't help herself from smiling back in return, even as her middle flipped about. *So handsome. And not so young. He's married, no doubt.*

She ripped her gaze away and stared at the ground, but a hair too late; heat was already rising up her neck and would soon color her face red. He had nice boots, but though newly polished, they bore signs of wear. Not at all what she would have expected from a rich man who could, no doubt, buy a wardrobe full of the most expensive boots if he had a mind to. She'd have guessed that he bought multiple new pairs of boots each year to stay up with the trends.

"Have a nice day," he said, tipping his hat.

She looked up again to acknowledge him—it would have been rude not to—and admired his handsome face before she bobbed a curtsy and headed back across the street.

Rich, but not so young, she thought as she entered the tea shop once more and remembered the faint signs of gray hair at the sides of his face and the lines about his eyes made from a mature life and much laughter. *And American.*

After entering the tea shop, she closed the door and then stepped into some shadows near the front windows so as to not be easily visible from the outside. She watched the man—Davis, he'd been called—hold out the iced basket to his companion, who'd exited the carriage, and the two of them partook of the orange-blossom treat.

I should have asked them something about America, she thought. *And I should have asked for her name. Is Davis his family name or his Christian one?* No Englishwoman would call even a close associate by his Christian name while in public, but did America have similar conventions?

She had so many questions about America.

Any one of them would have been most improper coming from someone of her station, but as she stood in the shadow of the shop and watched through the window as the man and woman ate spoon after spoon of ice cream, she couldn't help but hope that this Davis fellow would stop by the tea shop again.

Is he married? She did not care to examine the question closely, as such a path of thought inevitably would lead to happy ideas of matrimony for herself—something long since out of her grasp. At one and thirty, she might as well wish for the late Napoleon to ask for her hand.

With a sigh, she went to the door and hung the sign that read *CLOSED.*

Two

DAYS CAME AND went, but Anne simply could not keep her thoughts on her work. Every time the bells on the tea shop door jangled, her heart leapt to her throat. She didn't think the American would actually step into Gunter's Tea Shop, but the slim possibility existed, and her frayed nerves insisted on assuming that he would materialize before her, *and* that it would happen the one time she didn't look up at the sound of the bells.

He never appeared, of course. Not in the tea shop, and not in the park, either. While she couldn't see across the street from her post in the kitchen, she'd made sure that the serving boys knew to alert her in a trice if they saw the American again. As a reward, she promised a sweet to *both* boys if either one brought her news of the man.

Once more, she was closing the shop without buying the boys sweets. She drew the drapes and locked the front door.

Despite the shop's closure to the public, the day's work wasn't finished. Mrs. Argus had left half an hour before, and the serving boys would finish tidying up front before going home, per usual. Anne would stay at least another hour, decorating a cake to be delivered to the Millennium Hotel in

Grosvenor Square. She usually enjoyed decorating cakes in the evenings, when the bustle of the workday quieted, when she wasn't in the noisy boardinghouse, and when she could be alone with her thoughts.

She plopped a copper tip into a canvas piping bag, which she filled with icing. Each sound seemed amplified by the empty silence of the shop. As she worked, piping rose petals on a flower nail and sliding them into place onto the cake, her mind kept trailing back to the American and the moment she first saw him leaning against the carriage with his hat tilted over his eyes. His height when he straightened. His voice and contagious smile. The soft warmth of his hand when she plucked the coins from his outstretched palm. She did her best to banish every resurfaced memory, but they kept returning.

We exchanged but a few words over the course of perhaps a minute, she thought, frustrated with herself. She'd spent more time than that bartering with a seller at a flea market over an old ring. She had no memory of that man's voice or what he'd worn, yet she could remember every detail about the American, down to the navy stitching on his coat. Her mind homed in on the man's eyes—dark. Not brown, and not blue, but dark gray, like storm clouds or fog on the Moors. Her insides flipped at the memory, and then she promptly berated herself for conjuring the image at all.

She rotated the cake to an empty spot still in need of roses. With a sigh, she continued piping and carefully sliding roses into place, but she felt no satisfaction over the beauty in what she was creating. Rather, she wished for noise over solitude, something entirely unlike her. She wished for people to surround her and make noise so she could stop thinking about a specific—handsome—stranger.

He was being friendly, nothing more. Her thoughts were the sound and logical ones of a seasoned old maid. All the same, a crumb of hope, even if nothing but a fantasy, refused to be dislodged.

When at last she finished the cake, she stood back and admired it. She really did have a hand at such things. Oh, to have her own shop—her own piping bags and tips, her own ingredients and recipes, her own bowls and spoons and cupboards. Her own customers. Sometimes, if she remained alone in the shop, she could almost believe that she owned the place. The cake before her had been made by her hands, yes. But not with ingredients she'd purchased, nor baked in an oven that belonged to her.

Someday.

For now, she needed to get the cake to the Millennium Hotel. She glanced at the clock on the wall and amended her thought: she had to get it to the hotel *quickly.* Daydreaming about handsome strangers apparently made time rush by. The order indicated that the cake was to be delivered by nine o'clock, and it was already eight thirty. On a typical day, she could walk the distance in a matter of ten minutes, but with a cake in hand, even one like this, with only a few layers, she'd have to move slowly and carefully. That necessary care doubled the time required to cross the distance. And the hotel cook would require an opportunity to prepare it for its presentation to the guest of honor—a wealthy gentleman from the continent, she'd gathered.

She could get there in time, but just. She had no more than a few minutes to spare.

Quickly, she transferred the cake from the old pedestal to the center of an unfolded paperboard box. With the cake in the center, she scored the corners, folded the box about the cake, and tied the whole of it with twine for carrying. She left through the back door and headed into the alley, then down the street toward the back of the Millennium Hotel. Vigilance marked her every step until at last she reached Grosvenor Street and headed into the wide passage adjacent to the hotel stables. The way was paved by cobblestones, but that was the only real separation between it and the stables themselves. The distinction was enough to ensure that the section she had to pass through was typically clean, if visible from the horse stalls. The day had seen no rain whatsoever, so she had no need to avoid slippery patches of wet or muddy cobbles, which made her passage that much easier.

Halfway to the servants' entrance, she heard voices that made her stomach twist uncomfortably.

"Pretty little thing, she is," the first said. "Don't you think so?"

"Old, I'd say," the other said. "A bit too long in the tooth for my taste."

Those were the voices of the stable hands, Hank and Eric. They enjoyed taunting anyone who wore a skirt, girls and women alike. She'd known them long enough to be aware that they were mostly bluster, though she'd heard rumors that one or the other had been in a fistfight not too long ago.

Bluster or not, I'd like to be seen as someone other than an old maid good for nothing but teasing. She was certainly aware of her spinsterhood; she didn't need to be reminded or mocked because of it. With a party going on at the hotel, why weren't the hands busy? Whatever the reason, here they were, creating their own entertainment at her expense.

Hoping to get inside before the men decided to create any additional mischief, Anne increased her pace. She held the box securely with both hands, but she hadn't gone more than two steps before both men hopped over the edge of the stalls, ran ahead of her, and blocked her way to the short staircase that led to the entrance. She sighed, not in the mood to contend with young men who acted like boys or to be the target of their teasing. She leveled her best old-maid stare at them in the hopes that they might have had instilled in them some modicum of the value of respecting their elders.

"Hey, old lady," Eric said in greeting.

While the two had never caused her any serious harm, they were certainly regular burrs for her. They'd tripped her more than once, irredeemably staining her best work dress. *If they trip me tonight, the cake will be outright ruined,* she thought with dismay. *And they'll see it as a hilarious joke— might even eat the smashed mess. And I'll have to report to Mrs. Argus that the diplomats didn't get their cake.* She didn't want to think what Mr. Argus would say. His wife would be bad enough.

"I have a delivery for the hotel," Anne said evenly. "Let me through, or I'll take it up with the prime minister."

"Oh, ho ho," Hank said with exaggeratedly wide eyes. "The prime minister, you say?"

She had no idea which world leaders were in the hotel at the gathering, only that there were representatives from around the world, including important leaders of Great Britain. But mentioning the prime minister couldn't hurt, and after all, he *might* be inside. Instead of giving a yes or no answer, she simply leveled another look at Eric, and then a matching one at Hank. "Let me pass. The cook is expecting the cake now."

Instead of answering, Hank elbowed his mate. "She's *so* old." Both wore ridiculous grins as if they knew where to poke and prod to get the desired reaction from her.

She lifted her head and pulled her shoulders back, looking first Eric and then Hank in the eye. "You must excuse me, *boys*," she said, making a special point to emphasize the last word. "This old maid has work to do."

Hank jutted his chin out as if pointing to the cake box. "Who's it for?"

"Not for you." Anne took a step to the side, hoping they'd take the hint and move over to make room for her to pass.

"Just give us a peek," Eric said.

"Yeah," Hank chimed in. "And a small bite for me?"

"A bite for each of us," Eric clarified. They laughed uproariously at that. Anne groaned silently again and gripped the box even tighter even as Eric went down one stair and said, "Come, give us some."

A heavy step sounded on the hard ground behind Anne, followed by a deep voice she'd imagined hearing for days now. "Stop at once."

With a start, the boys' heads came up, and she turned to see who was behind them. Visible back a couple of yards to her right stood the American. Anne's cheeks went hot; matching pink was surely creeping up her neck. He couldn't have known that she'd thought of him hundreds of times over the last four days. She'd honestly believed she *wanted* to see him and had been genuinely disappointed every night when she hadn't. But now, there he stood, in a smelly stable, right before her, and she wished she were anywhere else.

"Get away from the young lady," the man ordered, stepping closer. He sounded tense, with each word clipped, as if he was holding back anger. "That's an order. Move away from her and allow her passage. *Now.*"

To an outsider, the situation likely did look much worse than it was. "Sir," Anne said, hoping to assuage his worries. "I'm quite—"

But before she could say another word, the man raised his walking stick and quickly walked past her, toward the stable hands on the stairs. "Get away from her now. And yes, she is a lady to you. I assume even sewer rats can grasp the basic decency involved in respecting a woman." As if to punctuate the seriousness of his threat, he raised his walking stick, this time holding it with both hands like a cricket bat.

113

At the sight, Hank and Eric scampered down the steps and toward the stables like startled mice. The American followed them to a stall where they apparently were hoping to go undetected. Walking stick still in the air, he said, "You two are a disgrace."

Anne couldn't see the hands anymore, but she could certainly hear tremulous fear in Eric's voice when he spoke next.

"P-please—" He sounded incapable of more speech so long as the black walking stick was held in the air above him.

The American squinted slightly as if measuring the mettle of the stable hands. He was older, clearly, yet in spite of a life that prevented calloused hands, he seemed plenty strong enough to take both men if the need arose. "You should know that I spent my childhood in a rebellious former colony, learning the ways of the world. Part of that means I never run from a fight. It also means I've been known to land plenty of punches and break my share of noses."

Hank made a strangled noise. For her part, Anne had to stifle a laugh. The American lowered his walking stick and made a show of tugging on his suit cuffs and smoothing his coat. "Truth be told, I rather miss fighting. It's been too long since I've had the opportunity to have a really good brawl. But alas, you rodents aren't worth my effort tonight. Unless . . ." The trailing off of his voice was accompanied by the tilt of his head and a silent implied threat.

In the gap between the stall and the ground, she could see Hank and Eric scooting backward, sending straw all over. They succeeded only in backing into the stall edge.

"We won't bother her," Hank said in a rush.

"We won't," Eric agreed. "I swear it on my father's grave." His tongue had apparently loosed.

The man drew nearer, his walking stick now resting over

his shoulder as if it were nothing of consequence. "Do you swear to leave this young lady alone? I mean not just tonight, but every moment hereafter?" His booming voice seemed to echo throughout the cavernous structure. "Both of you?"

"Yes," both men said at the same time.

"Good. Now get out of here." The walking stick swooped through the air and pointed toward the street.

The stable hands scuttled away into the darkness. Anne pressed her lips together to keep herself from saying anything, though she did wonder if they'd sneak back to finish their work, or if they'd simply run home in abject terror. After their footsteps had faded, the American lowered the stick and turned about to face Anne. She fully meant to thank him for his aid, though it hadn't been precisely necessary, and then hurry the cake inside to the hotel cook.

Instead, she stood there still as stone because he was walking toward her, closer and closer. She was quite sure her limbs had gone numb. She'd drop the cake to the ground at any moment. Yet she couldn't tear her eyes from the man, who was even handsomer than she remembered, which didn't seem possible. He stopped only an arm's length away and lifted his hat with a nod, as if she were of the upper class and not a woman whose every dress was old, whose face was becoming lined, and whose days were spent working so she could live another day.

"Th-thank you," she managed, as breathless as if she'd run a mile.

"My pleasure, I assure you," he said with a half bow. He glanced over his shoulder and shook his head. "Those scoundrels . . . did they hurt you?"

"N-no." Anne shook her head to emphasize the word, and the movement seemed to bring her out of her frozen state. "I'm quite well, thank you."

Except a bit addled in the head.

He extended a hand. "Davis Whitledge at your service."

She eyed his hand, surprised at the overture, but then, balancing the box in her left hand, reached out the other and allowed him to take it. "Anne Preston."

American etiquette had to be very different if a man could be so forward as to introduce himself in such a manner instead of being properly introduced by a shared acquaintance. And to do so in such a low place, alone, without a chaperone—

Her eyes widened with realization at how this situation might be interpreted by an onlooker—a single woman alone with a man. She tried to wipe her reaction from her face as quickly as it had appeared so as not to offend. "I truly must get inside." She nodded to the box bound with twine. "This cake is needed inside right away."

"Oh, of course," Mr. Whitledge said; but instead of leaving, he slipped past her, took the four stairs in two bounds, then held the door open for her.

No man, as far as she could recall, had ever held open a door for her. A warm spot bloomed in her chest. *He truly is a gentleman.*

She went up the steps and crossed the threshold, all the while oh-so-aware of how close Mr. Whitledge stood. Her dress sleeve brushed his coat, and the masculine scent of him came over her—far too briefly. One breath of it, and it was gone. It left every hair on her arms standing on end. Once inside, she turned about. "Thank you, Mr. Whitledge." This time, her voice sounded even and soft, perhaps because the intent behind her words was so sincere. He might assume she was thanking him for saving her from Hank and Eric, but she was really thanking him for treating her with the utmost kindness, as if she were more than a working woman or a servant. He'd treated her like a gentlewoman.

"It was my pleasure, Miss Preston." He gave one final half bow and tip of his hat, then released the door.

Anne stood there as if in a dream as the weight of the door settled into place and the latch clicked shut. She didn't want to move, not yet, so she stood there, letting her mind gather details of what had transpired as if picking up pebbles on a path. She needed to capture the moment, commit every detail about him and what had just happened to memory.

Whenever something pleasant happened to her, she made a point of doing that very thing—capturing and treasuring it. She did so partly because truly pleasant moments tended to be rare in a life such as hers, and partly because holding such experiences close allowed her to live them anew when reality grew dark and dreary. First when she grew too old to be considered a marriage prospect, and then when, one by one, she lost her family members, and later still, when she had to find a way to support herself in the world, she'd reexamined the cherished memories she'd saved and tucked away in her heart. During particularly lonely and hard times—like last winter, which was so cold that her little bottle of ink froze in her room at the boardinghouse some nights—she endured by selecting a memory, opening it slowly like a priceless gift, and reliving every second of it, down to the tiniest of details. Therefore, the more she memorized after something good happened, the better.

Still holding the cake, she almost felt as if she were embracing a loved one. She closed her eyes and relived the interchange. She might have added a few details that bordered on fictitious, ones that would certainly make the recalling of the memory that much happier the next time she needed a lift in spirits. The ritual wouldn't take long, but until she'd finished it, she couldn't make her feet move. When she finally opened her eyes, she had an urge to open the door, peer into the stables, and see if Mr. Whitledge was still on the other side. But no. That would serve only to pop the newly created soap bubble of a memory. And she wouldn't do *that* for the world.

She was vaguely aware of quick yet heavy footsteps along the stone corridor and a voice speaking to her. "There you are. I was getting nervous that the cake wouldn't arrive in time." A portly woman, whom Anne would have once upon a time called middle-aged or even old, but who was probably forty-five, took the box from Anne's hands and shuffled away with it.

With the cook's words and the movement, Anne's happy moment officially ended. She looked about, blinking, as if she needed to reorient herself to the real world. A grandfather clock nearby gonged, and she looked over at it. Nine o'clock. The cake would need to be transferred to a serving platter before being wheeled out on a fancy cart to be presented to the gathering of diplomats. It wouldn't appear at the party for another five minutes at least.

Anne leaned back against the door, smiling slightly as she let the warmth of Mr. Whitledge's smile and concern wash over her, not caring in the least that the party guests would need to wait for their cake.

Three

DAVIS WHITLEDGE MAINTAINED his gentlemanly composure only until the door to the servants' entrance had securely clicked into place. For the sake of woman on the other side—Anne, her name was—he'd tamped down his righteous indignation, but knowing that she was now safely inside the hotel, he couldn't keep still. Those stable workers needed to be taught a lesson. Plenty of places in London were dangerous. An upper-class place like Grosvenor Square and its surrounding streets shouldn't number among them.

Not that Davis knew London all that well; he'd come with his best friend from their Harvard years, Peter Cowley, who now worked as a diplomat for the American government. Davis hadn't come along merely to see the sights, but to conduct business: find investors, widen his connections, and hopefully find other businesses he could work with for importing and exporting goods between England and the United States.

He'd heard plenty of horrifying things about the dirty, dangerous districts of London, which he hoped were exaggerations. He'd heard equally broad statements about the elite and expensive Grosvenor Square and its environs. People described them as the place where the highest in Society gathered and where to find the most elite—which meant the most expensive—places to dine and shop. Supposedly, this was where one could find the world's latest fashions, best foods, and more all gathered in a relatively small area of London.

When he first alighted from the carriage that brought their company to the hotel, he'd assumed that the talk about Grosvenor Square and such were exaggerations. So far, however, he'd found them to be quite accurate, a discovery that made him worry that perhaps the descriptions of poor, sickly, and crime-ridden areas of the city were equally real. The very idea made his stomach turn at the injustice.

Which brought him back to Miss Anne Preston—or was it Mrs. Preston? How she'd been taunted and nearly assaulted by two men who could have easily overpowered her small frame. One of them alone could have had restrained her with hardly any effort; Davis had no doubt of that. What evil could the two, working together, have done?

Though born of English immigrants, Davis was American through and through. As such, he struggled to grasp the English mentality of class and the etiquette demanded of such things. While certain people in America were most definitely considered higher class, the reasons usually amounted to money or education, though the two often went hand in hand. But in America, a man could pick himself up by the bootstraps and change his status; he wasn't bound to the station he'd been born into.

That was precisely where he lost understanding with the English, no matter how much he admired their literature, architecture, and art.

All these thoughts flitted through his mind in a matter of

seconds. He was briefly tempted to open the door and check on Anne, to be sure she hadn't been unduly upset over the encounter, but thought better of it. While he knew little about the rules of English etiquette, Peter had pounded one lesson into him: that a man and an unmarried woman should never be alone together. Such a thing might taint a man's reputation, but it would utterly destroy a woman's.

So no, Davis would not open that door to seek out Anne Preston, for her sake. That didn't mean, however, that he was finished with the matter.

With the side of his walking stick, he tapped his palm several times. From the top of the short staircase, he scanned the stables, hoping to find evidence of where the hands were now. He suspected that they hadn't left altogether, though they'd run into the dark street. They'd likely return to finish their work tonight. Had they run home? Although, come to think of it, did they *have* a home that wasn't part of the hotel and stables?

When he saw no sign of them, he stepped down the stairs slowly, one at a time. They were probably hiding from him until he left. Let them think he planned to. With each step, he used his walking stick to announce his presence. He even cleared his throat once or twice to be sure they'd hear where he was and that he was heading toward the street. When Davis reached the shadows outside the mews, he secreted himself behind a burnt-out lamppost and watched the stables for movement, hardly daring to breathe in case the sound, or the puffs of white air, would give him away.

After a few minutes, the men appeared, first moving cautiously, looking about the stables, then toward the servants' entrance, and even over their shoulders toward the street. They gave no sign of spotting Davis. Seemingly confident of being alone once more, they returned to talking and laughing—and to referring to Miss Preston in the most disrespectful terms. Their language was not as foul as he'd heard on the docks in Boston, but anything ill spoken of a woman sent a surge of protectiveness through Davis, the kind he felt for his elder sister Bonnie, who'd seen to his upbringing after their mother passed away in his infancy. He'd heard men on the street spreading lies about how Bonnie earned the money that kept him eating and their small flat from freezing. He knew they were all lies, for he'd seen her take on jobs to make every penny—laundry, ironing, mending, and more, until her hands were raw and chapped.

By the time he was grown and strong enough to stand up for his sister, to protect her from such vicious lies, she'd already taken to her bed for the last time. He'd forever regret being unable to avenge his sister's honor, yet in some small way, all of these years later, Anne Preston had lit a similar protective flame inside him. A small but undeniable flame. He could not protect Bonnie, but this night, he could make certain that Anne Preston returned to Gunter's Tea Shop unmolested.

Minutes passed, with little happening beyond the stable workers mucking stalls, feeding horses, scraping muddy rocks from hooves with a hook, and doing other mundane tasks. From his position, Davis watched the boys, never taking his eyes off them except to check the servants' entrance for any sign of Anne. Small and wiry, no doubt thin from constant work, she looked perhaps thirty or so. Close to the age at which Bonnie had passed.

Of course Anne Preston was not Bonnie, but she re-minded him of her, and he'd vowed to spend his life trying to atone for his sister's death. No matter how many associates assured him that it wasn't his fault, he could never convince himself. He'd been so occupied with his university studies that he hadn't noticed Bonnie's one brief mention of a fever in a single letter, or at least, it hadn't concerned him. She'd always been capable of caring for herself and anyone else.

In her typical fashion, Bonnie didn't want to be a burden to him. By the time he learned of the nature and seriousness of the illness and flew to her bedside, it was too late for him to do anything but hold her hand and offer what comfort he could. If only he'd asked her about the illness or inquired of her neighbors. Even when he left Boston to go to her bedside, he had to search to find her, as she'd moved to a tiny flat several blocks away. The room was scarcely nice enough for vermin to live in. She'd gone without coal to cook with and warm up by, managing to survive on raw vegetables—mostly potatoes—and near-freezing water to drink and bathe with. She spent her days wrapped in blankets over blankets so as not to freeze to death at night.

She'd done it all to give every possible penny to Davis for his schooling. He'd had no idea. He'd assumed that their father had set aside a fund for his education—and while that was technically true, it had been a paltry sum that hadn't lasted more than a few months. Bonnie supplemented the rest however she could.

He'd sat at her bedside, shedding tears and begging her to stay, promising to care for her no matter the cost. He didn't understand the full sacrifice she'd made for him, and wouldn't until after her quiet burial. *That* was when the rumors caught hold and spread like a flame set to dry bushes. First it was the whisperings of men and women alike as he passed. He overheard their words, their degrading tones.

He'd never been a dandy who drank his money or spent it on lavish clothing, art, or the opera. But during his university years, he hadn't worried about money. He'd never felt a need to flinch at purchasing a new book. He'd never worried over hiring a laundress or housekeeper or eating meat at most evening meals. None of those things seemed frivolous. Comfortable, surely. But he had plenty of friends who drank their family money, gambled it away, and indulged in the darker side of humanity by consorting with the kind of women Bonnie had been accused of being. Even so, his spending had cost Bonnie everything.

More than fifteen years after her death, Davis still found his hackles rising at the insinuation. His nostrils flared at the attacks his innocent sister had endured, and he wished he'd known they were happening. She'd done it all in the name of keeping a promise to their mother that Davis would get an education. As the only living son, he would carry on the family name with honor and have a beautiful life and posterity. He would be able to care for Bonnie in her old age . . . if she'd lived to see it.

Here I am, almost forty years old, with no wife or posterity, and no sister to support, either.

But he did have that Harvard education. Unlike his classmates, he'd had no family to witness his graduation. He'd plunged into starting his own business, yet he found himself often distracted by situations like these—by women who, due to no fault of their own, could benefit from help the way his Bonnie would have. Women like Miss Preston. This world was not a safe one for women, not when men like those despicable stable hands existed, and he viewed it as his duty as a man to stop such abuses wherever he could. He wouldn't be in London long, but he most certainly would take action to be certain that she would not be accosted in such a manner by those two sniveling, vulgar men ever again.

He'd done similar things in other cities when he could, but he did not recall many faces or names. But Anne Preston held his fascination and stoked the flame of protectiveness more than any woman he'd encountered in his travels. He knew instinctively that he'd remember her long after tonight and for more than the protective surge that reminded him of Bonnie. There was something more about her that held him captive.

The wood door of the servants' entrance finally creaked open again. Suddenly alert, Davis peered around the lamp-post, waiting. The stableboys did the same, standing from their chores, wiping sweat from their brows, and watching Anne Preston as she walked, head high, gaze straight forward, along the stone-paved walkway from the door to the street. She didn't look the least bit afraid.

Good on her, David couldn't help but think. *She's got a fire inside.* He admired the tilt of her lifted chin, how her shoulders were pulled back, how she walked with a stately air that almost seemed to belong to one of the women in ball gowns inside the hotel.

The party. Drat.

Peter was certainly waiting for him, though few others would notice his absence. He wanted Davis there, however; somehow his presence among the London elite was supposed to help elevate both his business and marriage prospects. Part of his mind said he should care about such things, but he always snorted whenever Peter brought up the topic.

Not that Davis didn't admire women. On the contrary. And he wasn't opposed to matrimony. But to make that kind of commitment, he would need to find a very special kind of woman—one who saw the world and its problems as he did. One who would not protest their wealth being spent—squandered, in some people's minds—on small acts of kindness that might forever go unseen.

Davis highly doubted he'd meet such a woman at an upper-crust ball at the Millennium Hotel. Most women in attendance wouldn't have the slightest concept of what the world outside of their personal experiences looked like. "Charity" to them would mean sending money to some far-flung mission in Africa to convert heathens, not helping the poor, sick, and indigent on the streets of their own cities.

He watched Miss Preston reach the street, his eyes darting to the stable hands every few seconds. Fortunately, while they stopped their work to watch her, they didn't approach or speak to her. And when she entered the darkness outside the stables, she let out an audible sigh of relief. For a moment, Davis felt the slightest bit guilty for watching her unawares, though his motives were good. The gentleman in him wanted to make sure she was aware of his presence, but speaking up right now would likely only startle her into a fright. Instead, he remained silent and walked a distance behind her all the way to a back alley of Berkeley Square, where she unlocked a door and went inside. When he heard a bolt click into place, it was his turn to breathe a sigh of relief.

He wanted to stay, to peer through a window to watch her work for a moment, to admire her profile and gentle eyes, the confidence each of her movements spoke of. But he'd already stepped beyond the bounds of propriety by secretly escorting her. Not to mention that Peter would be wondering at his absence at the ball.

Time to change into his best suit and make an appearance. Not at all how he would prefer to spend his evening, no matter how fancy the caviar and wine. He suspected he'd enjoy an evening in the kitchen of a sweet shop, watching Anne Preston at work and learning more about her—perhaps making her laugh or smile. *That* would be an enjoyable way to spend an evening.

He hurried back the way he came, but when he reached

the stables again, his step came up short thanks to the laughter and conversation between the two stable hands.

"Did you see her face?" one said.

"You mean when she looked like this?" The other must have been mimicking poor Miss Preston.

"Next time, I dare you to open the box and eat whatever's inside."

"Care to make it interesting?" the other said. "What will you give me if I do?"

Standing just outside the yellow lantern light of the stables, Davis felt his heart beat double time. His fists involuntarily clenched.

"I'll muck out your share of stalls for a week."

"That long?"

"But you must eat at least two bites of her delivery *and* kiss her."

"Kiss that old thing? That's a lot to ask. Make it *two* weeks."

"That old thing"? And wagering on kissing her? How dare they!

As much as Davis wanted to march into the stables and pound the boys, he knew that one must play by social rules. Oh, he'd go to the ball. And while there, he'd ask Peter for how best to handle the situation with the stable hands.

Because one thing was certain: if Davis Whitledge had anything to say about it, those fiends would never again have the opportunity to harass Anne Preston.

Four

DAVIS STORMED INTO the stables and planted his walking stick firmly on the ground. The hands looked up in surprise.

"I will say this once and once only. You will never again bother Miss Preston in any manner whatsoever. You will not speak to her. You will not block her way. You will not touch her, nor anything she carries. For the remainder of your days." He paused to let his words sink in, then added, in a confident but less demanding tone, "I assume I have made myself clear."

The men seemed stunned into silence. Davis didn't wait for a response. He spun on his heel, this time striding quickly until he was engulfed by the darkness of the street. He almost felt as if he were covered in a vile smell from his interactions. As he reached a streetlamp, he slipped his timepiece from his vest pocket.

Blazes, he thought. He knew he was late, but not that late. Peter would be wondering what delayed him, though at least Davis wouldn't get an earful about schedules and showing respect to a country's leaders during a diplomatic visit—not during the party. He'd surely hear it all later, in their adjoining suites. Clara had a way of diffusing tensions between the two friends, who were as close as brothers.

He returned the pocket watch to its home and increased his pace to round the hotel and enter from the front. He passed the tall white columns that lined the hotel's facade and glanced into the night-darkened square. He'd rather spend the evening meandering the paths—a pleasant respite from the bustle of the city streets. That was not to be tonight. Peter expected him to appear at the ball.

Davis hurried to his room, where he changed into his best suit. Not for a moment did he stop thinking of Anne, reliving every detail: her voice, her words, the strong shoulders and raised chin that told the stable hands that she didn't fear them. Her smile. Her warm eyes. He hadn't been taken with a woman in far too long—and had nigh unto given up hope of ever experiencing such a thing again.

It'll be some time before I forget the fire in those eyes and the sweetness of that smile, he thought as he tied his cravat.

He'd tired of young women practically throwing themselves at his feet, batting their eyelashes, speaking in a falsely high-pitched tone that he half expected to shatter crystal. Despite their fancy dresses and jewels, he found none of them appealing, and he was quite sure that they did not find him attractive, either. They found his reputation and success attractive. If he lost those things, they would never again look his direction. The fawning was nothing but pretense, as if they wore masks to hide their true selves. Not to mention that most were so young that he could practically be their father.

No, he found himself drawn to the rare woman whom he could enjoy a long conversation with, a woman with opinions of her own even if they differed from his. He enjoyed the women who made him think and challenge his own assumptions and opinions. He could not bear the thought of spending his life with someone who batted her eyes but had nothing in her head. The brief interactions he'd had with Anne told him that she did, in fact, think for herself. She had a tangible inner strength that he'd rarely seen in women. He found *that* undeniably attractive. Such strength was created through life and experience—through maturity. Girls newly out in Society quite simply could not possess such a thing. No, Davis wanted a *woman* to share his life with, not someone who functioned as a pretty decoration on his arm but left his emotional home and hearth barren and cold.

The closest woman he'd found to that description was his cousin Clara, who, as fortune would have it, married Peter two years ago. She'd proved to be a delightful addition to his life, with wit, brains, opinions, and even a striking, almost dangerous sense of humor when she decided to wield it. What he felt for Clara was nothing beyond brotherly affection—and she certainly seemed to have entirely taken on the role of sister, to the point that they could tease each other mercilessly. While he didn't love Clara in a romantic sense, her existence proved that intelligent, mature, pretty women did exist. At least one did.

Once, fifteen years ago, he'd fallen madly for Angelique, a French girl visiting the States. She'd toyed with his heart and then casually tossed it aside after her eight-month tour of America. He hadn't heard from her since and had no desire to, either. He'd never again allowed flattery, outer beauty, and that irritating high-pitched manner of speaking to distract him again. As his business had grown and he became known as a successful, wealthy man, more women than ever sought after him—something he found neither pleasant nor flattering. No, if he ever married, it would be to a woman who cared for him for the person he'd been before he made money, and who would love him even if he were to lose every penny.

He'd practically given up hope that he'd ever meet someone like Clara for himself. Naturally, cruel as fate was, the very kind of woman he yearned for might well have appeared in his path, living on the other side of the globe.

Davis made his way back to the ballroom, where a doorman bowed slightly and held a door open for him. Davis returned the bow, then smoothed one hand across his hair to ensure it lay properly. He sauntered into the ballroom without drawing undue attention to himself. Better yet, he spotted Peter and Clara in full evening dress, standing a pace off, each holding a flute of champagne as they listened to the prime minister speak at the front of the room.

Passing a waiter with a half-full tray, Davis retrieved a flute of champagne for himself, then took a spot beside Clara and pretended to be deeply engrossed in the prime minister's words. Neither Peter nor Clara noticed him for several moments, which gave him time to, he hoped, calm his heart rate, warm up from the outside chill, and look as if he'd been there the entire time. With the official business over for the evening, the throng shifted, and a murmur seemed to buzz in the room as people conversed with one another.

"Davis, there you are," Peter said.

"Yes, here I am," he replied, raising his drink as if in a toast. He took a sip and looked over the room. "Beautiful event," he added, looking about for the cake that must have been recently rolled out and presented to the room.

Can I not go more than two minutes without thinking on Anne Preston? He cleared his throat as if that would somehow set his thoughts on a different path. All the effort accomplished was making him more curious than ever to seek out the cake and admire the workmanship of Anne's own hands. He felt a slight weight on his arm and looked down to find Clara's hand there.

She seemed to be studying his face. "Are you quite all right?"

"Y-yes," Davis stammered.

Clara folded her arms. "*Very* convincing." Her raised brows and challenging tone said more than a ten-minute speech from Peter ever could.

Davis never could hide his feelings from Clara. She was better at divining them than Peter.

I cannot very well say that I'm enamored with the woman who made that cake. He took another sip of champagne. *But perhaps I can mention my concern for her.* Not for a moment did he believe that his command to the stable hands would be obeyed for longer than a few hours. No, much stronger action needed to be taken to ensure Anne's future safety.

"As a matter of fact, something is on my mind." He stared at the rim of his glass.

Peter must have heard, because he stepped closer, his arm circling Clara's waist, his eyes growing hooded. "What is it?"

"Nothing of a diplomatic nature," Davis assured him. "At least, I don't think it would be, unless we decide to make it one." Now he was thinking aloud, and his words made no sense.

Peter and Clara exchanged glances. She squeezed his arm gently. "Tell us. Perhaps we can help."

At once, Davis forgot any cause for embarrassment, any fodder for teasing the revelations about Anne could create. All of those fell away as concerns for himself dropped and his concerns for Anne Preston's well-being took precedence. "I came across something tonight that distresses me," he began. "I fear that had I not been where I was at the very moment I appeared, things could have turned out vastly different for a local woman."

He tipped his head toward the front of the room, where the cake was now in view thanks to the thinning crowd. It sat atop a silver pedestal in regal glory, with iced roses and lace covering the whole. How one could create such beauty left him almost breathless, but he managed, "It was the woman who made that cake, actually."

Peter glanced that direction but then stepped forward and put a hand on Davis's shoulder. "What is it, man? Tell us."

So he did, including his order to the stable hands. "I'm sure my words were about as biting as a toothless dog. They're bound to cause trouble again, and as Miss Preston seems to be a favorite target of theirs, I worry about her. I've laid eyes on her but twice, and yet—"

"When was the other time?" Clara broke in.

Blame it all. He shouldn't have said that. She and Peter would be that much more likely to tease him now. But his genuine worry for Miss Preston outweighed any prospective discomfort from the two of them, so he pressed on.

"She's the woman from Gunter's Tea Shop who served us the other day."

"Oh, yes," Clara said. "Beautiful girl. I was quite taken with her."

As was I.

"Come," Peter said, for once not seeming eager to jump on an opportunity to needle his schoolmate. "Let's speak with the hotel manager right now."

"Are you in earnest?" Davis asked even as he set his half-empty glass on a passing server's tray.

Peter did the same. "Absolutely. We'll demand those hands are dismissed immediately. If the hotel manager refuses, we'll remind him that I represent the United States, and that we will not put our own women at risk by patronizing a business known to harbor criminals." His mouth widened into a grin. "You see, diplomats from many nations stay at the hotel, and they must all be assured of their safety. I'll have two of my security men talk to the manager tonight." He sighed, pleased with himself.

"I like the way you think, my dear chum," Davis said.

For once, Peter's innate ability to get what he asked for come what may would benefit Davis.

Rather, it will benefit Anne, he thought. *Which, in this case, is the same thing.*

Five

IN SPITE OF Anne's attempts to distract herself from thoughts of Davis Whitledge, hours of repetitive work allowed her mind to drift. As she stirred icing and smoothed it onto layers of cake, or stretched taffy, or washed dishes, or as she did a thousand other things, her thoughts always returned to the handsome American who had hints of gray at his temples and crow's feet by his eyes from smiling so much.

Over and over she replayed the night he had appeared behind her to rescue her in the stables. Only in her mind, it was not Hank and Eric but nefarious pirates that Davis had saved her from, and not only a destroyed cake he'd prevented but her very death by walking the plank. At times, she almost believed her fanciful imagination and the variations it created as to what had really happened that night. Almost, but never quite.

Daydreaming helped to fill what was otherwise a lonely void in her life. For a few minutes at a time, she could feel like more than an old maid with no family, with days so monotonous that they all blended together into a single shade of gray. Without such daydreams, she did not know how she would live one day to the next without losing her sanity entirely.

But she did wish that one dream would vanish like so much morning dew on the grass: the idea that Mr. Whitledge would ever return to Gunter's. Her nerves were nearly shot thanks to the jingling bells on the door that rang each time it opened for customers going in or out. Each time, her heart jolted just a little more. No amount of reasoning that the person coming or going had nothing to do with the American could stop her heart from jumping.

And so it was three days after the night of the cake delivery, as she drizzled flavored and colored syrups onto a cool slab of marble, on which the syrup would harden in various designs. The door jingled yet again. Anne gritted her teeth and focused on the dragonfly shape she was drizzling with the syrup. She would *not* ruin the design and waste precious materials.

It is not him, she thought. *He is likely on his way back to America even now. I will never see him again.*

America. Now that was something worthy of her distraction. She felt her mouth curve into a slight smile as her thoughts drifted away once more, but this time across the Atlantic Ocean. She let her mind roam to some town near the harbor. She could see herself on a busy little street, setting up her own shop and having her own bells to announce the door. No, she'd use something else. Something prettier sounding than the bells at Gunter's.

As she was finishing her mental inventory of the many tools and implements and ingredients her personal shop would one day have, one of the young boys raced back to the kitchen. Anne glanced up, her gaze returning to the marble and her work, only to jump back up as she realized that Freddie's eyes were wider than they had been the day Mr. Whitledge first visited Gunter's. Her airway narrowed, and she struggled to keep her hands steady. She tilted the syrup bottle upward so it wouldn't spill.

"What is it?" she asked Freddie.

It cannot be the American. Yet the look on the boy's face said otherwise. *Maybe it's another American, and that's why Freddie's so excited. Or some very rich Englishman, or a member of the Royal Family. Or . . .*

"It's him," Freddie said breathlessly. He held up a shiny coin between finger and thumb. "Look what he gave me! Just for coming into the kitchen to tell you that he's here—inside the shop!"

Anne froze and gaped, staring at Freddie until he pointed to the counter. "Um . . ."

The single word thawed her enough to look down at the marble, only to find a veritable puddle of red syrup and the dragonfly designs blurred into unrecognizable blobs. On the instant, she gasped and quickly righted the little earthenware pitcher of syrup. Her normally quick reflexes seemed to have abandoned her, however. She could not think how to save the syrup. Indeed, the necessity of doing so seemed to have fled her mind, likely accompanied by her reflexes, wherever they'd gone.

"Will you go out to speak with him?" the boy asked, eyes sparkling. "He promised me two more pennies if you do."

"What does he want with me?" She stood there half-thrilled, half-terrified, her gaze lingering on the door to the front of the shop, as if she could see through it to see Davis Whitledge standing on the other side.

"He didn't say, except that he has something he wanted to speak with you about."

Freddie's reply drew Anne's attention back to him; she hadn't realized she'd spoken the question. She swallowed against the sudden knot in her throat, then reached for a damp dishcloth and wiped her sticky hands with it. They shook as if she were about to beard a lion in its den. Had she done something to unwittingly offend him? Should she go out to meet him? Would that be wise, or terribly foolish?

As if I have a say in the matter.

"Come," Freddie said, sounding a bit too much like a governess coaxing a child. He rounded the counter, then pushed her toward the kitchen door.

She didn't resist, at least, not much. Not that she could have, so weak were her knees, and her heart hammered against her chest like a bird trying to escape a cage. Before they reached the door, she took the boy's hands off her and handed him the dishcloth. "I can handle it from here," she said. Though truth be told, she wasn't all that sure she could. But she was not about to let Mr. Whitledge see her being pushed from the kitchen by a young boy.

The child gripped the cloth in one hand and gestured toward the door. "Go on, then." Again, he used a tone he must have heard from adults demanding behavior of him, which sounded strange and sweet all at once.

She smiled and ruffled his hair. "I'm going."

"Don't mess up my hair!" he said in the first and only instance of vanity she'd ever seen in him.

"I beg your pardon," Anne said, glad for the excuse to return to some levity. "I'd never wish to hinder your prospects by making you look any less distinguished."

"That's all right," Freddie said as if she'd been in earnest. With one hand, he tried to smooth any misplaced hairs, then added, "His lady friend said that when it lies flat, I look grown up."

The simple statement made Anne's step come up short. Her hands were already pressed flat against the door, ready to push it open, but she froze. *His lady friend.* A sudden flare of envy rose within her—a foolish, illogical emotion, considering how little she knew Davis Whitledge. She had no claim at all on him, other than the one in her daydreams.

She dared not encourage the boy to reveal anything more, as that would only make her more nervous. With bold steps, Anne pushed the door open and stepped through. Hopefully she did not look as flushed and nervous as she felt. She casually looked about the shop until her gaze landed upon Mr. Whitledge and his lady friend. Anne could not be sure, but the woman looked very much like the one from the carriage the first time she'd seen Mr. Whitledge.

If my brothers could fight Napoleon, I can face two unarmed Americans.

Anne strode bravely across the room. "Mr. Whitledge, it is a pleasure to see you again."

"And you," he said tipping his head in her direction. He held his top hat in one arm, his gloves draped over the edge, and gestured toward the lady with his other. "May I introduce my cousin, Mrs. Clara Cowley. I believe you crossed paths once before but did not get a proper introduction."

The jealous heat in Anne's breast retreated, and she smiled broadly at Mrs. Cowley. "A cousin. Indeed?"

Davis made the pretense of shock with a false gasp. "Hard to believe, I know. Who would've thought that my foppish university mate could fool such an intelligent lady as my cousin into joining him in matrimony?"

Mrs. Cowley lifted one eyebrow and tilted her head in challenge. "I am not entirely sure if that statement is more of an insult to my husband or a compliment to me."

"Perhaps I misspoke about the intelligent part," he said, eying Anne with a chuckle.

His cousin playfully swatted his arm with the back of her hand, then extended it toward Anne. "A pleasure to see you again," she said. "And a pleasure to be properly introduced, even if it had to be by my rather ridiculous cousin." She leaned forward slightly and mock whispered, "We tolerate him and let him think he's the smart one."

"Ah," Mr. Whitledge said, placing an outstretched hand on his chest. "I am deeply hurt."

The banter completely melted whatever ice had previously frozen Anne, and she laughed warmly—something she hadn't done with such freedom in some time. To think she'd ever felt a moment's envy of Mrs. Cowley. Unfortunately, the moment had only made Mr. Whitledge that much more admirable and attractive.

"I understand you asked for me," Anne said. "How may I be of service?" She forced herself to look between the two Americans, even with her cheeks heating into what had to be a remarkable shade of pink.

"Let's chat elsewhere," Mrs. Cowley said. "Come with us for a turn about the park. But please, call me Clara. I am not used to the British rules of etiquette and prefer to hear my Christian name. To my ear, 'Mrs. Cowley' will always be my husband's mother."

"Very well, *Clara*, but then you must call me Anne."

"Agreed." Clara slipped her arm about Anne's elbow. "You'll walk with us, then?"

Anne had never felt such inner turmoil at making a quick decision. Oh, how she would *love* to go outside and walk with Clara and Mr. Whitledge. But she could not up and leave the shop if she hoped to remain employed. "I would love to, truly, you have no idea how much. But I'm afraid that I must work—"

"Surely the shop can spare you for a few moments," he said.

What would it be like to never fear the consequences of such choices? To him and his cousin, the invitation involved nothing more than a walk. To a member of the working class, and a woman besides, it could mean losing more than she could afford to risk.

"Mr. Whitledge," she began.

"Don't you worry about that little detail." He walked toward the counter but slowed his step enough to turn slightly and speak over his shoulder. "But I must request that, hereafter, you call me Davis."

Anne thought she nodded agreement, but once more she couldn't move. Mr. Whitledge leaned against the polished wood and spoke with Mrs. Argus. "What is he doing?" Anne asked Clara.

With a pat on her arm, which was still in Clara's grasp, the latter said, "He is addressing the situation."

A moment later, Mrs. Argus took several coins from Davis and slipped them into an apron pocket. Straightening, Davis tossed two more pennies to Freddie, who'd waited patiently by the kitchen. The rotund Mrs. Argus patted her pocket and blushed, clearly pleased with the attention from Mr. Whitledge as well as the money he'd offered. As she turned to the next customer, Davis walked back to the women as casually as if bribing people were an everyday occurrence for him. Perhaps it was.

He clapped and rubbed his hands together. "Now, do I have the pleasure of escorting you two fine young ladies about the park?" He held out his elbow, offering it to Anne. Unsure, she took it, highly aware that she was about to exit the shop, in public, walking with each of her arms taken by a wealthy, influential person. Davis held the door open for them, and they passed through, after which they crossed the street into Berkeley Square, and he wound her arm about his again. Anne had long wished to be escorted somewhere—anywhere—by a man such as Davis Whitledge. But in all of her daydreams, she hadn't considered the small details of what such an event might feel like.

Now, a thousand little things about the new experience felt exciting, from the warmth and heft of his arm beneath her hand to the sound of his heavier footfalls beside hers. The reality of his tall, broad self. His very masculinity, which seemed both natural and powerful at once. She focused on every detail, committing them to memory, intent that when this day was over, she would be able to recall every moment and every sense—the sound of his voice and laugh, the scent of his soap, the rumble of his laughter in his chest.

As they walked about the park, she mostly listened to Davis and Clara talk about their home in Boston, the sights they'd seen so far in England, their observations and opinions on English food, and more. The longer they walked, the more Anne became aware of others staring as they passed. Rather, staring at *her*.

I must look like a dandelion trying to blend in with red roses.

Her boots were old, and she could not remember when last they'd been shined. Only her toes peeked out from her hem, which itself was thready and ragged. She couldn't bear to look at the upper-class people about the square; their expressions would ruin the moment—and future daydreams—for her. So she lowered her eyes and kept them trained on her feet. Soon she was aware of every crack and scuff on her boot tips. Each imperfection seemed to call out another way she did not belong in Berkeley Square or anywhere else in the Mayfair district of London.

As they rounded another corner, Clara stopped speaking—about what, Anne couldn't have said—and furrowed her brow, halting their progress and turning to Anne. "My dear, whatever is the matter?"

"Nothing," Anne said quickly, regretting her clear inability to hide her emotions. "I am quite well. That is, it's nothing—"

Thanks to Clara's words, Davis looked at her and leaned in. "It most certainly is something," he said. Then, addressing his cousin: "I'm not sure how this is possible, but she looks both feverish and peaked at the same time."

Before Anne could protest that she was not ill in the traditional sense, Clara said, "Come. Let us go sit on the bench over there. You must have some shade and some rest."

Anne nodded and followed their lead, grateful for the concern as well as for their literal support on both sides of her. "Everyone is watching me," she said under her breath as they reached the bench and sat on it, Anne still in the middle. "They're staring at me as if they know I don't belong with folks like you."

While in many respects, this moment was something out of a daydream, and she didn't want it to end for that reason alone, she also knew she couldn't bear the stares and shocked faces much longer.

For a moment, none of them said another word. Then, "Hmm," from Clara.

Davis leaned forward to look around Anne's form and asked Clara precisely what she was thinking. "What, pray tell, does that mean?"

"Oh, I don't think you could tolerate hearing my thoughts."

"I am a grown man, dear cousin, and older than you are. I believe I can withstand *an opinion*."

"Very well," Clara said. "I was going to tell Anne that I believe I know the reason for most of the stares, and I am quite sure it has precious little to do with Anne's position."

"Or lack of one," Anne said quietly.

"I believe," Clara said, gazing about the square as if taking in every glance and stare of every passerby, "that all of those women see you on the arm of my cousin, someone I have been told is considered to be quite handsome, debonair, and attractive, though he pales in comparison to my husband, of course."

Anne appreciated the gesture of loyalty, while Davis chuckled at it.

"I believe," Clara continued, "that most of what you are seeing is envy, and that, if given the option, they'd quite happily exchange places with you."

If Anne had felt flushed and weak before, she felt nigh unto fainting now. She kept her gaze on Clara, absolutely unable to look at Davis to see his reaction to the speculation. She expected him to laugh off the idea as a ridiculous notion.

He did laugh, but this time, it came out as a nervous, stuttering thing. He cleared his throat—twice—before saying, "Let's discuss something else, what say, dear cousin?"

Clara looked at Davis, then shifted her focus to Anne, grinning. "I do believe we've embarrassed him. Or I suppose *I* have. Though every word I said is true. They envy *you*, and not only because you are with him. You are far prettier than I believe you know."

Staring at her lap, clasping and unclasping her fingers, Anne said, "You are very kind, but I know quite well—"

"Clara is right." Davis spoke the words—just three— quickly and quietly, as if self-conscious, but also sincerely.

In surprise, Anne turned to him, mouth half open, unsure what to say.

Davis pressed his lips together as if in thought, then lifted his gaze to hers. "I don't mean about anything to do with me," he said quickly. "I mean the other part. Too many women with all the means in the world dress themselves up yet lack the very inner beauty that makes a truly beautiful woman glow from the inside. You, on the other hand, I must say, are the reverse: a diamond wrapped in a dress far below what is suited to your beauty." He tilted his head to one side. "To mix metaphors."

"Th-thank you." Anne had no idea what else to say, or if she could say another word at all. Her day had shifted once more into something entirely unexpected. A sliver of doubt inside her wondered if this was all part of an elaborate daydream she'd concocted. She'd blink and come back to the present at any moment, only to find herself icing a cake or drizzling images of fireflies on the cold marble slab. For a few seconds, a moment that felt suspended in time, she looked into Davis's eyes, felt their warmth, and let that warmth flow through her down to her toes. He meant the words he'd said.

He thinks I'm beautiful. She would definitely remember this day.

Clara's voice pierced the bubble of the moment. "I suppose we should tell her why we came today, don't you think?"

They hadn't come to walk with her about the square? Embarrassment snaked through Anne like a finger of ice, dousing the previous warmth. Of course they hadn't come to take her for a turn about the park and some lively conversation. They had some sort of other business. Perhaps they wanted to order a cake or another ice. This was a business transaction. Why had she thought otherwise for even a moment?

"What can I do for you?" she asked, hoping to return to her typical businesslike self. She prayed her face and voice would not betray her disappointment.

"It is not what you can do for us," Clara said, "but rather, something Davis here has already done for you."

Her head spun seemingly one direction and then another. Clara and Davis had surprised her several times already and were about to do so again. What could Davis have possibly done for her—bought her a copper bowl? She turned back to look at him, her brows raised in silent question.

He licked his lips before answering, seeming nervous suddenly. "Those stable workers will never again bother you. I made sure of that."

Anne's eyes narrowed in confusion. She looked back and forth between Davis and Clara. "I don't understand."

"After what he witnessed in the stables, Davis came to the reception at the hotel visibly upset."

"He ... he did?" Covering her mouth with one hand, Anne was almost too scared to hear what was coming next.

Clara nodded, looking pleased at being the bearer of such splendid news. Davis gave Anne a sheepish smile and a one-shouldered shrug. "I could not bear the thought of those scoundrels bothering an innocent woman again. Especially not you. It did not take much to convince the hotel to find other stable hands. They have much to gain by maintaining a good relationship with the United States, and the manager knows that Peter and I have some sway in the government back home."

He shifted on the bench to look at her better, and his face was one of sincerity and gravity. "It is wrong for any woman to have to fear simply while going about her work. I pray that whoever replaces those boys will be kinder and gentler. That they will treat you with respect. And if they don't, say a word, and they will be dismissed."

So many questions swirled in Anne's head, like colored sprinkles falling from a jar, tumbling into a jumbled pile.

Davis rested his hands on his knees. "That's what we

came to tell you today. Those boys have been dismissed, and you need no longer fear them."

How precisely did one tell one's rescuer that he'd overstepped his bounds? That he might have ruined the lives of those poor, if annoying, stable hands? That they might struggle now simply finding food to eat and might never secure another position of employment? To have been dismissed from a position at a place as respected as the Millennium Hotel would be a disgrace. They would not have letters of recommendation to take to prospective employers. They might wind up on the streets, surviving by committing deeds far worse than teasing an old maid.

But Davis does not know any of that. Goodness, life in America must be different.

He'd done only what he thought was the right thing to do. He was a good man, trying to protect and help.

"That was very kind of you," she said. "I appreciate your efforts to keep me safe." She stood, then clasped her hands once more—they were trembling but for entirely different reasons now, and she couldn't well explain to them that it was due to an unease in her middle at the thought of Hank and Eric's dismissal. "I am sure the shop will be expecting me. Thank you for taking me out to experience some fresh air. And for the pleasant conversation. This was most enjoyable."

Six

THAT EVENING, ANNE opened the front of the oven. Protecting her hand with a thick dishcloth, she took out the last of tomorrow's breakfast scones—these ones made with blueberries and lemon zest. They smelled delicious, making her stomach rumble. As if one of the fates knew how tempting they were, Anne watched, first in dismay but then with a little glee, as the smallest scone, one at the corner of the baking sheet, slipped off and landed on the dirty floor. She slid the baking tray onto the wood counter, then picked up the hot scone. She blew on it several times, inhaling the deliciousness, then set it aside. That one wouldn't be able to be sold; aside from any dirt that might have gotten on it, the scone had broken apart. Blueberry filling marked the floor, and the flaky pastry was dented.

What a shame. It would serve as her supper. She hadn't managed to find the time to eat this evening, but more than that, having food she didn't have to pay for meant she could stash the saved pennies into her saving jar. With every coin that pinged as it fell into her jar, she imagined what she could purchase with it. A whisk, a wooden spoon, a tablecloth, a table. One chair, then two. An apron. And on and on.

With the scones cooling, she turned to the ice cream mold that she'd set to harden earlier. It was another order for foreign officials gathered this week in Grosvenor Square. Soon enough, she had the ice cream basket completed and prepared to make the walk as quickly as she could to the Hampton mansion, which was in Grosvenor Square proper. She didn't have to go walking through the mews behind the hotel. That meant a more pleasant walk but also a slightly longer one. She'd have to hurry, or the detail on the ice cream would become blurred as it melted. She carried the treat in a pail and locked the back door of the shop behind her.

She'd long been used to walking alone in the dark; she'd had to do so most months of the year thanks to the distance to the boardinghouse. Sometimes she could afford to pay for a ride, but she rarely did, and even when she could, she preferred to stash the pennies into her jar. This walk was more comfortable, however; while her boardinghouse didn't sit in the worst part of London, it wasn't the best area, either. Thieves, robbers, and ladies of the night were known to take up there. But the Mayfair district was one of the best. This was where the upper crust of Society spent their time. Poorer folk couldn't afford to eat, let alone live, in Mayfair.

This district had a greater number of streetlamps, for which she was grateful, as they provided fewer shadowy places for unsavory individuals to hide in. Tonight, the nearly full moon brightened her surrounding all the more, almost as if she carried a lamp. Of late, her imagination had gotten the better of her, and she'd envisioned horrible things hiding in the darkness, waiting to pounce on her. She rounded the corner that put the Millennium Hotel stables in sight. A faint lantern glowed from somewhere inside, reminding her of the night earlier that week. Where was Davis now? Would he remember her in six months? She'd remember him, no question. He was forever bound to her daydreams.

Heavy footfalls sounded behind her, and a slight jolt went through her. Anne increased her pace, trying to make no sound so she could instead hear whatever—or whoever—was behind her, all the while keeping her chin up and her shoulders back to make a show of confidence. Only silence met her. She continued walking. There it was again. She stopped altogether and whirled about. The sound had stopped again. She saw no one. Heart pounding, Anne turned forward again, determined to make her delivery quickly and get to the boardinghouse right away.

There it was again. Or *almost* the same sound. A gentleman appeared ahead, moving her direction with purposeful steps. Her breath caught in her throat, and she gripped the pail handle tighter. The man, however, simply acknowledged her with a slight nod, started whistling, then bounded up the steps of a townhouse, which he entered without the slightest to-do.

My blasted imagination, she thought, moving ahead once more. She breathed out heavily, hoping her nerves would exit with the air. She hummed a folk tune to help keep her distracted and to prevent her from hearing imaginary and innocent noises.

At last she reached Grosvenor Square. Stepping onto one of the manicured paths made her relax and let out a sigh of relief. She checked the address on the order and headed to the row of grand mansions facing the square. Upon finding the correct door, she mounted the front steps, feeling nervous as she always did when delivering to the main door rather than a servants' entrance. That was the request, so there she was. She used the heavy knocker hanging from the center, then stepped back and held the pail handle with both hands as she waited. When the door remained unanswered, she rapped with the knocker a second time, but with more force.

Leaves on the bushes and trees behind her moved.

Someone followed me, she thought, but once more chastised herself for being so sensitive as to border on paranoia. After all, a slight evening breeze could have easily created the same whispered flutter.

At last the hinges creaked, and the heavy door opened. On the other side stood Davis Whitledge. His eyes widened, surely matching her own, though she felt quite sure that hers were larger than tea saucers.

"I—I thought you were staying at the Millennium," she said lamely.

"I am," Davis said. "I'm here with Peter and Clara—"

"On government business," Anne finished. "Of course. How silly of me."

"Not precisely." Davis smiled at her apparent confusion. "Peter was invited to this ball. It isn't necessary for his duties, but he felt certain that important businessmen would attend, so he brought me along. I came in hopes of being introduced to some of them, but the prospects so far are minimal." He gestured toward the pail, which in her nerves, she'd almost forgotten about entirely. "I imagine that is for the guests?"

"I suppose." But her brow furrowed. "Seems like an awfully small refreshment for a ball." She handed over the pail.

Someone important stayed in this townhouse, likely the minister from another government, but she could not recall who it might be, or whom the ice was intended for. Befuddled at having Davis answering the door—what rich man does such a thing instead of allowing the servants to do their jobs?—she couldn't formulate another coherent sentence.

Someone came up from behind Davis, calling his name— a woman. She sidled up to him and slipped a hand through the crook of his elbow. "There you are," she said, stroking his coat sleeve with her free hand. "I've been looking for you. Never imagined I'd find you performing the butler's duties." She laughed, a tinkling noise, like crystal.

"I was just trying to be helpful. It didn't appear that Mr. Oaks heard Miss Preston knocking on the door."

"Oh, you know each other," the woman said, leaning her ringlet-bedecked head to rest on Davis's sleeve.

"Yes, we do," Davis said, straightening. Perhaps pulling away from her slightly. "Miss Hampton, this is Miss Anne Preston. Miss Preston, Miss Eliza Hampton. She is the daughter of Mr. Hugh Hampton."

The famous tea merchant. *Rich, indeed.* No wonder Davis had come in hopes of being introduced. He clearly hadn't anticipated the attentions of Hampton's daughter.

Eliza laughed again, this time a brief staccato thing that sounded only a shade away from a scoff. "I do believe she's awestruck," Eliza said, looking at Anne but speaking to him as if she weren't right there. "Quick, let's let her be on her way before our wealth and prestige overwhelm her entirely and she faints right there on the front step." Another tinkling laugh floated out the door.

Anne's face flushed hot, and her stomach twisted uncomfortably. At least Davis hadn't laughed, too. "I should go now. Thank you." Anne curtsied and turned.

"Wait," Davis called to her.

She stopped but daren't do more. She could not bear to see Eliza's amused, patronizing expression again, nor Davis's look of pity.

"Have you been paid?"

Upper-class folk never paid in advance. Gunter's made sure to collect payment separately. On the other hand, deliveries such as tonight's typically did garner her tips, something else she hadn't received—and noted only now, when Davis alluded to the subject.

His footfall sounded behind her, and soon he stood at her side on the step, which barely had room enough for the two of them. He held out one hand, palm filled with coins as it had been the day they met. "Take what's fair. For the ice cream, but also for your trouble."

The girl seemed to have flounced off in a huff. She smiled softly at that realization, glad he'd left Miss Hampton inside. The coins glittered slightly from the light spilling out the door. "This appears to be becoming a habit."

Davis held them out farther. "Please."

"Mrs. Argus will be sure the correct amount is collected from the housekeeper." She made a move to take the next stair, but Davis stepped in front of her and looked at her with pleading eyes.

"Please? For your trouble."

Somehow, she couldn't bear the thought of reaching out and feeling his hand under her fingertips again, though she felt mighty tempted. She was not, however, accustomed to others' pity and did not plan to be part of such a thing now or ever. "I don't need anything," she said, meaning coins, of course, though even that statement was false. As soon as the words slipped past her lips, she caught her breath. She needed so many things, *wanted* more. She'd resigned herself to not getting most of them, or at least of dreaming she'd have them sometime in the future. She was tired of resigning herself.

"Here." He reached forward, opened the mouth of one of her apron pockets, and dumped the entire handful of coins inside.

She gaped as they clinked against one another, and then she looked up, mouth hanging open. She simply could not comprehend the generous gift. "I—I don't understand."

"I wish I had more with me."

She didn't doubt his sincerity. At first, she doubted his understanding of how much money he'd given her, but the intensity of his eyes told her that he knew quite well what he'd given her. "Thank you," she said again, somehow getting the words out through a tight chest and throat even as her mind flew through the many items such a sum could buy.

Part of her screamed inside, yelling at her to give the money back, that she had indeed been nothing more than an object of pity, something she despised and did everything to avoid. Until now. How could she give this gift back, when all by itself, it could almost pay for her passage to America? The rest of her savings could go toward room and board, food, and even getting a start on her shop. Davis smiled at her once more, a sight that melted her heart like butter on a skillet. In a trice, he was back at the top of the stairs. He didn't go inside, just waved her direction. With the interior light behind him, she couldn't make out his features any longer. She waved back, turned, and headed for the pathway, keeping her hand protectively over her bulging apron pocket.

Seven

ANNE COULDN'T HELP but walk practically sideways as she stole glances at Davis with every other step. He didn't go back inside until she'd left the light of the yellow glow of the gas lantern outside the door of the Hamptons' impressive residence. The facade had columns between window bays, making for a powerful-looking building.

When she crossed into the full dark of night, she turned back one last time just as the front door clicked shut. As when Davis and Clara had visited her at the shop and taken her for a turn about Berkeley Square, her mouth opened wide in a smile, a feeling both foreign and welcome, and she savored the accompanying sensations of gooseflesh breaking across her skin and delicious shivers of joy. As she walked into the center of Grosvenor Square, following one of the well-tended paths of the gardens, she slowed and wished Miss Hampton hadn't appeared; perhaps the conversation with Davis would have lasted longer. He seemed to enjoy speaking with her and find her agreeable.

Might he even think me a little pretty? The thought made her mouth widen farther. She must have looked ridiculous smiling so wide that the paddle from a butter churn could have fit in the space. She retraced her path through Grosvenor Square, but in such a dreamy state that she failed to notice the leg of a bench that was askew. The toe of her right boot caught the curlicue metal, pitching her forward.

A cry of surprise escaped her throat, and she was in the air just long enough to realize that on crashing to the ground, her precious coins would go flying in all directions. Most would be lost to her forever, as she had no way to hunt them all out in the nighttime, and by the time she returned at daylight, others would have already pocketed them. She remained airborne long enough for those thoughts to flash through her mind, and then she landed with a heavy thump. Her arms bore the brunt of the force. They stung even as she grimaced, first at pain, but then at the thought that the blow might have ground mud stains into her sleeves or dress, though hopefully her apron had protected some of it.

Shakily, she pressed herself off the ground and got to her knees, then reached for the pocket, afraid she'd find it empty. Indeed, the pocket lacked most of the money, though by some good fortune, a few coins remained. Through the fabric, she could not tell which coins remained. Shaking her head to clear it, she reached for the rogue bench and clung to it as a support to get back to her feet. She'd only just regained her footing when something—or rather, someone—shoved her back to the dirt path with such force that her face slammed down and scraped against the surface. A hand gripped the side of her face with a viselike grip and pressed her cheek into the rough path. The man's fingers felt like hot pokers digging into her skin.

He pressed his weight onto her, flattening her under his heft. So compressed were her lungs that she could not get a full breath, could not call for help. After a shuffle of footsteps and some whispered orders, she felt another weight, this time on her legs, as a second person sat on the backs of her knees and tied her ankles together.

Are these highwaymen? The thought came to her with no small measure of panic. *What will they do to me? Who will ever think to inquire after me?* With no family or friends, who would miss her? If she didn't appear at work in the morning, Mrs. Argus might wonder at her absence, but would likely replace her instead of notifying a constable of Anne's disappearance. Such was the life of an old maid of no name or consequence.

"Please," she managed, so quietly she wasn't sure her captors would hear it. "Let me . . . go."

"Not likely, *Miss Preston*," the first man sneered directly into her ear. Hank. As she lived and—sort of—breathed, it was definitely Hank. That meant the other man was almost certainly Eric.

She tried to look at them, but Hank pressed the side of her face into the ground even harder.

"You're not getting away that easily, you aren't."

Eric chuckled at that. "No, indeed. Not after what you did, and not after this." He yanked the rope tight, drawing her ankles together with such force that the bones slammed together. She whimpered.

Eric continued working the knot and then tucked in the end. "Cry all you want, old lady. It won't do you a bit of good."

Hank leaned down to her ear again, and when he spoke, his words were breathy, as if a snake were whispering in her ear. "After getting us thrown out of the hotel stables with nothing, you'll deserve everything you get."

Anne pressed her eyes together, tight, as if blocking out her sight would also block out reality. "But I didn't—"

But Hank's weight cut off her words as well as her breath. He ground her face into the dirt so hard that she prayed her face wouldn't be permanently marked from cuts and scrapes. She didn't try to speak again.

"There, all tied up," Eric said, and he wiped his hands together, as if he'd completed a project to be proud of.

She'd done nothing that would have led to their dismissal. While she found their teasing to be vexing, she'd never want to do anything to send someone to the poorhouse or debtor's prison. Ever. The rich did that to the poor. Those with power and influence. The stable hands knew as well as she did that no person of money or nobility would have listened to her on such matters—she didn't have the influence to get them relieved from their positions.

They blame me because of Davis. Her eyes opened in fear, and she stared into the darkness, hoping they'd let her go. She tried to ignore the yellow glow of lanterns along the edges of the square—especially the one visible if she looked in the direction she'd come from.

He'd had no idea what he was doing. He just wanted to help me.

When she stopped struggling and trying to speak, Eric and Hank got off her. Before she could relish inhaling a lungful of welcome night air, Hank grabbed her under her arms and lugged her to her feet. He held her in place with an iron grip on her shoulders. She tried to wrench away, but Hank grabbed the back of her hair and yanked her backward into his chest. She gasped at the pain.

"Don't. Move." His tone was so dark that she wouldn't have recognized it as Hank's if she hadn't already known it was him.

Anne managed a nod—rather, several half nods in succession, due to her weakness and utter terror. He shoved her back to standing, then released her hair. She got no reprieve from pain, however, as he didn't release her shoulders but rather held on even tighter. She'd be covered in bruises by morning.

"No talking, neither," Eric said as he proceeded to tie her wrists behind her back.

Fully restrained, her feet together at an awkward angle, Anne tried to maintain her balance, but Hank raised a boot and shoved her with such force that she fell to her knees and rolled onto her back. Her arms flared with pain, twisted and bound as they were with her own weight upon them.

Through shock and the threat of tears and burning anger, she managed, "Why?"

"Why?" Hank repeated in a voice of disdain. "Why? As if you don't know."

"I—I don't. Honest." Her eyes burned with welling tears. Would she be alive tomorrow? Would she live another day to ice one more cake? Would she live long enough to dream one more time of opening a shop in America?

Eric squatted down before her, but his face was little more than various indistinct dark shapes. Even so, she'd have recognized the voice and tilt of the head anywhere. "What did you expect us to do when you had your American friend demand our dismissal, with not so much as a penny to buy our next meals with and no scrap of recommendation? Did you think we'd be happy to starve on the streets?"

"We did consider that option," Hank said, now walking slowly around her, as if circling a prisoner ready to be tortured. "But seeing as such a plan is only too likely to succeed, which would mean our imminent deaths, we thought that first, we'd enact vengeance on the old lady who brought this fate upon us."

"Yes," Eric agreed. He grinned; she could tell by the moonlight reflecting off his crooked teeth. "Consider it our own brand of vengeance, as it were."

"What are you going to do with me?" She tried to sound brave but failed. Her voice trembled with each word. She tried to wriggle free of her bonds, tried to kick the men in the kneecaps, anything to get free, but with each attempt, one of them kicked her hard with the sole of his boot. In her stomach, in her ribs, in her head. All until she saw stars and wondered that she was still conscious, or alive.

"Let's show her what we'll do," Hank said.

"Yes, let's," Eric agreed.

"First we do this . . ." Hank kicked her in the ribs again. Pain exploded through her side.

"And this." Another kick, likely from Eric, this one to a soft spot on her lower back. She cried out, certain she was about to die.

"*That* is what we will do to you," Eric sneered again. "And this!" He kicked her in the stomach, making her bend in half.

She retched onto the path, shaking. She hadn't eaten in hours, and hunger, combined with such an assault, made thinking clearly impossible. As much as she prayed for the kicks to stop, she tried to stay awake, for if they succeeded in knocking her out cold, she wouldn't be able to make any protest at all. They'd find transporting her elsewhere that much simpler.

And who knew what they'd do to her then.

Eight

SOMEWHERE IN THE periphery of her mind, Anne sensed that she should call for help. Not that she could. Each breath took effort and sent shocks of pain through her. She couldn't get enough air to so much as say a word of protest or pleading for the boys to stop. And who would hear her, even if she could cry out? If they'd cornered her behind the mansion, plenty of drivers waiting to take their lords and ladies away from the party would have been witnesses.

Precisely why they did this here instead. They must have placed the order at Gunter's. They'd even requested front-door delivery.

The quietness of the night was broken by a carriage pulling into the square. Hank's hold on her tightened, and Eric stepped forward, searching the street beyond Grosvenor Square, where the clopping of hooves seemed to be approaching from.

"Someone's arriving late," Hank muttered under his breath.

"Stupid, rich fools," Eric added.

"You'll keep your mouth shut and hide behind that hedge." Hank spoke the words into her face so that spittle landed in her eyes.

Not reacting with disgust took everything in her power. He jerked her to her feet by one arm and pulled her forward to the hiding place. But he must have forgotten that she couldn't walk with her ankles bound, let alone run. She pitched forward and nearly landed on the ground. When her entire weight hung from her arm in his grip, the pain was so intense that she wished she *had* collapsed to the ground. The carriage entered the square. Hank and Eric froze in place for a moment, then dropped to the ground. Anne ducked of her own accord.

Let them be distracted by the carriage. She needed time to think and catch a breath, then find a way to escape.

The driver alighted and opened the carriage door. A man and woman exited, and then the carriage was back on its way, heading around back to the mews, as the couple climbed the short staircase. The man used the elaborate brass knocker, and the couple waited. Anne ached. Oh how quickly her fortunes had shifted. But a moment before, by that very door, a handsome American had smiled at her and treated her with so much kindness that she'd descended the stairs with a pocket bulging with coins. Now she was the prisoner of two men she'd once thought of as mischievous and troublesome but not dangerous.

She felt a trickle at her temple and realized she must be bleeding. She licked her lips uneasily and tasted blood. From her nose? Her mouth? She didn't know. With her hands bound behind, she couldn't touch her face to find out.

"Don't you think about yelling," Hank snarled in her ear. He must have seen her mouth open when she licked her lips. He reached into his ragged coat pocket and pulled out a short blade. He held it just high enough for the dim light to gleam off the sharp edge. Anne's stomach soured with fear. "Are we understood?"

She nodded several times, not taking her eye from the blade. Her heart beat so hard and so fast that it was a wonder she hadn't fainted.

The door to the mansion opened, and her chest expanded with a drop of hope. *Please let it be Davis answering again,* she thought—begged—the heavens. Hank narrowed his eyes at her and twisted the knife nearer to her throat.

She swallowed hard, still sending her plea heavenward. Hank returned his attention to the mansion, and Anne began working at the knot binding her wrists. She'd already managed to loosen the rope slightly with twisting and pulling motions. If she could loosen it a bit more, she'd be able to wrest the rope free of one hand. But she couldn't allow Hank or Eric to know that, so she kept her attention on the mansion door or on Hank's blade.

The door finally opened. The face illuminated by the lantern was that of a sixty-year-old man. He bowed and gestured for the couple to enter. Not Davis, then. The butler. Her soaring hopes crashed, creating a heavy pit of fear in her middle. She worked the rope over her knuckles, and her left hand came free. But how could she flee the situation without help? She couldn't outrun Hank and Eric on a good day, and certainly not tonight when she was weak and in pain all over from what they'd done to her.

The couple entered the mansion, and the butler moved to close the door. She willed it to stay open, for somehow it seemed that if it closed entirely, her doom would be sealed.

"Ho, Mr. Sainsbury," a voice said from inside. The door hadn't closed all the way yet, only partially.

Like a butterfly testing its new wings, Anne's hope fluttered, but hesitantly, unsure. That voice. The door continued to move, cutting off light from inside as it did so. Only a slice of light a few inches wide. Time and opportunity were both nearly spent.

"Mr. Sainsbury," the voice—clearly Mr. Whitledge—said.

Knife or no knife, she had to act. *"Davis!"*

"Have y—" His voice cut off, and the night stilled as if a heavy blanket had been draped over the square. Even the crickets had silenced as if on cue.

Anne glanced at Hank. What would he do now? He looked stunned into paralysis; he gaped at her as if he'd forgotten he had a weapon—as if *she* were a weapon. Almost as if he feared her.

Davis stepped outside, onto the top stair. "Miss Preston?" he called into the darkness.

"Here!" she yelled, fully expecting Hank to grind her face into the ground to silence her.

Hank pressed the point of the knife against her throat; she sucked in her breath and held it. He leaned close, the stench of alcohol hitting her as he spoke. "Make one more sound . . ."

With one hand held over his eyes, as if shielding them from the noonday sun, Davis took each of the four stairs slowly, then stopped on the walkway and peered forward, searching the dark square again. "Miss Preston?" he called once more. "Are you there? Are you well?"

Once again, Hank pushed the blade into her skin. A high-pitched whimper escaped her. Hank slapped his hand over her mouth, almost covering her nose and cutting off most of her air. But he'd acted too late; Davis's attention snapped toward them. He'd heard her.

"Who's there?" Davis said. "Whoever you are, release Miss Preston at once."

She wanted to yell again, knife notwithstanding. If it were daytime, he'd have easily spotted them only a stone's throw away. But the darkness, the extra shadows cast by foliage, and the light behind him all made seeing into the paths of the park difficult. With his beefy hand still over her mouth, Hank wrapped his other arm around her and held her fast to his chest. Would he notice that her hands were no longer bound?

She slowly moved her left hand to her pocket and wrapped her fingers about the remaining coins. Only the briefest of regrets crossed her mind at the thought of losing them, too. Better to lose them than suffer who knew how much more at the hands of these filthy scoundrels.

Anne withdrew her fist from her pocket, the coins folded inside. With all her might, she threw them into the darkness. Hank started with a jerk. Startled, Eric jumped to his feet, looking ready to run for his life. Precisely as she'd hoped, her aim went true. At least a few of the coins went far enough to ping against the cobbled street.

Davis's attention snapped that direction, and he ran toward the park, calling over his shoulder. "Sainsbury, fetch Mr. Cowley's security!"

He scanned the area left and right but still squinted, clearly not seeing well, as his eyes adjusted to the darkness.

Careful, Anne thought, wishing she could tell him to watch for two men, one with a knife. And while Davis wasn't lacking in strength, he hadn't made his way in life through physical labor as Hank and Eric had, something their thick arms bore witness to. Two of them and a knife against the American did not seem like good odds. But then Davis reached across to his left coat pocket and withdrew the smallest revolver Anne had ever seen. Relief washed over her in a wave.

"A gun!" Eric said urgently and with not a little fear.

"Shut your mouth," Hank retorted.

Davis's even boot steps calmed Anne's heart as he approached, even as she feared the unknown. When he reached the gravel-covered pathway, he planted his feet and waited, his revolver at the ready. Hank and Eric's attention was fully on Davis.

Should I yell again? Try to grab the knife? The stable hands could very well be bluffing ... except they'd already hurt her, and they seemed every bit as likely to continue doing so.

Four men hurried out of the mansion door, two holding lanterns. They rushed to Davis as they drew their own weapons—much larger pistols. While their clothing was clean and pressed, it didn't look expensive or formal like Davis's.

"What's going on?" one said. He had a strong American accent. The men flanked Davis, two on each side, offering their support to whatever threat lurked in the darkness.

"I heard something in the park up ahead. I'm quite sure a young woman of my acquaintance is in trouble."

Eric scrambled to his feet, arms raised. "Let me go, and I'll tell you every—"

Hank yanked Eric down by the belt, but even he knew it was too late. They'd been found. He angrily thrust his boot into Eric's stomach, then got to his feet, pulling Anne with him, the knife still digging into her neck. It had moved slightly, leaving scratches that stung in the night air. Were any of them bleeding?

"Come close, and I'll kill her!" Hank called. "Don't think I won't!"

The five Americans looked ready to charge headlong into the gardens, but Hank's words made them hesitate.

"Where's your friend?" Davis said.

"The sniveling rat. You can have him." Hank nudged Eric's form, and the other man scrambled out of the way, then ran as fast as he could to the line of security. One of the guards promptly restrained him with some kind of leather bindings.

"You won't get away free," Davis said. "There are five of us, and we already have your friend. Surrendering now will be much better for you."

Hank let out a scoff of a laugh. "Better than what? You think I'm afraid of a few Yanks? It's you who should be scared. One little push with my knife, and this pretty face dies." With his free arm, he tried to pull her close again, back to his chest.

This time, she didn't allow it. In one swift movement, she reached up with her now-free hands, grabbed his forearm with them both, and twisted his arm down and out. Before he could recover from the shock, she grabbed his shirtfront and held on for leverage, then thrust her knee as hard as she could into his nether regions. Hank bent over with a grunt of pain. His eyes seemed to bulge out of his head. Anne grabbed the knife from his hand and ran. But after expending such effort, and being beaten, her legs felt no stronger than custard. A pace away from Davis, her step faltered, and he caught her before she could fall, but she gasped as pain shot through her, for his arms held her exactly where Hank had kicked her ribs. Davis gently lowered her to the ground.

"Better?" he asked gently.

She wasn't sure if she replied, but she tried to nod. She shook head to foot at what might have happened even as her head, stomach, and back throbbed with pain.

Somewhere in the back of her consciousness, she heard the guards make chase, and soon after that, both Hank and Eric cussing up a storm as they were led away to a constable, both bound and no longer a threat to anyone.

She could not bear to think beyond this night. Whether they'd broken her nose, turning her plain features downright ugly. Whether her reputation would be ruined for having been alone with two men at night, regardless of the circumstances. Whether when she returned to Gunter's covered in bruises and one or both eyes swollen shut, she'd be able to keep her position or be forced to find work elsewhere.

But I'm alive. Thanks to Davis, I'm alive. Tears of relief built up in her eyes and spilled onto the sandy soil below her, made worse as the excitement of the events wore off and the pain of her injuries reared its head. She couldn't breathe without pain.

He knelt beside her and gently smoothed the hair from her face. "What did they do to you?"

She tried to look at him, but the slight movement brought with it more pain than she could bear. *I'm too weak to walk home. What will become of me?*

"I knew those men were trouble," Davis said. "And they're not so bright—attacking a lady at a diplomatic event that's bound to have plenty of security about."

Carefully, he slipped his arms about her—one under her arms, the other under her knees—and stood, cradling her like a child. He adjusted his hold, which sent more stabbing pains up her right side. She hadn't realized she'd winced until Davis stilled and said, "I'm so sorry. I'll be gentler."

Feeling genuinely safe for the first time in years, Anne relaxed into his arms as he carried her away.

Nine

ANNE'S BODY SUDDENLY went limp in Davis's arms. He stiffened, and his step came up short as he looked her over. An inexplicable fear gripped him, and as he held her close, he wished for a free hand with which to pat her cheek and otherwise attempt to rouse her.

Cheeks pale as death. She needs a doctor.

Her chest rose and fell, a sight that made him let out a huge sigh. She was alive, if unwell. He looked about the square, suddenly aware of movement and voices in every direction. The ball must have been disrupted, as the square was filled with guests in their finery.

"She needs a doctor," Davis called toward some bystanders as he walked their way. "Please help." He gestured toward Anne's unconscious figure in his arms. "Where can we find a doctor?" He'd reached the edge of light spilling from the mansion door. Several people turned their attention from the arrest of the stable hands toward Davis. An older lady gasped and turned away, pressing her face into her husband's shoulder.

Another man looked at Davis and held out a hand.

"Stand back, sir. You cannot expect ladies of the *ton* to look upon such things."

Davis looked about and only then realized that most of the women also had their faces covered, whether by a hand, a fan, or, as he'd noticed with the older woman, a gentleman's shoulder. Did they truly not want to help? Was looking upon a fainted, injured young woman so grievous? He looked down at Anne and fully realized why those gathered—including several men—looked horrified. An entire half of Anne's head was covered in blood, including her hair, ear, and sleeve. Some had dripped onto his boots. He looked over his shoulder and found a trail of blood he'd left behind.

His worry only intensified. Unsure where her wound was but disturbed by the sheer amount of blood, he set Anne onto the walkway as gently as he could, then pulled off his suit coat, rolled it into a ball, and propped her head on it in lieu of a pillow. He searched for the source of the blood, wiping her face and hair with a handkerchief until he found a cut over her ear. He pressed the cloth against it to stanch the flow, then searched the crowd. He spied a boy standing alone some feet off.

"You."

The boy pointed at himself, eyebrows raised.

"Yes, you. Do you know where to find a doctor?"

The boy nodded. "Dr. Spencer is staying at the hotel."

"Good. Go fetch him," Davis said. The boy glanced about as if unsure whether he should be taking orders from this American instead of the Hamptons, or whomever he worked for.

"*Now,*" Davis implored.

The young man jumped into action, his legs pumping as he disappeared into the night in the direction of the hotel.

"I need a shawl or wrap or something," Davis said next,

this time scanning the women decked out in fine attire. He tilted his head toward Anne, indicating her wound and the now-blood-soaked handkerchief that he held to it. His was bright red from blood, and his coat under her was covered, too. "Please." He understood that any wrap worn at tonight's event would be an expensive one. He also knew full well that the women who attended this event had the means to replace them, too.

From inside the door, Sainsbury called, "Make way!"

The group parted, and the butler ran through, carrying what looked like a worn but clean blanket. He dropped to Anne's side and held out the blanket. Davis took it, wadded it up, and pressed the fabric to her wound. "Thank you," Davis said softly.

"Of course," Sainsbury said.

"Is there a place we can take her?"

The butler looked at Anne and then at Davis, clearly sizing up their positions in life and what that would mean for proper accommodations. "There is room in the basement," he said. "An extra bed, too, where a former scullery maid used to sleep."

"That will do nicely, thank you," Davis said. He moved to pick her up again, and the butler grasped the blanket to keep pressure on the wound.

"Are you . . . " Sainsbury began, but his voice trailed off. His gaze darted to the onlookers and then back to Davis. He turned his back to the group, which prevented Davis from moving forward. The man looked in earnest.

"What is it?" Davis asked.

The butler's expression bore such intent that Davis felt as if the servant had a critical message that he was trying to convey silently. Sainsbury lifted his eyebrows and asked in a deliberate, oddly slow tone, "Are you a relation of the poor

girl's?" His brows remained up, and his eyes widened, empha-
sizing his secret message.

Davis scrambled to determine what the correct response
would be. Of course he wasn't a relation; he could scarcely be
called an acquaintance. *How can that be so, when it seems as
if I've known her for so much longer?*

"Are you a relation?" the butler asked again, this time
leaning forward.

He wants me to lie. Davis looked over Sainsbury's
shoulder at the other guests, whose attention, now that the
ruffians had been carted away, was focused on the American
and the English girl. Davis had never understood all the
proper rules of British Society and their class system. His
father had come to America from England and raised himself
from a lowly station to a respected, relatively wealthy one—
something nearly impossible to do in England. *They see Anne
as below them. And ladies' reputations are as fragile as
feathers here, it seems.*

"Mr. Whitledge?" the butler said, bringing Davis's attention back to him. "Is she a relation of yours?"

"Yes," Davis said, lifting his chin slightly. The butler's
mouth softened into the hint of a smile. Encouraged, Davis
raised his voice so everyone else could hear. "In fact, she is my
wife."

A murmur of surprise rippled across the gathering. Miss
Hampton looked most displeased, folding her arms and lifting
her nose into the air and deliberately looking away from him.
He half expected her to stomp her foot like a child. He hadn't
encouraged her attentions, but rather the opposite. If she had
thought that he sought after her in any way—or was available
for courting—that assumption was entirely on her. Married
men often danced with other women at balls; that was seen as

the gentlemanly thing to do—preventing women from having to sit out if the numbers of bachelors was not in their favor.

Even if I were married, she'd have no basis to complain.

"Your wife," Sainsbury said with a nod. "Very good, very good. I'm sure Lord Hampton will be most pleased to see to her care." With that, the butler led the way inside, still holding the cloth to Anne's head.

Let's hope none of them recognize her from Gunter's, he thought as they walked by. *It's dark enough that they might not see her features well.* Now that the rush of initial panic had subsided, Davis noted that Anne looked a bit more polished than usual. She wore a more delicate-looking apron than he'd seen on her at Gunter's. Those ones were thick canvas, with a myriad of stains across them. This apron was torn in several places from the attack, and streaks of dirt surely bore witness to more of what she'd endured. Though the twist in her hair was askew now, it was a much more elaborate style than he'd ever seen her wear. She must have arranged her hair in the evening and changed her apron, at least, all to improve her appearance for her important front-door delivery. And look what it had gotten her.

Mr. Sainsbury led him through a hall and then down a short flight of steps to what was clearly the servants' quarters. Another hall—spare and stark, if clean—was lined with doors.

"Here." The butler opened the fourth door on the left and ushered Davis, who yet carried Anne in his arms, inside.

As Davis gently laid Anne onto the bed, a wiry woman with a gray bun swooped in. "What is this?" When she saw Anne, she gasped. "Oh my." She turned to the butler for an explanation.

"Mrs. Fripps, this young woman was attacked in the square. Fortunately, the culprits have been caught." He paused and eyed Davis, who'd pulled up a chair so he could sit at the head of the bed. He took Anne's hand in his. The butler nodded toward at him. "Her *husband* here . . . stopped the attack, and Lord Hampton's men are fetching a doctor."

The housekeeper clearly didn't believe much of what she'd heard. She said not a word as she took in the room and everyone in it, including Anne. The fact that only one of them had been a party guest did not escape her. Even a child would have been able to tell, from the style of her clothing to her worn boots and tanned face. She did not belong to the class of people who attended aristocratic or diplomatic events. She'd likely never seen servants' quarters this fine.

At last, Mrs. Fripps clasped her hands. "Well then. How providential that you happened upon your wife at such a time." She smiled, but it was tight-lipped.

"Indeed," Davis said, not daring to say more.

Let me stay, he thought, stroking the back of Anne's hand, careful not to touch the raw scratches. A bit of hair had gotten stuck to her temple, and he gently brushed it aside.

"Mrs. Fripps," the butler said from his position holding the blood-soaked blanket to Anne's head, "would you fetch some warm water and clean rags?"

"Of course, Mr. Sainsbury." The housekeeper's face softened as she looked at Anne. "And I'll make some broth for her for when she wakes."

"Be sure to send the doctor in when he arrives," Davis said as she headed out the door.

"Naturally."

Steps sounded outside the door, followed by the appearance of a young male servant—a footman, Davis guessed.

"Mr. Sainsbury," he said, panting, "With the perpetrators caught, Lord Hampton is asking for you, and the constable is asking to speak to you."

"Of course."

The butler checked the bleeding, which had slowed considerably but hadn't stopped.

The events of the evening had happened so quickly that Davis hardly had time to know what was happening. Somehow, he felt more alive and at ease right this moment, in a servant's room rather than in the fancy ballroom he'd spent most of the evening in. He didn't want a fancy, expensive life like Peter had—and enjoyed.

He wanted the comforts of life, certainly—but for many years, he'd felt empty, as if something large was missing from his life. He'd long assumed that traveling, with and without Peter, and making a success of his own importing and exporting business would fill that void.

And for several years, he'd believed that the void was indeed filled.

But now, as he sat at the bedside of Anne Preston, he felt an overwhelming warmth and desire to care for her and a knowledge that without someone to care for—someone to give his life meaning—he wouldn't be fully happy. No amount of wine, no number of balls, felt as pure and *complete* as did this feeling he had now.

Who would have thought I wanted a wife? He'd long assumed that he would be perfectly happy to remain a bachelor for life. After his heart had been broken by Angelique, he'd believed he could never love again. And after all, he had friendly companionship with Clara. He had means. He had family. That should have been enough.

I could come to love someone like Anne Preston. The thought—the truth—landed in his mind and heart together with such force that he could not deny it, though he tried to resist the notion. *I hardly know her.*

You know enough, his mind—or his heart, or was it fate?—replied. *You don't have much time. Act now. The rest,*

175

including love, will follow. Indeed, Anne was the first woman in over a decade to turn his head and awaken the desire for a feminine half to come into his life. He hadn't known how big the hole was until she'd appeared and seemed to fit it perfectly.

Perhaps we can spend our lives learning about each other and learning to love each other all the more.

Mrs. Fripps returned with a bowl of warm water and a sponge. She gestured for Davis to move off his chair. "Need to tend to her wounds, sir."

"I can do it." Davis reached out for the bowl and sponge. "After all, she is my wife."

Ten

ANNE CAME TO, blinking her heavy lids in spite of their desire to stay closed. Where was she? This bed did not feel like her lumpy one in the boardinghouse. Nor did the sheets feel right; these were far too new and crisp. Even the air in the room smelled different, but not at all unpleasant. Rather, she had the sense that somewhere nearby was a kitchen where a cook was at that moment working magic. The scents made Anne's mouth water.

She pressed her eyes closed briefly, trying to think, then opened them again and focused on the unfamiliar ceiling. Had she gone home last night? She tried to sift through her hazy thoughts to find the most recent memory but couldn't pull one out. Out of habit, she reached up to smooth back her hair, only for pain to shoot through her head at the slight touch. She sucked air between her teeth as she pulled her hand away, then realized she'd touched something foreign. Carefully, she probed the spot again and felt what seemed to be a bandage.

"You're awake." It was a man's voice.

Dread filled her—not a memory, per se, but the sense of clear danger and a need to escape. Her *inability* to escape.

She clung to the bedclothes and held them against her body. "Please, don't hurt me."

A face entered her line of vision.

"Mr. Whitledge?" She could not have been more stunned if she'd seen a unicorn.

After the sound of a chair scooting closer, he sat beside her, wearing a warm, disarming smile that belied the dark circles under his eyes. "I thought we agreed that you'd call me Davis." His smile widened to show his teeth.

She chuckled, but the small motion sent stabbing pains through her side. "What happened to me? And why are you here . . . with me . . ." Her voice trailed off as her mind cleared enough to grasp the situation. No matter how well-meaning Davis Whitledge might be, a man staying with a woman alone in a room, while she *slept*, simply wasn't done. As an old maid beyond thirty, she had very little in life, but she'd maintained at least a shred of dignity and a proper reputation. Until now.

She didn't fear Davis, but another fear stole through her, snaking through her middle like a hungry beast ready to consume her.

"Where are we?" she asked again.

"The Hampton mansion." Davis leaned forward, resting his arms on his legs in a most casual manner, almost as if they'd known each other for years.

While her mind said that such behavior was inappropriate and rude, her heart could not believe it. The whole felt utterly natural, and knowing that Davis was here, at her side, made her initial sense of imminent danger dissipate.

"The hotel's stable hands attacked you last night," Davis said. "You'd come to make a delivery to the Hampton party."

The cobwebs in her mind were beginning to clear bit by bit. "Yes. You met me . . . at the door," she said slowly.

"That's right."

The picture grew clearer. "As I left, Hank and Eric ..." The next moments rushed back with such force that she felt as if a wave from the sea had knocked her feet out from under her. She closed her eyes again, hoping to block out the memory, but while she could not recall vivid details of what had transpired, she could remember the fear and agonizing pain that resulted from those events. What all had she forgotten? She opened her eyes again and turned her head, oh so slowly, to look at Davis directly. He gently rested a hand over hers, which clutched the bedclothes. His touch made her relax, breathe more easily, gave her the means to broach a most difficult question.

"Did they—I mean, was I—were—"

"No," Davis broke in. The single word was accompanied by a firm shake of his head and what appeared to be a distinct flash of protective anger in his eyes. "I am most grateful that I came upon the incident soon enough to chase them away. They have since been apprehended." His thumb softly stroked the back of her hand. Not since childhood had anyone touched her with such gentle tenderness.

More cobwebs cleared, and with them came more worries. "What time is it? Surely I should be at work by now."

"I sent word that you were unwell and needed to convalesce," he said. "I might have implied that you will need up to a week's rest—with pay."

That would be a relief beyond expression, but she didn't know if it was at all possible. "What did they say? They may well decide to not let me return at all after this," she said, avoiding the subject of being attacked. Davis had to know what she meant, and that a tarnished reputation could be grounds for dismissal.

"I don't know," he said honestly. "But Peter has not an insignificant amount of influence. I'm confident that we can ensure that you will have employment, if that is what you wish."

Of course she wanted employment. But she also knew that plenty of women vied for positions such as hers. Her skills were good, but another woman with lesser skills could replace her for less money and learn as she worked.

"Do others know that you've been here . . . with me . . ." She refrained from saying *during the night*, for she didn't know for certain how long he'd sat watch, though the disheveled and rumpled appearance of his clothing and hair, and again, those telltale circles under his eyes implied enough.

"Yes," he said, then held up a finger. "But."

But what? What did he mean to say next? How could he possibly explain away the situation to look acceptable to anyone, let alone the *ton*, her employer, or her landlord? Yet he seemed so optimistic that she didn't retort with her arguments about how the life she'd carefully built for herself would soon shatter into a thousand shards like sugar syrup cooked too long.

She prompted him, repeating his last word. "But?"

His cheeks flushed pink, and he wore a sheepish smile, making him look like a boy of fifteen even with the hints of pepper-gray hair above his ears.

He dropped his gaze to their hands. He still stroked the back of hers with his thumb—warm and strong and twice the length of her thumb. It made her feel feminine. Noticed. Worth being cared for. After having to be strong for so long, after having to watch for her own safety at all times, for years on end, no longer having a father or brothers to tend to that duty, that simple act by Davis made her feel safe and protected. She waited, but he didn't finish his thought.

"Why are you doing this?" she asked. "All of this, I mean. I'm no one."

"What I was going to say," he said, clearly returning to the previous question instead of the one she'd just asked, "is that they all believe that you are my . . . you see . . . that is . . . they are under the impression that . . ." He cleared his throat. "That you're my wife." Only after completing the declaration did he look at her, and then it was with one eyebrow raised in an expression of trepidation.

Anne didn't know what to think, aside from assuming that she must have heard incorrectly. "That I'm your . . ."

"Wife, yes." He said it quickly now that the truth was out. "It seemed to be the only thing to do in the moment. I couldn't have lived with myself if your reputation had been injured beyond repair after what happened, especially seeing as I had a hand in making it come about."

She shook her head, which made it throb. "It wasn't your—"

"Then I added to the problem by not wanting to leave your side, but I couldn't. I had to stay here and make sure you received proper care and . . ." He shrugged helplessly. "I hope you don't hate me for the lie. It was told with good intentions."

"That was rather ingenious of you." The dread of what her life would become without a reputation intact faded like fog in the morning sun. If she really were married, Gunter's wouldn't need to worry over her fallen reputation tainting the shop's good name. A married woman would be able to stay on at the boardinghouse—and perhaps have sympathy if she'd been abandoned by a supposed American husband. The situation seemed to be turning out quite well after all.

"Being a married woman would provide many advantages, even if my alleged husband is a continent away."

Davis released her hand and ran his fingers through his hair, then got off the bed abruptly and paced the little room.

Had she said something wrong? "I'm sorry. I assumed

that you were going back to America. Are you planning on staying in England?" They could certainly live out such a ruse here, although the details would be a bit more complicated.

"You asked why I was doing this," he said.

"Yes . . ." She had the feeling that she was about to hear something that might well shake the ground beneath her feet, and she didn't know whether to hope for it or run from it.

"I care, Anne. Though we've known each other but a short time, I genuinely care about you." His pacing ended at her feet. Davis pulled up the chair and clasped his hands, leaning forward as if making a plea. "I feel quite strongly that with time, that affection . . . will only increase."

Anne felt ready to faint, though that was because his words had made her stop breathing, not due to her injuries.

He leaned closer and encompassed both of her hands between his. He slid off the chair and knelt beside the bed, his face only inches from hers. "Come to America with me."

He couldn't possibly be in earnest. She tried to laugh, but it came out as a near sob. "You're mad," Anne said, though in her mind's eye, her future shop already had a handsome man of Davis's description working at her side. "Has someone given you laudanum instead of me?"

"I may be mad, but you're wonderful," he said. "You have no family here, correct?"

She'd told him and Clara as much, but she confirmed it. "None."

"You've long wanted to go to America to begin anew."

Reluctantly—oh, so reluctantly—Anne extricated her hands from his, though she immediately missed the contact. "I'm a proud woman, Mr. Whitledge," she said, returning to the formal name. "I earn my way. I am not one to take charity, even from those with good intentions." She did not add that she refused to be obligated to anyone.

For a charged moment, they sat there in silence. She stared at her hands in her lap. Davis didn't say a word, but at length, he reached out with one finger and lifted her chin until their eyes met. The dark-gray depths would not release their hold; she couldn't look away again.

"I do not offer charity, Anne Preston. I offer myself, my life, and anything I am capable of providing to make you happy and comfortable."

What, precisely, was he implying?

"While you were sleeping, I consulted the papers and learned that the *Soteria* leaves the harbor tonight. I can secure us passage in a private cabin. That is, if you're feeling well enough to travel, and—"

What a kind, if uninformed, man. She smiled sadly. "I have a feeling that even in America, a single woman traveling with a bachelor would be scandalous." She wouldn't jump from one frying pan if it meant landing in another fire.

His eyes suddenly twinkled. "Oh, but that wouldn't be the case." Davis lifted her hands to his lips and pressed a kiss to her fingers. A flutter in her stomach erupted into a flurry of heat and happiness inside. "A ship's captain can marry his passengers. Or, if you'd rather, I can find a preacher to handle the matter before we depart. Whichever you would prefer."

Anne's insides felt ready to burst with any number of conflicting emotions. "Davis, I don't know what to say."

"Say yes." He held her hand so close to his lips that she could feel his breath tickling her skin.

Kiss them again, she wanted to say. The sensation was bliss even with one of her eyes swelling, her body covered in scratches, and some ribs cracked, at least.

"We'll have at least six weeks aboard to become better acquainted. If, after we arrive in Boston, you'd prefer to never see my face again, I will make the necessary arrangements immediately." His brow furrowed, and he stroked the back of her hand again. "Though I would like to think that having me as a husband would not be so terrible, and I will do everything in my power to make you happy." He took in and let out a big breath, then went on. "Say you'll marry me, Anne. I'll help you set up your shop. I can do the books. Or I'll scrub the floors and dishes. Do deliveries. Anything you ask of me."

Anne couldn't bear to be lying down any longer. She eased herself to a sitting position, wincing a few times at the pain in her ribs, until she was upright. She scooted until her back leaned against the wall and her feet dangled off the edge of the bed.

The way he looked at her seemed to say that his very happiness hung in the balance and that she had the power to determine his fate. She took a steadying breath of her own before replying.

"We'll hire help to scrub our floors."

He seemed to think through her words once, twice, three times before answering, making sure he understood her meaning. He rose from his knees and climbed onto the bed, sitting beside her, their legs out straight, parallel to one another, both of them leaning against the wall.

After a moment of silence, he asked, "Does that mean yes?"

She felt herself blushing. "I cannot believe I'm saying this—or sitting on a *bed* with a man I've spent less time with than some cakes . . ." Her voice trailed off.

"But?" He reached for her hand and squeezed it.

If that moment could have been frozen in time, she would have happily lived there forever, leaving her hand in his, even if it meant never again piping with a bag of icing.

"Yes," she said. "I'll marry you aboard the *Soteria*. Let's go to America, and you can make a proper woman out of me."

Davis leaned close and whispered, "Anne?"

She leaned in, too, to hear . . . and to draw nearer to him. "Yes?" she answered with the only breath she could manage. To her ears, her heart sounded like an army marching inside her, so loud that customers at Gunter's could have heard.

He brushed his lips against her temple. "I hope that one day, I'll be more to you than a man who made you a *proper woman.*"

Anne summoned her courage to do something she never would have imagined herself capable of. She held her face to Davis's stubbly cheek and pressed her lips to it, slow enough to breathe his scent and feel his warmth against her skin before she pulled back, but not far.

She looked up at him, his gray eyes so deep that she could have drowned in them. "I believe that can be arranged."

Annette Lyon is a *USA Today* bestselling author, a 6-time Best of State medalist for fiction in Utah, and a Whitney Award winner. She's had success as a professional editor and in newspaper, magazine, and technical writing, but her first love has always been fiction.

She's a cum laude graduate from BYU with a degree in English and is the author of over a dozen books, including the Whitney Award-winning *Band of Sisters*, a chocolate cookbook, and a grammar guide. She co-founded and was served as the original editor of the *Timeless Romance Anthology* series and continues to be a regular contributor to the collections.

She has received five publication awards from the League of Utah Writers, including the Silver Quill, and she's one of the four coauthors of the *Newport Ladies Book Club* series. Annette is represented by Heather Karpas at ICM Partners.

Find Annette online:
Blog: http://blog.AnnetteLyon.com
Twitter: @AnnetteLyon
Facebook: http://Facebook.com/AnnetteLyon
Instagram: https://www.instagram.com/annette.lyon/
Pinterest: http://Pinterest.com/AnnetteLyon
Newsletter: http://bit.ly/1n3I87y

Little London

-HEATHER B. MOORE-

One

Somewhere outside of London, 1826

HARPSHIRE VILLAGE WAS a far cry from London in both architecture and entertainments, and the type of people who lived
in the village were simple folk. The only time a member of the
ton was sighted was when they stayed at the Harpshire Inn
while *en route* from London to some vast country estate.
Never to actually visit Harpshire itself.

Yet there were advantages to not living in London. One
didn't see the poor and destitute lurking in the streets, clothed
in rags and begging for shillings. One didn't have to breathe
the foul air. One didn't have to fight through masses of people
and carriages and horses just to walk down the street.

One also didn't have the opportunities of visiting museums, attending the opera, or browsing a shop that sold only
hats.

Missing out on all of this meant Ellen Humphreys had
plenty of time to be bored.

For whatever reason, Ellen's father had given in to her
mother's whims nearly fifteen years ago and moved the entire

family to the country. The entire family consisted of her father, her mother, her older brother Gerald, and Ellen. There had also been an aunt and uncle in there somewhere, but they had both died years ago. Her mother promptly became the world's most reclusive recluse and therefore desired her only daughter to be at her side. Fortunately for Gerald, he'd escaped the confines of the country and gone to Eton. After Eton, he took up residence in London with no apparent thought for his sister.

Ellen rarely saw her brother, and for that she would never forgive him. Ellen considered herself abandoned much like a wood nymph lost and forgotten in a dark wood. Her father traveled almost constantly, selling this or that, journeying back and forth to America to sell more things. He was a tradesman and owned his own factory in London, of which Gerald was an overseer.

Ellen had begged more than once to go with her father so that she might live in his townhome. She could bring along her governess, since her mother would never consent to living in London. But the answer was always no. Her mother forbade Ellen from going to the wicked city and mingling with rakes and debauched women. When Ellen had asked, at the age of eleven, what rakes were, her mother had called for the smelling salts. Ellen was grateful she hadn't asked about debauched women since they didn't sound much better.

Her family's property bordered Harpshire, and since it was miles and miles from civilization, Ellen had no choice but to walk to the village each day. It was the only place her mother allowed her to travel. At first, Ellen went with her governess, but by the time Ellen was fourteen, her governess preferred to stay in and take afternoon naps. So Ellen started walking on her own, and that's when she found the most enchanting meadow. The place wasn't far from the road, and she could usually hear an approaching carriage or a group of riders.

Ellen named the meadow Little London.

It was her escape. Her private world. And now, at eighteen, Ellen still went there every day. Sometimes she brought along a sketch pad and drew the wildflowers among the grasses. Other times she brought one of her father's books—his forbidden books—which Ellen delighted in sneaking out of the dusty library. Her governess had once discovered one of the books in Ellen's room but had said nothing.

It was like an unspoken agreement between the two—the governess took afternoon naps, and Ellen sneaked her father's books.

Other times, Ellen would pretend the meadow was an elegant ballroom belonging to one of the fabulously wealthy members of the *ton*, whose daughter just happened to be Ellen's best friend. This imaginary best friend had an older brother who was devastatingly handsome, and of course he was a marquess or an earl or a baron at the very least. He broke the hearts of all the women who met him, yet Ellen alone had the power to command *his* heart.

Despite the fact that Ellen was now a grown woman, this was still her favorite game to play. And today was the perfect day to play it. The breeze was light, the sun none too hot, and her governess had just gone upstairs for her nap. Mother never called for Ellen until the evening, when she asked for a report on all that Ellen had accomplished in a day. It used to make Ellen furious, since her mother spent day after day doing nothing in her rooms and expected Ellen to learn French, history, geography, embroidery, music, and art.

But one holiday, her brother had set Ellen straight. "Mother is like an infant who takes great care and patience. But she is still your mother. She brought you into this world, and you need to honor her for it. You should be more grateful."

Perhaps Gerald was right, perhaps he wasn't. Whatever the case, he got to leave Harpshire, so Ellen didn't put too much stock into his opinion.

Now, finished with her lessons for the day, Ellen slipped out of the house by the back door and stopped to pet Scruffs, her favorite cat. He purred and rubbed against her legs as if she were going to give him some sort of treat. "I have nothing for you, Scruffs."

She hadn't brought her sketching pad or a book today; she'd brought a shawl and her gloves instead to attend the ball in Little London.

Even though the sun was three-quarters across the sky, she pretended it was the fashionable hour of eleven o'clock in the evening. She hurried along the road until she reached the path that led to the edge of the meadow, where she paused. She imagined herself being handed down from an elegant carriage her father had purchased. Coming out of the carriage behind her was her best friend and her best friend's mother. Their names weren't important.

Ellen pulled on her gloves, which had never been worn to a real event, and then she spread the shawl out on a large rock at the edge of the meadow. She sat on the shawl, pretending it was a silk upholstered chair. Her first dance partner, the aforementioned marquess or earl, had promised her some lemonade before it all began. She'd heard of a Kenworth family which had two sons. Either of them would do for this scenario. And for her purposes, she decided that Lord Kenworth was one of the most eligible bachelors of the Season. Yet he'd sought her out for the first dance.

"Oh, thank you, Lord Kenworth," she murmured as she opened her fingers to receive the phantom crystal goblet. She took a sip. She imagined the sweet liquid with a bit of tartness blended in. As a delicate female, she couldn't possibly finish the entire glass. When the next servant passed by, she handed off her glass to him. He bowed, his quick gaze appraising her ensemble.

Even the servants appreciated her new dress.

As the music struck up, Lord Kenworth bowed before her. "Shall we, my lady?"

Ellen flushed at his address. So formal and sweet. She let him draw her to her feet, then placed her hand on his arm as he led her to the dance floor.

She had to look down only once to make sure she didn't trip on an ant knoll. In the center of the meadow, Ellen put her hand on what might have been a tall man's shoulder and let her other hand pause where the marquess might have held it if he were a real man. Then, Ellen began to hum a waltz. She knew, of course, from reading Society papers that she'd pleaded with her governess to fetch, that the waltz was a fairly new addition to the ballroom floors of London.

Ellen had never seen an actual waltz performed, but she knew it meant dancing in a partner's arms for the whole of the song. She continued to hum as the sun warmed the top of her head and the tips of her shoulders. Although she in reality wore an average dress, she'd tugged down the sleeve caps so that the form would better resemble a ball gown.

Turning first to the right, then to the left, then taking a few steps forward, and another few steps back, Ellen found her own rhythm. Her hummed song didn't follow a particular composer but jumped around a little. That was the beauty of her own meadow to dance in. Her imagination could become as large as she wanted. Perhaps it was due to her humming, or due to her focus on dancing and not tripping over the grass knolls and avoiding the rocks, but Ellen didn't hear a rider coming along the road. Neither did she hear footsteps coming through the thicket of trees. Nor did she see the man who watched her from the edge of the meadow until he turned away.

Two

QUINN EDWARDS, THE Marquess of Kenworth, cursed for the umpteenth time that day. His cursing streak had begun when he'd discovered that his younger brother had taken the carriage, along with Quinn's favorite stallions, back to London two nights before. His brother's errand was not to be complained about, though—he had gone to check on their ailing mother. And, when word came this morning that she had not improved, Quinn prepared to follow in his brother's wake. He didn't want to be encumbered with a carriage, so he'd been forced to take a second-rate horse, and now said horse was limping.

If memory served him right, up ahead was a small village, and he hoped he could switch out his horse at the local inn. He wasn't sure if he had a mile to go or two or perhaps three. Quinn dismounted the horse to walk alongside it. He might be anxious to visit his mother, but he wasn't going to be cruel to an injured horse, and he hoped the beast wouldn't have to be put down.

As it was, the day was pleasant, the sun not too hot, and if he weren't riding to be at his mother's bedside, he might have spent a night in the village. Quinn wasn't truly worried about his mother's condition—she had the habit of falling ill whenever she was lonely. But she would certainly worsen and give in to greater hysterics if he delayed his arrival by another day. Having his younger brother there now would undoubtedly help. Yet in his mother's mind, there was no substitute for the oldest son, simply because he was the title owner.

As Quinn walked along the quiet road, leading his limping horse, he thought of how his father must have been the most patient man in all of England. Although he'd been gone for over three years, if someone were to gauge the passage of time by his mother's reactions, one might think that he'd been gone for only three months. Quinn wasn't sure if his parents' marriage was such a close love match as to warrant his mother's continued despondency.

But what did Quinn know? His interactions with the female sort hadn't been entirely favorable. Sure, he'd always been the heir, but once he inherited, it was like the floodgates had opened. Mothers became brash about making sure their daughters secured an introduction to him at social events, and if he didn't ask those very daughters to dance—every single one of them—one would have thought a family death had occurred. Sometimes Quinn wished the mourning period were five years. He was no longer Lord Quinn Edwards, lover of science and mechanics; he was the Marquess of Kenworth. A commodity. A focus of gossip.

He was embroiled in his disgruntled thoughts when he thought he heard his name spoken. By a woman.

How was that possible? He stopped walking, and the horse stopped as well. He listened to the expected sounds one might find on a country road—wind pushing through the trees above, a couple of insects buzzing, a bird or two.

"Thank you, Lord Kenworth," the voice said. "It was my pleasure."

A laugh—light and cheerful.

Then, "Of course you may escort me into supper."

Another laugh.

Then humming.

Was he hearing things? Had the stress of his new responsibilities and his mother's illness finally cracked his mind? Quinn drew his horse off the road, pointed it to a nice section of wild grass to munch on, then started through the trees toward the woman's voice. Soon, he arrived at a clearing or a very small meadow. Yes, there was a woman, who was *not* a phantom of his imagination. This fact brought him much relief.

The woman was perhaps nineteen or twenty, and she wore a white dress, pulled off the shoulders so that there were no guesses as to the gifts of her gender. Her eyes were closed as she hummed a song that he wasn't familiar with. Her light-brown hair seemed burnished gold by the sun, making it appear as if she had a halo of light about her head. Strands of hair had escaped her updo, and wavy tendrils trailed along her rather elegant neck.

Quinn always noticed a woman's neck. Perhaps because it was the supporter of what might be a lovely face, as well as the beginning of what might also be a lovely physique. This woman had both.

She continued to hum a fractured tune, and then she lifted her arms as if she had a dance partner and . . . began to dance.

Quinn couldn't take his eyes from the sight of this ethereal creature dancing by herself as if she were in an entirely different world. A pang of envy shot through him. Had Quinn Edwards ever spent an afternoon, nay, even a few moments, in such an unfettered manner? The young woman was completely oblivious to everything else outside this meadow—it was like she was drunk on ambrosia in a Shakespeare performance. Quinn half expected fairies and sprites to leap about the clearing as she danced.

He was puzzled, though, about her dance moves. He'd heard of traveling dancing troupes that did performances, and wondered if she belonged to one of those and was rehearsing for an upcoming event. He'd never seen her particular moves, although she was repeating them over and over, as if she were mimicking a more traditional dance style.

Quinn then realized that he was spying on an unprotected woman. What might she think when she spotted him? She would certainly not be pleased, and he didn't want to frighten her. As much as he wanted to stay, he knew he should return to the road. Otherwise, he might be tempted to offer himself up for a partner. She could practice with him and then perhaps be more prepared for her upcoming performance. It sounded reasonable at first thought. At second thought, he knew it would never do. They hadn't been introduced, and he had no idea who she was. If she was a dancer, or an actress, he could only imagine the added hysterics his mother would entertain if she were ever to find out.

So, reluctantly, Quinn took a final, rather long gaze at the woman dancing on her own, then turned from the scene to head back to the road and rejoin his horse.

That was when she screamed.

Three

ELLEN'S HEART STOPPED for a full beat, and then she did the only thing natural upon seeing a strange man spying on her through the trees. She screamed.

Her scream was impressive, really, and she didn't know she had such a scream inside her. Not having previously had the opportunity to scream at anything before, she shocked herself as much as she must have shocked the man watching her.

She hoped to the good Lord that he was alone, although she would still be defenseless against any single tall, broad-shouldered man, if he indeed was a brutish type. Living in the country had taught Ellen that not every lone man, or band of men, were out to ravish women they might come upon in the road. Of course, Ellen wasn't in the road, but her private meadow, her Little London.

And this man with his hair dark as night, his brow pulled together in shock, his mouth half-open as if he might scream or yell himself, was still standing yards away. Staring.

Ellen shut her mouth. She debated on whether another scream was needed or if she should just hightail it back home.

She was quite a fast runner, and she knew every hill, rock, and tree from here to home.

"Please accept my apologies," the man said before Ellen had made up her mind on whether to scream again or to flee.

His voice was low and urgent yet somehow warm, like the melted chocolate that Ellen's governess was so addicted to. He was also turned out like a member of the *ton*. Pale-blue waistcoat, dark-gray overcoat expertly tailored, fitted breeches over muscular thighs that Ellen really shouldn't be noticing, and high polished boots.

And he kept talking. "I have a lame horse and was walking along the road when I thought I heard someone call my name."

Ellen blinked. Then blinked again.

"*Lord Kenworth,* you said," he continued. "That's my name, and I don't know of another Lord Kenworth unless you meant my father, which would be quite impossible. And my younger brother is Lord Robert, who is currently in London with my mother. But when I saw that you were ... play-acting ... I realized you probably didn't mean to address me at all. I didn't mean to startle you." He waved his hand with little purpose. "Preparing for your performance or whatnot. I didn't intend to dwell and watch—especially since we are not acquainted."

Heavens, this man could talk.

"But I was captivated," he continued. "You are a very convincing actress. I actually found myself wishing that I could be a part of whatever world you were living in."

His face flushed. Actually went red. Ellen was quite fascinated. This gentleman, clearly of the ranks of the *ton*, and goodness, a *titled* man at that, was blushing.

He'd stopped talking at last.

"I'm sorry I screamed," she said, because the silence was

much more awkward than his previous rush of words. "And I'm not an actress."

His brows raised, and Ellen decided they were perfectly shaped brows. Dark, thick, and expressive.

"I didn't mean to assume," he said. "I hope that I didn't insult you or your family."

"I can see how you might have assumed," she said, smoothing her dress to give herself something to do. "My father owns Rosecrest Estate, thus I've lived in the country most of my life. Being confused for an actress might be considered a compliment in some circles around here."

The edges of his mouth lifted as if he were about to smile.

Was he amused that she wasn't an actress or that she'd answered him in such a fashion? "And I'm sorry about your horse," she rushed to say.

He seemed surprised at that. "Thank you. Do you know if the inn at the next village keeps extra horses?"

"If you mean the inn at Harpshire, then yes, they keep horses for travelers to change out." Ellen wanted to ask him more questions—like his full name, where he was from, where he was headed. Would it be rude to inquire after his mother? But a breeze had kicked up, stirring her dress about her and reminding her that she'd tugged down her sleeves. She must look a fright, not to mention having acted fool enough so that he thought she was an *actress.*

"Thank you," he said again. "And might I trouble you with one more question?"

She wanted to smile. He was so formal. But she didn't smile, because that might seem too friendly toward a complete stranger. Well, she did know he was Lord Kenworth, something or other.

"How far is this Harpshire?"

"Less than a mile," she said, grateful she could aid him in this. "You're nearly there—you'll see it around the next bend. Is your horse badly hurt?"

"I am not sure," he said. "He's started to limp, so I climbed off."

"I hope it's not serious." Now she was the one chattering.

The man didn't seem to mind; in fact, he took a step closer. For some reason, Ellen thought this action might make her feel nervous or wary. She felt neither. He was still in line with the trees, but now the sun reached him.

"Can I ask you another question before I go?" he said.

She nodded, fully prepared for him to ask her name, even though there was no one to introduce them.

"What's the name of the dance you were performing?"

Ellen blinked. Then she tilted her head. "The waltz."

He seemed to straighten his already-straight posture. "It must be a variation danced in Harpshire."

Ellen exhaled. She knew she'd been off, but how far off she wasn't certain. "I didn't intend for it to be a variation. In truth, I've never seen the waltz performed—only described in the papers."

"Do they not dance the waltz here?" he asked.

"I am not sure, exactly," Ellen said, feeling the earlier enjoyment she had when humming and dancing about the meadow fade into a dull regret. "I've never been to a dance."

"Oh, you're not out yet?" At this he took a step back.

She realized that he thought her a young miss. "I am of age," she said. "Eighteen this past month. But my mother is in delicate health and needs my company."

His face didn't give way to any telling expression. In fact, he went very, very quiet.

The breeze was not cooling off the warmth spreading

through Ellen's body. She'd confessed too many personal things to this Lord Kenworth. She looked away, wondering if it was too late to run back home after all.

"Would you like me to instruct you in the waltz?" he said.

She turned her head to look at him, knowing that she was gaping in a very unladylike fashion. "I do not think that would be proper."

"You're right," he said. "I suppose all of this fresh country air is making my mind addled."

There was nothing addled about this man in the least. "And we have not been introduced," she added.

He didn't turn to go. In fact, he took a step closer. "No, we have not, and unless my horse suddenly starts to talk, there seems to be no one about to do the honors."

"Ellen Humphreys," she said. "Although everyone calls me Ellen."

His mouth curved into a rather nice smile. "Quinn Edwards."

"You mean Lord Kenworth?"

He lifted his brows and looked about the meadow, then his gaze landed back on her. "Quinn will do for here and now, in this meadow of yours."

Ellen scoffed. As soon as the sound came out, she realized it was very unattractive. "I can't very well call you *Quinn.*"

He tilted his head, amusement in his eyes. "You just did." It was as if he were enjoying bantering with her.

She almost scoffed again, but she caught herself in time. She wondered if this man would have ever spoken to her if they'd met at a ball or musicale in London. Out here, where there was no other female within sight, she could almost believe he thought her pleasing. Or perhaps he was one of those rakes whom her mother had forbidden her to even mention.

Before she could stop herself, the question popped out of her mouth. "Are you a rake, Lord Kenworth?"

He nearly missed a step, then his brows pulled together. "I've . . . I'm not . . . a rake."

"Wonderful," Ellen said. "Then I think I would like you to teach me the waltz, provided that we view it only as an instructor teaching a pupil."

He visibly swallowed. "I could be that instructor."

"Very well," she said, holding back a laugh. Was this man of the *ton* actually nervous? "Then I can be the pupil."

Four

MISS ELLEN HUMPHREYS was certainly of age to be out in Society, Quinn decided as he stepped into the meadow. Upon closer and fuller inspection, he saw that she was not as young and innocent as he'd first surmised. No, there was a bit of mischievousness in her pale-green eyes. And her curved lips turned up just so, making him think she might be an accomplished flirt, even if she hadn't been to a dance before. He also realized she was not fairylike at all. She was beautiful, sturdy, and warm.

He'd danced plenty with women whose hands were cold even through their silk gloves. Quinn wondered if Miss Humphreys's warmth was due to her being raised in the country. Or more likely because she'd just been dancing herself beneath the afternoon sun. As it was, he felt her warmth travel from her hand to his and form a sort of cocoon about them.

For when Quinn set his hand at her waist, then took her other hand in his, he felt something he hadn't felt in a long time. Or ever. He felt completely content. As if he were in a place that he never wanted to leave and with a person he never wanted to stop talking to. He didn't want to instruct this woman how to dance. He wanted to ask her about her childhood. What she did with her time in the country. How often she came to this meadow. Which composer was her favorite?

"At least I got the position right," she said, pulling him from his thoughts.

He had been staring at her, and she seemed to be staring right back. Openly. As if she found him interesting. He found that he didn't mind her inspection—it wasn't like the women of the *ton* who inspected him for good teeth, the amount of his hair, and the size of his bank account.

What were they talking about? "You did get it right, the position right," he said, fumbling over his words. "This is the right position after the gentleman leads you the dance floor." He didn't mind speaking to her, but he found that his words seemed to come out wrong. He exhaled. "There are three steps to a waltz. When I learned, the instructor counted out *one, two, three.*"

"Only three steps?" Miss Humphreys said, still looking into his eyes.

How did she do that? How did she make him feel like he wanted to touch the rose blush of her cheek or trace the softness of her gold-brown hair? "Yes, only three steps."

Were they to talk of nothing else but how many steps in a waltz?

"Let's begin," he said, explaining how they would both step at the same time, yet he would step forward while she stepped back. After they survived a few jerky movements, they fell into a rhythm. *One, two, three. One, two, three.*

"Should I hum, or should you?" she asked him.

Quinn laughed. "I think you should hum. You don't want to hear my scratchy voice."

"I think you have a nice voice, Lord Kenworth."

He shook his head, smiling. She couldn't know how he was a horrible singer, and he wasn't about to enlighten her. It turned out he didn't have to argue his point any further, because she started to hum.

Whatever she was humming, it wasn't any composer he knew, but he wasn't about to complain. Her voice was sweet and light, and if he allowed himself to close his eyes, he would fall into another world. He kept his eyes open because truthfully, the ground wasn't all that even, and he didn't want her to trip and then tumble into his arms.

They were close enough as it was, and Quinn was already having trouble keeping a proper distance. One part of his mind knew he was bewitched by the lazy, warm air, the scent of grass and flowers, the separation from all of his worries and concerns . . . The other part of his mind didn't want to leave this meadow or this entrancing woman. He smiled to himself and then quickly learned that Miss Humphreys didn't miss anything.

"Am I doing this wrong?" she asked. "Is that what you find so amusing?"

"Oh no," he said. "You are becoming quite proficient. I was just thinking of the unexpectedness of our situation. Moments ago, I was walking my lame horse on a dirt road. Now, I'm dancing with a beautiful woman while she hums. You have a lovely voice."

Miss Ellen Humphreys laughed. The sound went straight to Quinn's heart, and he nearly stumbled.

"You are one of those accomplished flirts, aren't you?" she said, her pale-green eyes sparkling like early-morning dew.

It was Quinn's turn to laugh. "I do believe, Miss Humphreys, that the term 'accomplished flirt' is used to describe a woman."

Her smile faltered. "Not a man? Oh dear, I'm showing my naivety about Society matters."

"Please don't apologize," Quinn said, wanting the woman to smile again and hating that he'd caused her any distress. "I find you quite refreshing. Besides, I was telling the truth, not flirting."

"Hmm," she said, her cheeks growing even more rosy. "Thank you for the compliment, then. I apologize for doubting your sincerity, but I don't think you can blame me." She lifted her hand from where it had been resting on his shoulder. "As you can see, I don't have many others to interact with and teach me good manners."

Quinn looked about the meadow as if he were truly checking out their surroundings. Then he met her gaze again, hoping to coax a smile or another laugh out of her. "You are better for it," he declared. "You might think the ballroom scene is somehow a magical thing, but I can tell you that it is tedious to the nines. Everyone is so formal, all conversations stiff, about the weather or horses. And if you say something wrong or wear something not up to the latest fashion, you are cruelly dismissed in the gossip columns."

Miss Humphreys raised her perfectly arched brows, and Quinn wondered for a moment if she painted them. No, he decided, they looked quite natural.

"I should be a disaster in a ballroom, I fear," she continued. "It's one thing to imagine a grand ball in this meadow, and another to be surrounded by people such as yourself."

"Such as myself?" he asked.

"You know," she said. "A member of Society who fits in." Her smile returned, but it was sad. "I will probably spend the rest of my life in this place. Caring for my mother. Seeing my brother and father only at holidays. Their business in London keeps them there most of the time."

"Family is important," Quinn said, wondering if he should confess more himself. Miss Humphreys had been so open and honest. He wasn't used to it.

"Of course, I should not wish for the impossible," she said.

"I suppose we all wish that from time to time."

She smiled, and with her smile, another part of Quinn's heart was touched. One deeper than before.

"Thank you for teaching me to waltz, Lord Kenworth. I will never forget it." With that, she stepped out of his arms.

Quinn felt like a small child who'd just had his favorite blanket ripped out of his hands. "Is the dance over?" he asked, finding it hard to hide his disappointment, while wondering if he should be displaying his feelings so much.

"I must return home, and you must take care of your horse."

She stood only a couple of feet from him, but he could still feel her warmth. "You are a practical woman, I see," Quinn said. He was rewarded with another smile, this one a bit wistful. He didn't know a woman could have so many different types of smiles.

"My mother and brother are waiting for me in London. My mother has been ailing of late, although I suspect she will make a swift recovery once I arrive. Perhaps . . ." He hesitated, unsure of what he was about to suggest. "Perhaps I'll see you in a ballroom someday."

She gave a small laugh, her eyes sparkling again. "I don't think so. More likely you will come upon me in this very meadow again. Although, that would be quite a coincidence."

"Indeed." He didn't move, didn't turn to go. No, he was quite rooted to the ground.

He wasn't sure who moved first. It might have been him. Or it might have been that she stepped forward first. But when she closed the short distance between them and rested her hands upon his shoulders, he should have known what was about to happen.

Five

ELLEN HAD LOST her mind. At least that was what went through her thoughts as she pressed her mouth against Quinn's in a moment of insanity. She had taken it upon herself to kiss a man—a stranger—when she had never kissed a man before.

Lord Kenworth must have been surprised, although he did kiss her back, more ardently than she would have ever predicted. His hands went to her waist, and he pulled her so close that their bodies were flush, and Ellen could swear she felt his heart beating as rapidly as hers. He then proceeded to kiss her quite thoroughly—beyond any description she'd ever read in a book.

Eventually, they both had to catch their breath, and when his hold relaxed, Ellen stepped out of his arms. She couldn't look at him after he released her. His rapid breathing met her own in pace, and this embarrassed her even more. She'd stirred up things between them and made a complete fool of herself. What he must think of her boldness. Surely not even an actress or dancer would be so audacious toward a stranger.

Face hot and legs quivering, she turned from Lord Kenworth and hurried across the meadow, away from him and away from the road. Then she started to run. She should have run a long time ago, but instead she'd flirted and waltzed with a stranger. Then she'd kissed him.

Heavens.

Kissing him had been like partaking of the most delicious dessert.

She thought she heard him call after her, but she couldn't be sure over the pounding of her feet, the snapping of twigs, her labored breathing and frantic thoughts. If she stopped and faced him, that would only make things worse. She'd apologize; he'd apologize. And then what? They'd never see each other again, which was to be expected. They'd go their separate ways, both feeling guilty.

He was a member of the *ton*. She was a young woman who lived on a secluded country estate and had never even been to a Society event. She didn't even know about his background, where he lived, who he was connected to. All she knew was that his mother was ailing, that he had a younger brother, and . . . *Good heavens.* He could be married.

Ellen nearly stumbled as she groaned. To all that was good and holy, she hoped she hadn't just thrown herself at a married man. She reached the last line of trees before the sloping hill that led to her home and used the trunk of a tree to brace herself up. She scanned the area as if she expected a great change to have happened to the house and grounds. Everything looked the exact same. How could that be when Ellen felt like everything about her had completely changed?

Perhaps, she thought, perhaps Lord Kenworth had been accosted by country misses all the time. Perhaps he'd thought little of the kiss—maybe found it humorous, and that was all. Yet, even though Ellen tried to convince herself of that, she knew Lord Kenworth had definitely kissed her back. The way that his mouth had captured hers and the way that his arms had pulled her against him. She blushed again at the memory. Stronger than her boldness had been the way he'd responded.

It was clear that Lord Kenworth was an experienced man in the kissing department. Well, that made him a rake after all. Ellen lifted her head and straightened from the tree. No one but she and Lord Kenworth knew about the kiss anyway. She was certain that by the time he arrived at his destination in London, he wouldn't give her a second thought. So she determined to do the same. From the moment she stepped foot in her house, she would completely forget there had ever been a Lord Kenworth in her meadow.

Ellen began to walk with determination toward her home. She made her way down the hillside and then around to the front of the house. This new Ellen wouldn't skulk through the back door; no, she would enter the front door as any lady would do. If her mother found out that she'd been gone, or her governess noticed the late hour, then Ellen would face whatever the consequences might be. It wasn't as if she had any pressing matters to attend to.

In the foyer, Ellen paused when she saw a tray with the day's letters on the sideboard. Their housekeeper must not have delivered the letters to her mother yet. Ellen reached for the stack, noticing a familiar envelope that came every so often from her father's widowed sister, Aunt Prudence. The woman was a busybody to say the least, and her opinions could never be countered. As the wife of the younger brother of a baron, she also believed that she'd been accepted into the top ranks of the *ton*.

But Ellen's mother had clarified that although Aunt Prudence moved in some of the upper circles, it was only when they needed to even out their numbers. It was the one thing that Ellen agreed with her mother on. Ellen turned the letter over in her hand and scanned the elegant script addressed to her father.

What was she writing about, and why did she address it to the country home? Surely Aunt Prudence knew her brother was mostly in the London townhouse or even abroad.

The foyer was quiet, and although Ellen thought she heard a door shut on the second level of the house, she was quite alone. Who knew when her father would receive this letter, and what if it was urgent? Without thinking of what the consequences might be, Ellen broke the seal and pulled out the letter.

It took only moments of reading for Ellen to realize that the letter was about *her*. Yes, it was addressed to her father, but it concerned Ellen.

Dear Patrick,

It is with utmost urgency that I write to you about your daughter, Ellen. The other day, I realized that she had just had her eighteenth birthday and is not out yet. This will not do, Patrick. I know that wife of yours would turn her into a spinster given half the chance, but I cannot in good Christian conscience allow that to happen. I would like you to send her to me for the Season. I will make the appropriate introductions and secure her a good match. I know you have funds to provide a wardrobe, and it's the least that you owe Ellen. I have told you this before, and I'll tell you again, that this girl should not be tucked away in the country for the rest of her life. Who would she marry? The vicar's pimple-faced son? I expect an immediate reply.

Your sister,
Prudence

Ellen read the letter a second time, making sure she didn't miss any words. If this letter had arrived the day before, Ellen would have been ecstatic. She would have believed that she was the most fortunate girl alive. But, today, it was the worst thing she could imagine. For, if she went to London as she always dreamed of and entered the Society circles with her aunt as chaperone, Ellen would eventually run into *him*.

Lord Kenworth.

She could never see the man again. She couldn't even take the chance of possibly running into him. She had ruined herself, and she couldn't let another soul know about it.

Ellen slipped the letter back in its envelope and carried it to her bedroom. Thankfully, she didn't encounter any of the servants, or her governess, on the way. So no one saw her slip the envelope beneath her pillow to be later burned when the evening fire was lit in her bedroom hearth.

It was a letter that needed to go astray, a letter that could never be read by either parent. Ellen, at the age of eighteen, had just forced her fate.

That evening, supper was a quiet affair. Ellen's mother kept to her rooms, as always, and Ellen sat across the table from her governess, Miss Nebeker. The woman looked tired and wrung out, as if she'd had no sleep at all that afternoon. Her normally neat bun was falling out of its pins.

When Ellen noticed Miss Nebeker picking at her food, she said, "Are you feeling well?"

Miss Nebeker looked up, and Ellen was surprised to see the woman's eyes fill with tears. "I feel poorly," she said in a quiet voice. "I tried to sleep earlier, but I only tossed and turned."

"Well, then you should go and rest," Ellen said. "Should I send for the physician?" He was at their house often enough with her mother proclaiming she had one ailment after the other.

"I don't think I'm as bad as that," Miss Nebeker said. "I'll just go lie down, thank you."

Ellen shook her head after her governess left. The woman was at least fifteen years older than Ellen but sometimes acted like a much younger person. If one thing was certain, Ellen shouldn't have been the one ordering the governess to go and rest. Shouldn't her mother be doing that?

Now Ellen was picking at her own food. Eating alone was never favorable, and besides, her mood was becoming blue as she thought of all the things her mother should be doing. If her mother weren't always in such hysterical spirits, could they have a congenial mother-daughter relationship? If only Ellen hadn't kissed Lord Kenworth, then she wouldn't be so against having a London Season.

She released a sigh. She'd made the right choice to hide her aunt's letter, but it still hurt. Ellen had been mere hours away from redirecting her entire life, and she'd thwarted everything. Why did she have to kiss that man?

Six

"WHAT'S GOING ON with you?" Robert asked Quinn over supper.

Quinn looked up at his brother. "What do you mean?" They were dining together while their mother took her meal in her bedroom. She was feeling much better now and acting more cheery, but apparently dressing to eat in the austere dining room was still too much for her.

"Well . . ." Robert's brown eyes filled with their usual amusement. "You keep smiling to yourself. As if you're replaying a pleasant memory over and over in your mind."

Quinn tried not to act surprised at how accurate his brother truly was. For he had been replaying a memory, an event, in his mind. An event that took place only three short days ago, though it seemed more like weeks. The memory of dancing in a country meadow with an enchanting woman.

Robert set down his fork on the china plate so that the plate rattled quite loudly. "Confess what you're thinking of. It's a woman, isn't it?"

Quinn shook his head and was about to deny everything when Robert hooted.

"You can't fool me, brother," Robert continued. "Ever

since you arrived in London, your mind has been elsewhere—with *someone* else. Even the barbs Mother has thrown at us for neglecting this or that have had no effect on you. You've even laughed at some of the things she's said that were meant as stinging retorts."

Quinn was stupefied. He stared at Robert—who might have been the most observant human in the world. Had Quinn been so oblivious to all that his brother claimed? Yet, as Quinn thought about his meeting with Miss Humphreys, he didn't know if he could, or should, share such a bizarre encounter. Quinn didn't quite believe it himself.

"If you won't tell me, then I'll go read about it myself," Robert said, scooting his chair back and setting his napkin on the table.

"Oh, no you don't." Quinn was on his feet in an instant. His brother very well knew that Quinn was a meticulous diary writer, and if there was something to be said, *or* kept secret, it would go into his diary.

Robert made a move toward the hallway, but Quinn was faster. Soon the two brothers were barreling up the stairs, creating a thundering of noise as they raced to Quinn's bedroom. To some, they might seem like juvenile young men, but, distinguished marquess or not, Quinn would use any method of preventing Robert from reading about Ellen in his diary.

Quinn reached the door of his bedroom first. He tugged the door shut and stood in front of it, arms folded across his chest.

Robert came to a running stop and nearly fell against Quinn.

"Open the door," Robert said.

"Never," Quinn retorted.

A woman's voice sailed from somewhere down the hall, calling out to them. "Quinn? Robert?"

Both brothers ignored their mother.

"Who's this woman who has you so off-balance?" Robert asked, leaning close. He was only an inch shorter than Quinn and nearly as broad. "What's her name?"

Quinn hesitated, tempted to tell his brother Miss Humphreys's name. But he didn't want any speculation around a woman he'd never see again anyway. He released a sigh. "It doesn't matter."

Robert arched one of his thick brows. "I'll say it matters. She's in your every thought."

"Quinn? Robert?" Their mother's voice was louder, as if she'd climbed out of bed and crossed her room.

Quinn opened his bedroom door and ushered Robert inside, then shut the door again, secluding them in his bedroom. "She's not a member of the *ton*. Her father is a merchant of some sort."

"And?" Robert pressed. "Is that all?"

"Is that *all*?" Quinn tugged at his cravat. The thing was suddenly too tight. "I'm a marquess now, and according to Mother and every other person who tells me what I'm supposed to be doing, I need to marry above or parallel to my station."

Robert turned from Quinn and walked across the room.

At first Quinn thought his brother might search for the diary after all, but Robert stopped in front of the long windows that overlooked the back garden. "On the other hand, you are the Marquess of Kenworth now, so perhaps it's time you made your own decisions."

Quinn stared at the back of his brother's head. Had he just heard Robert right? "You think I should . . . court this woman?"

Robert spun around. "I think you should do what is right for *you*."

219

Quinn narrowed his eyes. Why was his brother being so conciliatory?

"Don't look at me like that." Robert waved a hand. "All I'm saying is that marriage is a great commitment—you are choosing the person you'll spend the rest of your life with. If you are in love, then that is a better start than what most of us will get."

"Whoa," Quinn said, holding up his hand. "I am *not* in love. I've spent only a short time with her, and it was under an unusual circumstance. Besides, how do you happen to have so much advice on the subject?"

Robert grinned and gave a shrug. "We're talking about you, Marquess. Explain this 'unusual circumstance.'"

Quinn released a sigh and crossed to the set of chairs in front of the cold fireplace. He sat down in one, and Robert took the other chair.

"Her name is Ellen Humphreys," Quinn finally said.

A loud knock sounded at the door, and their mother called through it, "Are you all right in there?"

"I'm fine, Mother," Quinn called back.

"I'm fine as well," Robert added, stifling a laugh.

Their mother paused, as if debating whether or not to believe them. "Don't you two cause any trouble," she said for good measure before she walked away.

Robert shook his head. "I'm so glad you arrived when you did. I was about to go mad being the only one here with Mother." He leaned forward in his chair. "Now, tell me about this woman who's bewitched my brother."

Quinn met Robert's gaze straight on. It was inevitable. If there was one thing about Robert, it was that he never gave up, for better or worse. So, Quinn told his brother about everything, from the first sight of Ellen in the meadow dancing by herself, to how he'd instructed her on the waltz, and then finally to the way she'd suddenly kissed him, then fled the scene.

Robert smiled throughout most of the story and even laughed a few times. "She *ran* away? Like a child runs from her governess?"

"Well, she wasn't walking," Quinn said, his mouth twitching into a smile, although he hated to think she ran because she was embarrassed—which she likely was. He didn't want her to feel embarrassed. She'd kissed him, at first, but if she'd waited even an instant longer, *he* would have kissed *her.*

Robert threw his head back and laughed.

Quinn shook his head at his brother's reaction, but he couldn't help but chuckle too.

"Oh," Robert said, catching his breath and calming. "I want to meet this woman."

Robert's eyes were too bright and eager for Quinn's taste. Quinn pushed out a breath. He had no doubt that once Ellen had her come out into Society, she'd have no shortage of admirers. She was just too . . . fresh, innocent, charming . . . The way her pale-green eyes had sparkled up at him and her soft lips—he knew firsthand how soft they were—curved into an amused smile . . .

"See, you're doing it again!" Robert cut in, his voice like a cold pan of water dashed over Quinn's feet.

He flinched.

"We have a situation, Lord Kenworth," Robert said in a formal and demanding tone, much like he was mocking their mother's stern voice. "You're besotted, and something must be done. The question is . . . what?"

Quinn groaned and tugged at his cravat. "I can't very well ride all over the countryside in search of her. I don't even know where she lives."

Robert barked out a laugh. "That can be fixed by a simple

inquiry. You know the woman's first and last name, and it won't be hard to find out her father's."

Quinn nodded, mostly to himself, because if he indeed did inquire after her father, then that would mean he was interested in Miss Humphreys. That perhaps the things Robert had accused him of were true. *Laws.* What would his mother think? Let alone *say*?

"Wait," Quinn said, not believing he'd forgotten this, or that he was about to tell Robert. "She said her father and brother have a place in London."

"Ah," Robert said with a wink. "What luck. How many Humphreys can there be?"

Seven

A SECOND LETTER had arrived three days later, and fortunately Ellen saw it on the side table in the foyer before the housekeeper could deliver the post to Mother. Ellen had just finished her morning meal, and her governess had gone to the library to ready the day's lesson. So it was that Ellen found herself in the foyer by herself. She snatched up the letter with the familiar hand and hurried to her room before opening it and reading Aunt Prudence's words. The missive was much like the first one, although the tone was a bit more demanding.

Ellen was flattered that her aunt was taking such an interest in her, although even if Ellen had wanted a Season, she didn't know if she'd be able to bear Aunt Prudence's company for long. Yet the sentiment was kind and generous. Ellen could just hear her mother's opinion now about how Aunt Prudence was just using Ellen to further her own position in Society.

Ellen tucked the envelope beneath her pillow once again. The first letter was long since burned, and she tried not to feel guilty about it. The other option would be to confess her crimes and then be faced with explaining the reason she didn't want to go to London after all, despite years of pleading with her father.

Ellen had tried to stay content since her life-changing event in the meadow. She'd tried to forget all about Lord Kenworth, and she found this was possible in only very few moments during the day. She knew she was being ridiculous. They'd spent less than an hour together, but that time had expanded in her mind while she thought about each and every action between them and each and every word.

Someone knocked on her door, and Ellen quickly straightened from the bed and turned. "Yes?"

"Your mother is asking for you, miss," her mother's lady's maid said.

"Thank you, Mary," Ellen called out. Then she took a moment to check her hair. If there was one thing that her mother didn't abide, it was a sloppy coiffure. Even though her mother spent her days in one location, she still demanded that protocol be followed.

Satisfied that her hair was neat enough, Ellen left her room to meet Mary, who was waiting to escort her. Mary was in her forties, but she still seemed spry and youthful. She was definitely the perfect lady's maid for Ellen's mother, since Mary always followed orders immediately and exactly. They walked along the corridor to Ellen's mother's quarters. A couple of years ago, her mother had had the end of the wing renovated so that her bedchamber also had two sitting rooms. One was her morning room, the other her evening room.

Mary opened the door to the suite and motioned for Ellen to enter.

One might say that Ellen looked like her mother, since both had green eyes and honey-brown hair. Although all the years of reclusiveness had paled and thinned her mother's skin significantly. Her mother reminded Ellen of a paper doll. All dressed up, but only on the outside. Inside, her mother was fragile. Their topics of conversation were mostly one-sided, and when Ellen did answer, she kept her answers as short as possible. Any elaboration would only lead to more questions and then eventually overdramatizations. Ellen had learned by age twelve how not to send her mother into hysterics.

As she walked with Mary into the morning room, Ellen wondered what her mother wanted with her so early in the day. Lessons with her governess hadn't even started yet.

"There you are," her mother said in her reedy voice.

Ellen had to admit her mother looked quite regal this morning—although it was rather early for her to be up and about. Her mother wore her hair piled on top of her head with a beaded headband laced through. Her morning dress was a pale lavender, embroidered with silver-thread flowers. If not for the wrinkles about her mouth and eyes and the sallow skin at her neck, she might pass for a much younger woman.

"Hello, Mother," Ellen said, dutifully offering a curtsy.

"That color is terrible on you."

Ellen looked down at her own morning gown of plain white. How did someone look poorly in white? It wasn't even a color.

"Mary," her mother continued without waiting for a reply from Ellen. "You must do something about Ellen's choices in white dresses. How many do you have?"

This last question was directed at Ellen again.

Ellen wanted to give an accurate answer, but she didn't exactly know how many white dresses she had. "Five or six," she said, hoping she hadn't delayed too long in her answer to annoy her already-annoyed mother.

"How did that happen?" her mother said, again looking at Mary. "You know she looks poorly in white, therefore she should not own any white dresses."

Mary visibly paled and swallowed. This was the first time her mother had criticized the color white. There had been plenty of criticisms about her clothing choices, her hairdos, her skin that was too tanned, and other things, but never before about the color white. Ellen knew it, and she knew that this was the first Mary had heard such a comment.

Yet Mary nodded her head as if she were personally responsible. "I will go through Ellen's wardrobe today and donate all of her white dresses to charity."

Her mother sniffed as her eyes narrowed. "See that you do." Then her attention swung back toward Ellen.

"I have had word from your father."

Ellen blinked. This was unexpected. She hadn't seen a letter this morning, or the morning before, from her father. Or had she missed it somehow?

"He feels that you should begin to mingle with other people your age," her mother said.

Ellen tried not to react, for her mother was watching every movement she made. Had her aunt gotten ahold of her father anyway?

"It seems that he's let London go to his head, yet again," her mother continued. "We both know what happens when he's away from home too long. He gets ideas and notions that I can never support."

Ellen swallowed. What had her father meant by 'mingling'? That she'd be allowed to go to the village dances? She'd been able to go to the village fair only twice yearly, never the dances. She wouldn't mind going to a dance—one in which she could be assured that no men named Lord Kenworth would be in attendance.

She tried not to bounce on her heels, but in truth, that was exactly what she felt like doing.

"Your father thinks you should attend the village dances."

Ellen wanted to smile, but she quickly schooled her features. She could tell that Mary was surprised at the conversation as well, but like Ellen, Mary was a master of not reacting.

Her mother paused. "Well, what do you think? Your father insisted that I get your opinion on the matter. Once you've given me yours, I'll give you mine."

Ellen had to tread carefully. If she said she would like to attend the dances, and her mother wanted her to stay home, then her mother would fly into a tirade about how she had an ungrateful daughter. But if Ellen said that she didn't want to go, and her mother determined that she should go, then her mother might write back to her father about how ungrateful their daughter was.

So, Ellen said, "I will do whatever you think is best, Mother." Ellen hated herself for her compliance, but she hated her mother's temper more.

Her mother smiled. It wasn't a sweet smile, though; it was more of a calculating smile. "Have I a raised a daughter who has no opinions? Are you so weak as to have no capacity to make up your mind about a simple village dance?" Her gaze snapped to Mary. "Fetch the governess. I need to find out what exactly has been taught in the schoolroom these past eighteen years. Perhaps it is time to look for a new employee."

Ellen felt sick to her stomach. Her mother's threats were never idle. How could a simple question, and a very vague answer, lead to Miss Nebeker's dismissal? Ellen wished she could run to the library and warn the poor woman. Ellen believed that the afternoon naps her governess took were a direct result of having to answer to her mother.

"Right away, my lady," Mary said, then hurried from the room.

Ellen was left to stand alone before her mother. Until she was invited to sit, Ellen was required to stand.

Her mother turned her head toward the windows. "You will not attend any village dances. No daughter of mine will stoop to socializing with those beneath her. Your father will agree once I explain things to him."

Whatever Ellen's hopes might have been, she should have known this would be the outcome. Perhaps later, the disappointment would sink in. But for now, she gave no reaction, no answer.

"And," her mother continued. "I cannot abide any more white dresses."

Typically, Ellen would pacify her mother, assure her that the offending white dresses would be sent out. Then Ellen could leave her mother's rooms. But Miss Nebeker was on her way up, and Ellen sensed that her mother was still spoiling for a fight, which left Ellen feeling particularly desperate.

"What does it matter what color I wear if I am not to go to any village dances or anything in the village for that matter," Ellen said before she could think better of it. "I don't see anyone, and no one sees me. Changing the color of my dress won't change anything in my life. The only two people I see outside of this household are the postman and the milkman. They certainly could not care less if I'm wearing white or blue. Besides, *I* like white. And that's *my* opinion. Does that count for anything?"

When Ellen took a much-needed breath, she realized her mother was staring at her, open-mouthed. Her mother's face had flushed a deep red—so red, in fact, that Ellen worried she'd gone too far, said too much. If only she could go back a handful of minutes in time and not say anything at all.

Her mother slowly rose to her feet. Then, just as Mary escorted Miss Nebeker into the morning room, her mother pointed a long, narrow finger at Ellen. "Leave me now! You are to be locked in your room for the next two weeks. I will not have this defiance in my household."

Before Ellen could comprehend all that had happened, her mother turned her fury on the governess. "You are to pack your things and be gone by tomorrow morning."

The tears started despite Ellen's resolve to keep her emotions hidden. She didn't want to see Miss Nebeker leave, but her mother's words had frozen Ellen.

Miss Nebeker's face had drained of all color, and she looked as if she were about to be ill.

Ellen knew the woman had nowhere to go. Would she beg for a job at the village inn? Would she become a maid at one of the other country estates? Being turned out so quickly didn't even give her time to write letters or put out a notice.

When Miss Nebeker started to back out of the room, Ellen took a deep breath and said, "Wait!"

Everyone in the room stilled.

Ellen didn't dare look at her mother, but she could feel the anger coming from the woman. "What if I hired you?"

"You'll do no such thing," her mother said.

Ellen finally looked at her mother. "I have been saving my pin money for two years," she said. "And since I'm eighteen, I should probably have my own lady's maid."

Her mother's lips pressed together into a thin line. Everything about her mother looked thin right now. "This is still my house, and you are still my daughter. I am the mistress here, and you will do as I say." She looked at Mary. "Take Ellen to her room directly. I will deal with Miss Nebeker on my own."

Ellen tried to catch the governess's eye, but she was

looking down at her clenched hands. Ellen knew the best thing was to let everyone's emotions calm down. The women needed to separate. So she let Mary lead the way back to her bedroom. There, she sat on the bed and listened as Mary turned a key in the lock from the outside.

Eight

MORNING MEALS WERE never pleasant at the London town-house, Quinn decided as he joined his mother in the dining room. Somehow, his brother was able to get out of them and sleep longer. Quinn was naturally an early riser, though, and his mother's tendency to call for his presence in the morning anyway meant that Quinn had started taking meals with her. He'd been here a full week and was already making plans to leave even though the Season would be starting soon. He would tell his mother that he'd return in a couple of months—when most of the matches had been made. He didn't want to be caught up in the frantic pace of everyone speculating.

His mother Josephine wore her usual black widow's weeds today, and when he complimented her on her dress—as any gentleman would do—she pursed her lips.

"Thank you, son," she said, her tone begrudging, as if it pained her to be polite. "But we have more important matters to discuss this morning."

"Does this have anything to do with the stack of letters at your elbow?" Quinn asked, helping himself to the food lain out on the side table. He piled on cold eggs and ham, then added two scones. The marmalade was already set out on the table.

"Why, yes it does." She smiled and tapped the neat little stack. "We're going to find you a wife."

Quinn was grateful that he'd already swallowed the juice he'd poured, or else he would have spit out the entire mouthful. While his mind raced to find an answer, his brother came into the dining room.

"Oh, hello, dear," his mother said. "You're awake early."

Quinn looked at Robert—the man was fully dressed and presentable, which meant he was up to something. Robert kissed his mother's cheek and then turned to the sideboard and proceeded to fill his own plate with enough food for two men.

"What's this about finding Quinn a wife?" Robert said over his shoulder.

Laws. Robert had heard their mother's comment.

"I've got a full two weeks' worth of invitations here," his mother said. "I'm sure that one of them there will be a woman equal to the task of becoming a marquess's wife."

"Hmm," Robert said, walking over to sit next to his mother. After setting down his plate and pouring himself a glass of juice, he picked up one of the invitations. "Lady Helen Anderson is pleased to invite you and your sons to an intimate ball at her home in Grosvenor Square."

Nothing about Grosvenor Square is intimate, Quinn thought. The houses were posh and elegant. Only the upper crust of the *ton* owned homes in the area. He'd overheard his own mother coveting the estates more than once.

"Do we know this *Lady Helen*?" Robert said in a teasing, pretentious voice.

Their mother laughed. Quinn did have to admit that it

was good to hear her laugh. Robert was quite skilled at coaxing it from her.

Robert continued to read. "In honor of my esteemed daughter, Lady Amelia, who is of age this year."

"See, a debutante ball," their mother said. "It will be just the thing for Quinn." She smiled at Robert. "*You* might even start looking around if there are any heiresses present."

"Lady Amelia . . ." Robert mused. "Do I know her from any childhood events?"

"She's about six years your junior, so I doubt it."

All this talk of "Lady Amelia" was bringing another woman to mind for Quinn—Ellen.

"Still, Lady Amelia Anderson sounds familiar," Robert continued. "Does she have a brother?"

"She does!" their mother said. "I'd almost forgotten. He would have been a year or two ahead of Quinn at Eton. Do you remember August?"

Quinn looked up from biting into a scone and met the gaze of Robert, who promptly winked at him.

Quinn narrowed his eyes and shook his head at his brother to warn him off whatever he was up to.

"I do remember August," Robert said. "Do you, Quinn?"

Quinn thought the name did sound familiar, but no face came to mind.

Remarkably, during this conversation, Robert had managed to eat his entire meal.

"Well, Mother," Robert said, rising to his feet. "I must be on my way. I have some business to do with Mr. Humphreys."

Quinn snapped his head up and stared at his brother.

Robert purposely kept his gaze on their mother.

"Who's Mr. Humphreys?" she asked.

"A man who I'd like to discuss some investment advice with." Robert kissed her on the cheek. "Nothing to concern yourself with. I look forward to hearing which invitations you will be accepting."

Quinn tried to keep the scowl off his face so that his mother wouldn't see. But he wasn't about to let Robert get away without some sort of explanation. As Robert left the room, Quinn told his mother, "Excuse me for a moment." Then he hurried after Robert, catching him just as he was opening the front door.

"What are you about?" Quinn said in a hushed voice, although he felt like yelling.

Robert grinned, settling his hat upon his head with a flourish.

Quinn grabbed his arm.

It was Robert's turn to narrow his eyes. "I've done the investigating and found the father of the woman you are so enamored with."

"Robert," Quinn said in a warning voice, tightening his grip.

"I'm going to have a simple conversation with the man." Robert's smile dimmed. "Don't worry, I won't bring up your name, or heaven forbid, his daughter's. It's a fact-finding mission. I'll report back what I learn."

Quinn exhaled. "I don't like it."

"I think after my conversation with Mr. Humphreys, we can determine our next course of action."

"*Next* course of action?" Quinn said.

Robert paused. "Do you trust me or not?"

Quinn eyed him. "I don't know."

"Come on, brother," Robert said. "You know I have only your best interest in mind. If this Miss Humphreys is a woman worth pursuing, then you'll need me on your side when Mother finds out."

Quinn released his brother's arm. "True." He stepped back, then gave a nod.

Robert flashed a smile and was outside in a blink.

Quinn schooled his thoughts for a moment, then returned to the dining room. He sat down and continued to eat methodically, without really tasting his food. His mother read through the stack of invitations, accepting Quinn's occasional nod as good enough for her.

It seemed that every evening over the next fortnight would be filled with Society affairs. Quinn wasn't sure exactly what Robert thought he was going to accomplish, but Quinn hoped that whatever it was, he would be forgiven if he decided to return home and leave Robert to accompany their mother himself to each function.

Quinn found much to occupy himself with the rest of the day while he went through account ledgers in the library, although his thoughts were never far away from what Robert might be doing, or more to the point, what a certain young woman was doing out in Harpshire. It was a fine day, full of sun and light breezes. The sort of day on which he'd first spied her in the meadow. Was she there now? Was she practicing the steps of the waltz on her own again?

The thought made him smile, and he took a break from the ledgers to fetch his personal diary from his bedroom. Back in the library, he sipped on a glass of brandy while he narrated the week's events in brief script. Then he reread the entry he'd written down the night that he'd first arrived at the London house—the night after he'd danced with Miss Humphreys.

His own words brought back her image, the sound of her humming, and the honey-gold color of her hair. If he closed his own eyes, he could imagine the pale-green of hers gazing directly at him.

"Have you been in here all day?" Robert's voice cut into Quinn's thoughts.

Quinn looked up to see his brother leaning against the doorframe of the library. He hadn't even heard the door open.

By the amused and knowing look on Robert's face, Quinn knew his brother brought news. Quinn realized he was holding his diary in his lap, and he quickly shoved it into the drawer of the credenza. He then closed the most recent ledger that he'd been working on in order to give his brother his full attention.

"So?" Quinn prompted. "What's the news?"

Robert smiled, then pulled the door shut behind him. He crossed the library and settled into the chair opposite Quinn. "I spoke to Mr. Humphreys. He's what we'd call country gentry, although he is a man of trade now. Quite successful, I'd add."

Quinn nodded. "What is it that he does?"

"He runs a textile factory," Robert said, folding his hands in his lap. "And his son Gerald works as his business manager."

"They sound respectable enough," Quinn mused.

"The *ton* will turn up their noses." Robert shrugged. "But a marquess shouldn't have to care what others think."

"Slow down," Quinn said. "You act as if I'm about to propose marriage to Miss Humphreys."

"Right, sorry," Robert said, but the amusement remained on his face. "I have another bit of news . . . well, several things, in fact."

Quinn leaned forward. "What now?"

"I've been to visit our old friend August Anderson," Robert said.

"Whatever for? Are you interested in his debutante sister or something?"

"No," Robert said. "At least, I don't know because I haven't actually met her. But I might have suggested that *he* suggest to his mother that she send out a few more invitations. Among my recommendations was the Humphreys family. One to Mr. Humphreys and one to Mr. Humphreys's sister. Apparently the father's sister lives in London as well—widow of a baron's brother—so she's all right and proper. Thought if more than one person in the family received an invitation, there would be a good chance of Miss Ellen Humphreys showing up at the Anderson ball."

Quinn blinked. "You did . . . what?"

"I told August—"

Quinn held up his hand. "You've been meddling like a woman!" He hadn't meant to shout, but it came out that way. He hoped to high heaven his mother hadn't heard. The last thing he needed was for her to come into the library and set in with her own questions.

Robert's eyes widened a fraction, then he chuckled. "I might have started a bit of gossip, but who doesn't from time to time?"

Quinn tugged at his cravat and stood. He paced to the tall windows overlooking the gardens. What had his brother done? And why would August agree to pass on such a message to his mother?

Quinn whirled and faced his brother. "You didn't."

The smile on Robert's face said everything.

Quinn knew then and there that Robert had told August, and who knew who else, that Quinn had a *tendre* for Miss Ellen Humphreys. The heat of anger flooded him and threatened to overboil. "If you weren't my brother, I'd call you out."

Robert leaped to his feet. "It's a good time for me to leave you alone, then." He took a comical step backward as if he were a child tiptoeing into the kitchen in the middle of the night. "Just remember, it's only an invitation. We can't predict if her father and aunt will accept or even bring Miss Humphreys out of hiding to attend the ball." He took another step back, arriving closer to the door. "If she does appear at the ball at Grosvenor Square, then the rest, my dear brother, is up to you."

Nine

ELLEN HAD CRIED her eyes out until they were red and swollen. She'd also developed a sniffly nose. It didn't help that her mother had stayed true to her word, and the day after her mother had threatened Miss Nebeker, the governess had indeed left.

The only saving grace was that Ellen had sent a letter with Miss Nebeker, addressed to Aunt Prudence, begging her to give Miss Nebeker residence until she could secure another position. Not only was Ellen crushed at the punishment of being locked in her room like a willful child, but she missed her governess. She'd been a friend and someone to talk to. Really, the only friend she'd had.

"Miss?" Mary's voice called through the door. "I have your supper."

Supper on a tray. That's how Ellen had been eating her meals for two days.

Ellen crossed the room to open her bedroom door. There stood Mary, her eyes lowered like usual and a tray in her hands.

"Thank you," Ellen said, taking the tray. She had barely walked across her room and set it on the edge of her bed when she heard the door lock turn again. Ellen sighed, then sat next to the tray and picked up the fork. Today, it appeared she was eating thinly sliced roast beef and boiled potatoes.

She took a few bites, then heard a commotion outside in the front driveway. Ellen crossed to the window and looked down to the driveway. A carriage had arrived, and she watched as her father climbed out of it . . . followed by her Aunt Prudence.

Ellen's heart nearly stopped. Their appearance had to be about her—there could be no doubt. She watched her aunt's skirts sweep up the stairs behind her and then heard the door shut downstairs. In the quiet of Ellen's bedroom, she could hear the buzz of conversation coming from below. Then silence. Ellen crept to her bedroom door and tried to listen for any further sound.

Footsteps coming up the stairs, then walking swiftly down the hallway.

Another voice carried—that of Ellen's aunt—then all went silent again.

Ellen wished she could see through the door and find out what was going on. If both her father and aunt had arrived at the same time, then surely her aunt had questioned Father about receiving her notes. And now . . . Ellen heard her mother's voice coming from down the hall. Father must have gone in to speak with Mother, and based on the volume, they were in a fierce argument.

Ellen couldn't move; she could barely breathe.

She couldn't distinguish the words of the argument above the beating of her heart.

Ellen closed her eyes and leaned her head against the door. The words eventually faded, then footsteps again. Someone knocked on her door, and Ellen jumped back.

"Ellen," her father called out. "Come to your mother's rooms."

Ellen swallowed against the lump in her throat. "Can you unlock the door?"

The silence was thick. Moments later, the lock turned, and a pale Mary opened the door.

Ellen's gaze swung from Mary to her father. She'd never seen him look so furious. His face was stained red, even reaching into his gray-streaked hairline.

He exhaled as he looked her up and down. Apparently satisfied with her appearance, he said, "Come with me."

She followed her father along the corridor. Mary remained at the doorway of the bedroom. Ellen wondered what state her mother might be in and what was about to be said. It was clear her father wasn't pleased to find Ellen locked in her room, but he had rarely interfered with Mother's decisions.

The door to her mother's chambers had been left open, and her father walked through. Ellen couldn't help being shocked at her mother's appearance. She wore her night rail with her robe as if she hadn't even dressed at all that day. Her hair was unpinned, and she looked at least ten years younger.

Her father turned to face Ellen. "Your aunt Prudence has invited you to her home for the Season. Your mother and I have consented to this arrangement."

Her mother made a sort of scoffing noise, but Ellen didn't dare look at her. Every part of her body had grown cold. She was being sent to London to attend Society events with her aunt. It was all of her dreams coming true in the most awful way.

"I . . . don't have a wardrobe for London," Ellen said, even though she hadn't meant to speak at all. For how could she explain that she didn't want to run into a certain member of the *ton*?

Her father didn't hesitate before he said, "Your aunt will take care of choosing your wardrobe. We are to leave first thing in the morning." He glanced at her mother, then looked back to Ellen. "Prudence is waiting in the parlor right now to discuss all that you need to prepare for."

When Ellen didn't move, her father added in a softer tone, "Go on now. I'll be there shortly."

Ellen practically fled her mother's chambers. She shut the door that connected to the corridor, then she made her way to the stairs. Her mind spun as she tried to comprehend all that was changing in such a short time. One part of her felt exhilarated to be leaving the estate and going to London. The other part of her wanted to go back into her room and lock herself in. She would just have to ignore Lord Kenworth if she sighted him. He would likely ignore her as well.

Ellen began to descend the stairs. She couldn't hear any arguing coming from her mother's chambers, so she took that as a good thing, though she wasn't looking forward to facing an audience from Aunt Prudence.

Aunt Prudence was standing before a fire in the parlor, which she must have ordered lit. She turned when Ellen came into the room.

"Oh, my dear," Aunt Prudence said, rushing forward with her arms outstretched. Her lemon-colored dress ballooned about her, adorned with what must be yards of lace and ribbon. "When Miss Nebeker showed up at my doorstep, I knew I couldn't stay away another minute. And you, you are a sight!"

Ellen embraced her aunt and was immediately enveloped in the heavy scent of expensive perfume. She had to force herself not to sneeze.

"Has your mother starved you as well?" Aunt Prudence said, grasping Ellen's upper arm. "You are as slender as a rake."

Ellen was not slender, and she knew it, but compared to Prudence's ample curves, Ellen supposed she was slender.

"I sent letter after letter," Prudence said, "but there was no reply from your father. So I finally had to visit that townhouse of his and demand to know what was going on. I found out that he'd just returned to London an hour before my visit and that his letters had been forwarded home."

Prudence stepped back and scanned Ellen from head to foot. "It seems I've come just in time. You're a lovely girl, but your wardrobe is atrocious. I don't know how your mother thinks she can—"

"Prudence." Ellen's father had arrived. "There will be no backbiting."

"Of course not," Aunt Prudence amended with a rather regal sniff. "There is a lot of work to be done—that was all I was saying."

Her father came into the room and folded his arms. He narrowed his gaze as he peered at Ellen. Why, this week of all weeks, did her parents decide to pay attention to her?

"I cannot believe that your wife hasn't planned a coming out for Ellen," Prudence continued. "It's a shame, really."

Her father looked over at his sister. "Not everyone lives and dies by London Society. We are quite content in the country."

"Hmph. You mean your *wife* is content," Aunt Prudence said. "You have a lovely daughter here who is just wasting away."

"Prudence . . ." Her father's voice held warning.

She placed her hands on her hips. "Well, I don't need to reiterate my feelings." She cast a sidelong glance at Ellen. "We have a lot of work to do upon our arrival in London tomorrow. Best get to sleep and rest those swollen eyes."

Ellen felt her eyes start to burn with tears again. She

didn't want to cry, but Aunt Prudence's words were the kindest she'd heard in a long time. Her father gave her a nod, his lips pressed together as if he were holding back on further conversation.

By the time Ellen reached her room, her thoughts were full of new worries. Not only would she possibly have to face Lord Kenworth and her embarrassing actions, but she knew her manners were far from polished. Until she'd met Lord Kenworth, she didn't even know how to dance a waltz. And she hadn't danced other dances with a male. Her governess had been her only companion. She hadn't known that conversation between a man and woman was supposed to be about the weather and horses.

Lord Kenworth had been a kind man, a kind man who was probably amused at her country-girl antics, but what about other men whom she might speak with? Would they even pay attention to her? Would they consider her worthy wife material?

Ten

"HAVE YOU SEEN Mother's calendar?" Robert asked, maneuvering his stallion alongside Quinn's as they rode through Hyde Park.

Quinn kept the galloping pace he'd set as soon as he'd arrived at the park. Tonight was the Anderson ball, and he knew there was a chance that Miss Ellen Humphreys would be there. To take his mind off things, he'd decided to attend a hot air balloon launch on the other side of the park. Only a few people were invited so that word didn't spread to the police.

Quinn wasn't in a hurry to arrive at the launch location, but riding hard through the park helped to distract him.

"I take it by your silence and the hard set of your jaw that you know what tonight is," Robert continued.

Quinn shot a glance at his brother. "It's all Mother talked about at supper last night."

Robert chuckled, then slapped his reins. His horse was starting to lag. "Sorry I missed supper; I know that you were hoping for my company."

Quinn released a sigh, then pulled back on his own reins.

They were within sight of the launch area, but the conversation Quinn needed to have with his brother should remain private. "I feel as if Mother thinks every social event will be magical. That the perfect woman and potential daughter-in-law with a large fortune is going to walk into the room, and birds will start singing or something."

Robert nodded, obviously trying to keep a grin off his face.

"My inheritance and title should be sufficient, but it's not enough for Mother," Quinn continued. He might as well get it all out, right now. "Even if I did find, and subsequently marry, the woman who our Mother thinks meets all of *her* criteria, I suspect she will find fault anyway. Perhaps it will be our children, or in the way my wife manages our household, or a number of other things. I'm about ready to pack my bag and return to the country despite the fact that I promised Mother I'd stay for a fortnight of events."

Robert laughed.

"Why are you laughing?" Quinn narrowed his gaze. His brother looked positively gleeful.

"You're nervous, aren't you?" Robert said. "For tonight."

Quinn didn't react. Rather, he tried not to react. He looked toward the hot air balloon launch. About a dozen people had gathered, and he could see their friend Carmel waving his hands as he explained his theory to those gathered. Quinn had read everything Carmel had written, and he hoped to add more to his own research by observing Carmel's launch today. But Robert didn't miss the fact that Quinn was pretending to be absorbed in the distant goings-on.

"August informed me that our 'friends' have accepted the invitation," Robert said.

This captured Quinn's full and complete attention. He looked over at his brother. " *Who* accepted?"

"August just said, 'your friends,' and I didn't press for anything more."

Quinn exhaled. Worst case, her father or her aunt would be at the ball, and he would see her relatives. Or . . . *she* was coming. Tonight. He might see Miss Ellen Humphreys tonight.

When he realized Robert was grinning at him again, Quinn shook his head.

"I'm not nervous," Quinn announced.

"You are so nervous," Robert said, letting a small laugh escape.

"Are you coming with me tonight?" Quinn asked.

Robert snapped his reins, and his horse lurched forward. "I wouldn't miss it for anything."

Quinn watched Robert gallop ahead for a few moments, then he set his own horse into motion. As he rode to where Carmel was kneeling on the ground, adjusting the burner, Quinn decided he'd blown his expectations out of proportion about Miss Humphreys and possibly seeing her at a social event. He didn't even know her, not really. If he saw her in a ballroom, she'd blend in with all the other women. In fact, he probably wouldn't even notice her unless someone pointed her out—which no one would. He could barely remember the color of her eyes and hair and the way she smiled at him with her curious gaze . . .

Quinn reached the launch site and reined in his horse, then climbed down. He greeted the men he already knew in the gathering, then introduced himself to the remaining few. He joined Carmel kneeling on the ground.

The Frenchman's eyes lit up as he saw Quinn.

"You've come," Carmel said, pushing his hair out of his eyes. It had come out of the ribbon that was tying it back.

Even though Napoleon's war had ended, Carmel had worked hard on reducing his French accent. In fact, he had been going by Carl in the several years he'd lived in England. He might have given up his name and his language, but he hadn't taken shortcuts on fashion. Now, Carmel made an interesting sight as he knelt in silk pantaloons, topped with a dark peach vest and intricately tied cravat.

"Almost ready," Carmel said, rising to his feet and brushing off his hands. "There she goes."

The balloon was quickly inflating with the help of a few men holding it just so to catch the blowing heat coming from the burner. Carmel climbed into the basket, a grin on his face.

Everyone cheered as the balloon rose above the ground. Quinn and Robert ran alongside it, then below as it rose higher and higher and moved across the park. There weren't many people in the park, but those who were there stopped and stared.

"Abort, abort!" Robert yelled.

Quinn looked back up at the balloon. One side was caved in, and it was descending fast. Then Quinn saw flames. He sprinted toward where the balloon was about to crash. A figure tumbled out of the basket and rolled on the ground.

Quinn slowed to check on Carmel as the balloon crashed to the ground a few yards beyond. "Are you all right?" he asked, looking for signs of flames. Thankfully, the man wasn't on fire.

"My balloon is destroyed!" Carmel said, his accent thick in his distress. He had leaves and twigs stuck to his clothing, and a fine bruise would soon color his cheek.

Quinn helped Carmel to his feet while Robert joined with the other men, using their coats to beat down the flame before it set any bushes or trees afire.

Carmel turned to stare at the burning mess, his face stricken.

Quinn clapped his hand on his friend's shoulder. "Look

at it this way," Quinn said. "You flew higher and longer than last time."

Carmel exhaled. "I panicked when I got too close to the trees, so I fed the fire too hot."

A shout caught Quinn's attention. A couple of men were riding toward them, and they didn't look happy. "We need a different location next time. We don't want to be reported to the magistrate."

"Right." Carmel brushed his hands off and went to speak with the new arrivals.

The fire had been put out, and all that was left was a smoldering, blackened mess.

"Well," Robert said, coming up to Quinn. "That was short and sweet. Hopefully those gentlemen won't be too cross. Although I know someone who can speak on his behalf to the magistrate if needed."

Quinn shrugged. "All in the name of research, I say."

Robert laughed, and Quinn found himself smiling. It had been exhilarating watching that balloon fly. They strode back to their horses and remounted. On the ride out of Hyde Park, the upcoming night started to become a reality. Robert had been right. Quinn was nervous. But he knew he was just nervous about the unknown. Once he saw her, or didn't see her, surely he'd return to his right mind again.

As they rode back together, Robert struck up an inane conversation, making the most annoying observations. Observations such as how many might be in attendance at the ball, how many young women might be seeking a husband, and how many ladies their mother would insist they meet.

Quinn urged his horse faster, pulling ahead of Robert.

Once he reached their townhouse, Quinn dismounted, handed the reins over to the groomsman, and entered the house well ahead of his brother. Silence at last. Fortunately, he made it to his bedchamber without encountering his mother either.

By the time his valet had shaved him and Quinn had dressed for the evening, the effects of the afternoon riding and the events of the balloon disaster had long since worn off, and all that remained was the anticipation for tonight. As agreed upon, Robert met Quinn in the foyer, and they had to wait for their mother for only a few moments.

Robert was sufficiently subdued, probably having decided to pass the mantle of wife talk on to their mother. And she didn't disappoint.

On the way over to Grosvenor Square and the Anderson's home, their mother talked nonstop about the families who would be in attendance and which ones had eligible daughters. She even narrowed down her list to the young ladies who were more accomplished than other young ladies.

Quinn supposed that was why the *ton* called these events a marriage mart. He felt as if he were on a shopping excursion.

He was the first to exit the carriage, and he very much appreciated the cool night air. If his valet hadn't tied Quinn's cravat so precisely, he would have been tempted to adjust it.

As it was, Quinn, his brother, and his mother all arrived at the Anderson's home uneventfully, without argument, and without further teasing from Robert. The ball was already in full swing, and the small orchestra was playing at one end of the ballroom while long tables of refreshments were set up on the opposite.

Quinn went through the introductions to the Anderson parents, then August—who he did recognize, thankfully—and then finally to August's sister. She was introduced as Lady Amelia Anderson, and Quinn supposed she was a pretty young woman. Although she must have been about eighteen, she looked three years younger than that.

As soon as it was polite to do so, Quinn separated from his family. He was thirsty, and what better place to observe the crush than from the refreshment table?

Once he had his glass of strong lemonade in hand, he scanned the room. Those on the ballroom floor were dancing the quadrille, and Quinn scanned through the women, looking for one who fit Miss Humphreys's description. No one matched the woman he remembered, yet his pulse was still thrumming in anticipation.

Perhaps she hadn't arrived yet, or perhaps she wouldn't be in attendance at all.

But then why was his heart beating so fast, as if he somehow sensed she was in the room?

"There you are," a man said, and Quinn turned to see Carmel. The bruise on his cheek didn't look quite as black as Quinn had expected. The man wore a dark-gray coat and lavender vest—not something every man could get away with, but Carmel could pull it off.

They walked along the edge of the crowd together, then they stopped to observe the party from one corner of the room. "Did you get reported to the magistrate?" Quinn asked.

Carmel laughed. "Oh, I talked those fellows down, I did." He winked, then took a sip of his drink. "Got them to agree to join me at my next launch."

Quinn shook his head. "You sure have a way with words—even with your accent."

"I'm doing so very much better, don't ye think, mon cheri?" Carmel said, sounding like an Englishman trying to imitate a Frenchman.

Quinn laughed. Perhaps he'd enjoy himself tonight after all.

"Ah." Carmel elbowed Quinn. "There are many beautiful women here tonight, eh? It is hard for a man to choose."

"Yes, it is hard . . ." Quinn's voice trailed off because not twelve feet from him sat a group of women on the couches and chairs that lined the wall. The women were a mixture of matrons and young misses, all chattering together, with the exception of one woman.

The dress she wore tonight was not a modified cotton dress from the country but a white sheath with silver embroidery. Even though she was sitting down, the dress flattered her curves, and the small sleeves did nothing to hide the slope of her smooth-as-cream neck and shoulders.

Her hair was not falling out in tendrils about her neck, nor was its honey color gleaming beneath the sun, but had been coiffed to rival that of the elite of the *ton*. The light of the thousands of candles about the room seemed to be drawn to her golden skin that fairly glowed.

Even before she turned her head in his direction, Quinn knew.

Miss Ellen Humphreys had indeed come to the ball at Grosvenor Square.

Eleven

THIS WAS ELLEN'S third social engagement in a week, which was remarkable because she had been in London for only eight days. She should be used to the conversation buzzing about her and the same questions asked over and over, and the *looks* from the other women . . . their silent assessments. Her aunt had spared no expense on Ellen's wardrobe, she even had new underthings. Ellen might be well turned out, yes, but that didn't mean she knew what to do or what to say. She had attempted to ask her aunt's lady's maid if she knew anything about the Marquess of Kenworth's family, but the maid had seemed too curious, and that might mean the maid was also very fond of gossip. The last thing Ellen needed was to be the focus of *ton* gossip. So Ellen had made some lame excuse as to why she had such an inquiry, then never brought up the name again.

She missed her governess, but Aunt Prudence had secured her another position. Ellen was grateful, yet she had also been left without any sort of person to talk to. So Ellen spent her time with her aunt, who, quite unexpectedly, she was becoming more and more fond of.

The Anderson ball had been an unforeseen invitation, according to Aunt Prudence. The Andersons were the cream of the *ton*, and Aunt Prudence had declared that heaven was watching over them. Which, of course, meant that Ellen's dance partners tonight would turn into ardent suitors.

Thus far, though, Ellen had danced only two out of the five dances. One partner had been an older gentleman, twice widowed. The other had been a young man about her age—definitely a fortune hunter—he'd asked her too many probing questions to leave her any doubt. And they'd been here right at the opening of the ball—something that Aunt Prudence had insisted on in order to show their deep appreciation to the Anderson family. She had been most particular about introducing her to Mr. August Anderson.

Ellen had known right away that she could never marry a man with a name starting with the letter *A*, not to mention his last name starting with the same letter. Not that she had the luxury or liberty to be finicky. The men certainly had the upper hand in this elite Society that Ellen was learning so much about, which made the women practically beggars—highly primped beggars.

Ellen was more than happy to sit out the quadrille. Her feet weren't quite used to the fashionable slippers she wore. They were French but might look better in a museum display than half-hidden beneath her gown. She had to admit that she had no complaints about any of her dresses. Aunt Prudence had brought in a dressmaker and her team, who had listened carefully to Ellen's preferences, then made a few suggestions of their own, and the result was more than she could have ever imagined. She just didn't dare eat or drink in any of her gowns.

"He is coming tonight, I've heard," a woman named Mrs. Livingstone was telling her Aunt Prudence. Mrs. Livingstone had three daughters to marry off. Two of them were already out, yet no proposals had been forthcoming. "Lord Kenworth is perhaps the most eligible man this Season."

Ellen stiffened. How many Lord Kenworth's could there be? And she knew enough now to know that a "most eligible" man meant he carried a significant title. Perhaps there was another Lord Kenworth. But if it was *her* Lord Kenworth, the good news was that she hadn't kissed a married man.

"He has a younger brother too," Mrs. Livingstone added, "but that doesn't signify as far as I'm concerned."

Aunt Prudence laughed. "You are too picky, my dear. A younger, and *only*, brother of a marquess is still a significant catch in my opinion. I would be happy if my niece gained the attention of the second son of any titled man. There is always a chance that the second son will inherit. And even if he doesn't, he will have a good income to take care of a wife and children."

Ellen couldn't move, couldn't breathe. She knew that Lord Kenworth had a younger brother. What were the chances that they were speaking of the same man? If they were, then that meant Lord Kenworth was a marquess.

"I am going to fetch a glass of punch," Ellen told her aunt. Her throat was so dry she wasn't sure if she could swallow.

"Oh no, dear," her aunt said, patting her hand. "Let's wait until the end of this dance. Surely a young gentleman will fetch you a glass."

Ellen tried not to let her disappointment show. There was always a protocol to everything. A young lady couldn't even fetch a drink on her own. She kept her shoulders straight so that no one would sense her inner turmoil, yet she allowed herself to look toward the refreshment table. But before she caught a glimpse of the refreshment table, her gaze connected with that of a man standing only a few yards away.

The man was dressed formally, all his tailored clothing of the latest fashion was perfectly neat and pressed and his cravat expertly tied. His hair wasn't windblown as it had been when she'd first met him. He was holding a drink while he stood with another man who was dressed like one of those flamboyant dandies who seemed to appear at every social event. The dandy was talking, but ... Lord Kenworth was looking right at her, a stunned expression on his face.

"Oh, mercy me," Ellen said.

"What was that, dear?" her aunt asked.

"Nothing," Ellen quickly corrected, turning her gaze back to the dancers. She could *not* let her aunt know that she'd just seen the one man whom she'd hoped to never come across. Although if she hadn't returned to speaking with Mrs. Livingstone, surely Aunt Prudence would have noticed Ellen's flaming blush.

He was here. Lord Kenworth was here. *Here.* In this room. Only *steps* away.

And, he had seen her.

Sweet heavens.

How long did Ellen have to wait before she could complain of a headache? One more dance?

"Oh my goodness," Mrs. Livingstone said, her voice falling to a loud whisper. "Lord Kenworth is here with his friend, some sort of a French count."

"Where?" Aunt Prudence asked.

No, no, no. Ellen wanted to close her eyes and block out every sight and every sound.

"Don't look all at once," Mrs. Livingstone said in a conspiratorial voice. "He's standing at the end of the row of couches, and what a fine figure he makes. As soon as the quadrille is over, I will fetch my husband and have him introduce us. I should like it if he'd ask one of my daughters to dance." She sighed. "Too bad they are both spoken for the next few dances."

"Ellen isn't spoken for," Aunt Prudence said. "But I cannot prevail upon someone with the title of a marquess, especially if your daughters are already enamored of him."

"You are such a faithful friend," Mrs. Livingstone said. "I think every marriageable young woman in the room is enamored of this particular marquess."

The women laughed quietly together, and out of the corner of her eye, Ellen saw her aunt look over in Lord Kenworth's direction.

"Well, I declare, he *is* a fine man," Aunt Prudence said. "I'm not too interested in his friend, the count, though. What about Lord Kenworth's brother? Is he here?"

Mrs. Livingstone looked about for a moment. "As soon as I spot Lord Robert, I will point him out."

Perhaps Ellen could swoon and faint dead away. What was the worst that could happen? The women would gather and fuss around her, then her aunt would send for their carriage. But could Ellen ruin the evening for her aunt? And what if heaven really was smiling down upon them and Ellen was asked by a perfectly nice gentleman to dance, one who wouldn't be opposed to marrying a country gentleman's daughter with a modest dowry?

She would just have to pretend that Lord Kenworth wasn't in the room. After all, he had seen her, and he hadn't come to speak to her. One part of her argued that it was because he didn't know the women she sat with and therefore couldn't make his own introductions. The other part of her knew it was because he was as equally surprised to see her and he'd determined to act as if they'd never met at all.

If that was his plan, then it would be her plan as well. And she would be satisfied with it.

"Oh my goodness," Mrs. Livingstone said, in a not-so-quiet voice. "My husband is bringing over Lord Kenworth and the French count. The dance is not over yet, though. Oh, where are those girls of mine? Can you see them in the crush out there on the floor? Perhaps we can alert them to leave their partners immediately."

If bees could talk, they would sound like Mrs. Livingstone, Ellen decided. If it was true that Mr. Livingstone was coming over to his wife in the company of Lord Kenworth, then Ellen had to think of a plan—and quickly. Something that her aunt wouldn't fully question.

"I am so hot," Ellen said, turning to her aunt. "Might I go onto the terrace for a few moments?"

Her aunt's gaze connected with Ellen's as if she were about to answer, but then Aunt Prudence looked past Ellen. Aunt Prudence's mouth opened slightly as she raised her eyes higher and higher.

Oh no.

"Mr. Livingstone, I thought you were at the tables," Mrs. Livingstone said in a rather loud voice.

It was as if she wanted everyone in the ballroom to know that her husband was keeping company with a certain person.

"Hello, my dear," Mr. Livingstone said, his voice filled with pride.

Ellen could not bring herself to raise her eyes, although she could very well see that there were three men standing in front of the couch she was sharing with her aunt and Mrs. Livingstone. She already knew that the middle pair of legs belonged to Lord Kenworth. She had observed enough of his clothing ensemble before hurriedly looking away.

Was it rude to stare at a man's knees . . . or thighs?

Heavens. Ellen's face was heating up faster than a wild brush fire. Why had she not fled when she'd had a chance?

The moment she saw Lord Kenworth in the room, she should have immediately left and dealt with any questions later.

"It's so lovely to meet you, Lord Kenworth, and Mr. Carl," Mrs. Livingstone pronounced. "This is my dearest friend, Mrs. Prudence Humphreys Fellows, and her niece, Miss Ellen Humphreys."

"It's a pleasure to make your acquaintance," Aunt Prudence said just as the music to the quadrille came to an end and the buzz of conversation escalated in the room. "My niece is from Harpshire, and I am chaperoning her this Season."

Ellen could not completely ignore the men—it would be unforgivably rude of her. She chanced the barest glance at Lord Kenworth, then settled her gaze on the French count. Without the frills and bright colors, he'd be a rather decent-looking man. No one compared to Lord Kenworth, of course. But he was an enigma—unattainable, above her in rank, fortune, and stature.

And . . . she could feel his gaze upon her, even as she kept her focus on the count.

"Are you engaged for the next dance?" Lord Kenworth asked.

Aunt Prudence uttered the smallest of gasps. Certainly he wasn't asking Aunt Prudence, or even Mrs. Livingstone. Which meant . . .

Ellen slid her gaze over to Lord Kenworth. His eyes seemed to gleam black as the night sky in this ballroom full of candlelight.

It seemed all conversation had hushed, and everyone was waiting for her answer.

Ellen swallowed, then swallowed again. Finally, her breathless answer came. "I'd be honored, Lord Kenworth."

One side of his mouth lifted into a smile as he extended his hand. She stared at the gloved hand until her aunt nudged her. Then, Ellen lifted her own hand and placed it in his. She rose to her feet with only the slightest support from him. She hadn't really needed his help; he was just being a gentleman. But her legs felt half-asleep as she stood and faced him.

"Shall we?" He nodded toward the dance floor where couples were starting to assemble, waiting for the next dance to begin.

She opened her mouth to say yes, but all she managed to do was nod. Lord Kenworth was taller than she remembered. More elegant. More handsome. More *everything*. And he smelled divine.

He continued to lead her by the hand to the middle of the dance floor. Shouldn't she take his arm? Were they attracting attention because he was being unconventional? Ellen couldn't ignore the stares that followed them and the heads that were turning as they passed by one person after another.

Finally, Lord Kenworth stopped just as the first strains of music started up from the orchestra. He looked down at her, his eyes studying her face as if he were trying to memorize it. "Do you remember how to dance the waltz, Miss Humphreys?"

Twelve

QUINN HAD THOUGHT seeing Miss Humphreys again would derail his obsessive thoughts, ground him back to reality, and make him realize she was just a woman from the country who happened to dance in a meadow and hum to herself. But from the moment he spied her sitting on that couch surrounded by Society matrons, he had one urge, and that was to rescue her and take her somewhere away from the prying eyes and wagging tongues of the *ton*.

But he was a marquess, an esteemed member of the elite, and he had to follow protocol. To do otherwise would disgrace his mother and ruin Miss Humphreys.

Seeking out Mr. Livingstone hadn't been a great chore, and fortunately Carmel hadn't asked too many probing questions. That was probably because he'd seen how Quinn's attention had shifted the moment he'd seen Miss Humphreys. With the formalities of an introduction over, Quinn had thought he could then walk away. But the more he tried to catch her gaze, and the more she avoided looking at him, the more he wanted to speak to her.

And what better way than to ask her to dance—the waltz.

The irony wasn't lost on him, and now that he held her in his arms again, he wondered how he'd ever thought he could forget her. The music filled the room, drowning out the conversations around them, and with one hand on her waist and his other hand holding hers, he began to lead her in the steps.

It wasn't the same thing as the meadow beneath the sun, but her arms were the same, her eyes were the same, and he could swear he smelled sunshine and wildflowers. She moved easily, even confidently, in his arms. She'd been practicing, that was clear. Or perhaps the floor was just free of grass and dirt and pebbles.

"I must apologize," she said, blinking those pale-green eyes of hers as if she were trying to hold back tears.

Blast. "Apologize?"

"For ..." She paused and looked about them as if she were worried about being overheard. "I must apologize for my untoward behavior. I did not act the part of a lady when I ... when we ... I don't know what I was thinking—or *not* thinking—but I am deeply sorry for my actions. I did not think you'd even acknowledge my existence after such a display—"

"Miss Humphreys," Quinn cut in. "Please do not be troubled over the events in the meadow. I understand that everything about it was ... unusual. Unexpected. I do not hold any ill feelings on the matter *or* toward you."

"Truly?" she asked, the light coming back into her troubled eyes.

"Truly." He wanted to say more. He wanted to tell her he wouldn't mind kissing her again, although he didn't want her to run away this time. But he must determine if his apparent infatuation with this woman was something of substance. For if it was, the battle with his mother would be fierce, and he'd have to be prepared to deal with whatever consequences followed.

"You've become proficient at the waltz," he said, hoping to steer the conversation before he got it into his head that taking her out onto the terrace and maybe going for a stroll in the gardens beyond would be a good idea.

"My dancing has much improved." Her tone was steady now.

And as sweet as he remembered it. His diary entries hadn't been able to do the sound of her voice justice.

He wondered if she might smile at him if they weren't in such a crowd. He would see what he could do to coax one from her. "Have you found a partner to replace me?"

"No," she said, and a blush stole upon her cheeks.

Quinn had the sudden urge to lean closer and kiss her cheek, but he focused on their rhythmic steps: *one, two, three.*

"I've had quite a bit of time to myself to practice what you taught me," Miss Humphreys said.

"I can see you've been practicing." He tried to keep the teasing tone out of his voice. She was breathing rather fast, and they had only been dancing but a few moments. He didn't want to scare her off for any reason. "Did you have someone play music for you, or did you hum your own song?"

This brought the anticipated smile.

Quinn's heart fluttered like a blasted butterfly.

"I hummed," she said, the edges of her mouth still turned upward. "But I counted the steps out so that I could keep in rhythm."

"Ah, counting always helps," he said.

She laughed. Paradise couldn't have sounded any better.

"How is your mother's health?" she asked him.

He shouldn't have been surprised that she asked, as unfettered as she was.

"My mother . . . How should I explain?" he began. "She does much better when her two sons are at her beck and call."

She looked down, her expression contemplative. He expected her to laugh or maybe return a light quip. Instead, when she met his gaze again, she said, "I think our mothers are a lot alike. I am not in London with my mother's blessing."

Interesting, Quinn thought. And enlightening. It would explain why she'd never been to a dance before, until recently. "Have you been in London long?" he asked, feeling a bit uncomfortable at the personal turn in the conversation. It wasn't that she was untrustworthy; it was that the more personal they became, the harder it would be to make an objective decision about what was going on between them.

"Eight days," she said, her eyes brightening.

This lightened Quinn's heart, which made him wonder when his emotions became so tied with hers.

"It's all been amazing," she said. "I mean, I don't know what I'm doing half the time, and my feet hurt all of the time, but . . ." She looked down at her white-and-silver gown. "These clothes are divine."

Quinn couldn't help but follow her gaze. *She* was divine. The clothing had little to do with that, and at this thought, he knew his face was turning red. He'd let his gaze stray for too long. He had to think fast in order to redirect his thoughts about the clothing she was wearing. "What has been your favorite part of London?"

Again, she didn't give him a flippant reply. Something he was quickly learning to love, er, like, about her.

"Before coming, I had thought of only the parties, social events, museums, parks, the clothing and hats . . ." She seemed to hesitate, then gather courage once again. "My favorite part about London is spending time with an aunt whom I've learned to appreciate. Even though she can be quite opinionated and domineering, she truly wants the best for me, and she will fight for me to have it."

"Your aunt sounds like a determined woman," Quinn said.

Her laughter was light, perfect. They danced a few more steps, then she said, "You know, Lord Kenworth, you were wrong about something."

"Oh?" he asked, enjoying the amusement in her eyes. "What was I wrong about?"

She released the barest of sighs. "Balls really are magical."

Quinn smiled. "Ah, that. I think this ball might be the exception."

The music had come to an end, and Quinn hadn't realized they were still waltzing while other couples were beginning to mingle and even leave the dance floor.

Reluctantly, Quinn released Miss Humphreys. He couldn't let the conversation end here. He wanted her to explain what she meant by magical. He wanted to know why her eyes held depths that he was just beginning to understand. He wanted to know why just before he released her, her hands had been trembling.

He took a step back and gave a small bow, sure that others were watching and would notice if something were amiss or if he were too forward.

Miss Humphreys flashed him the smallest of smiles, but he didn't like what he saw in her eyes—sadness. What was going through her mind? What did she think about him?

"Thank you for the dance, Lord Kenworth," she said as he escorted her off the dance floor.

Her aunt and other acquaintances watched them as they approached, and Quinn knew that his time with Miss Humphreys was over for now. He didn't know when, or if, he'd be able to find out where the deep sadness had come from that he'd caught a glimpse of.

"Hello, Quinn," a man said before Quinn had delivered Miss Humphreys to her aunt.

Quinn turned to see Robert. His broad smile and curious gaze told Quinn one thing. *Laws.* His brother wanted an introduction. So Quinn introduced the two, and before he knew what was happening, Robert had asked Miss Humphreys to dance the next set. She agreed, of course.

Moments later, Quinn found himself standing, arms folded, as he watched his brother dancing with the only captivating woman in the room, or in London, for that matter. Quinn knew he was scowling, but he couldn't help it. Robert was making her laugh. He was also talking a lot, probably about Quinn, if the many glances turned his way were any indication.

"She is a beautiful woman," a voice spoke next to Quinn. He didn't need to turn to know it was his friend Carmel. "You may need to call out your brother."

Quinn narrowed his eyes as he studied how Robert was openly flirting with Miss Humphreys. "We don't fight duels anymore in England."

"Not even in the rural parts?" Carmel asked, his tone sounding innocent, but Quinn knew better.

Quinn looked over at him, and Carmel grinned. "My brother wouldn't dare."

Carmel lifted a brow as if he were challenging Quinn's statement.

He snapped his gaze back to watch his brother again. Narrowing his eyes, he wondered if perhaps Robert would be a better match for Miss Humphreys. Their stations were more compatible, and his mother would most likely welcome a country gentleman's daughter for the wife of her second son.

Next to him, Carmel chuckled, but Quinn ignored his friend. He didn't need someone to tell him how far gone he was, and it didn't help that Robert was only adding more fireworks into the mix.

"How about we go get you a drink?" Carmel suggested. "Something stronger than the lemonade? We could play a few rounds of cards with the other men. Take your mind off things."

The dance was finally coming to an end. If Quinn remained, he'd be forced to watch another man dance with Miss Humphreys. There had already been plenty of glances her way, both when he was dancing with her and now during the dance with Robert. Perhaps retiring to the lounge to play cards was a good idea.

"Ah, there you are," a woman's voice rang out.

Quinn exhaled before turning. "Hello, Mother."

She latched onto his arm, smiling up at him. "Why are you not dancing? You're the most eligible man here." Her gaze flitted to the count, then back to Quinn. "Lady Helen, our hostess, has just shared many delightful stories about her daughter. I think it would do well for you to ask her to dance."

Quinn clenched his teeth. He had lost sight of Robert and Miss Humphreys as the dancers dissembled and reconvened with different partners. Where had they gone? Then he saw the shimmer of her silver dress as she accepted an offer from another gentleman—August Anderson.

"Lead the way, Mother," Quinn said, casting a regretful look at Carmel.

Carmel just nodded, a smile on his face, as if he were enjoying an amusing theatrical production.

And so it was that Quinn found himself dancing with Lady Amelia Anderson. It was all that he could do to carry on the thinnest of conversations with her when his every sense was aware of each movement of Miss Humphreys and her dancing partner.

He did not know how he made it through the set with Miss Anderson, but as soon as it was over, he took Carmel's advice and made himself scarce. He didn't join the older men to play cards but instead went out into the gardens and walked by himself and let the cool night air clear his mind.

Tomorrow, he decided, tomorrow he'd return to his country estate and throw himself back into other pursuits. Miss Humphreys had temporarily distracted him, and if he were to stay in London, he'd find himself hunting her down at every social event. His mother would be on his heels, and his brother would be right there in the mix.

Mind made up, Quinn strode to the terrace. Through the open glass doors, his gaze seemed to be drawn to Miss Humphreys again. She was standing with her aunt, but they were surrounded by four gentlemen, all of them seeming to soak up every word Miss Humphreys spoke. She seemed to glow, and her elegance had caught the attention of even the titled men in the room.

Perhaps she'd have a proposal before the week passed, Quinn mused. But there was nothing amusing about that, and he suddenly loathed every man in the circle. Without letting himself reason anything out in his mind, Quinn strode into the ballroom and approached the group. With only the barest apology for interrupting the conversation, he asked Miss Humphreys to stand up with him for the next dance number.

Thirteen

EVEN ELLEN KNEW that dancing two numbers with the same gentleman would become fodder for speculation and gossip. Three dances would be akin to a proposal. Quinn had hardly even looked at her—it was as if he were asking her out of duty ... but *what* duty? They'd already danced the waltz together.

His jaw kept flexing as he stole glances as her. They could not converse easily as they had during the waltz, so when the few opportunities came, Ellen was surprised he didn't say anything. She attempted a little conversation, but his answers were so short that she quickly gave up. She did not understand what he was all about. She knew only that he seemed to be totally focused on her, and in the process, warning other men off.

Which made no sense at all. They had no understanding, and she could hardly hope for one. He was a marquess and she many steps below him on the ladder of Society. As the dance came to a close, frustration had replaced the exhilaration of Lord Kenworth asking her to dance for a second time.

He bowed before her, then lifted her hand to his lips. He

269

didn't kiss the back of her hand but instead spoke. "I hope you enjoy your stay in London." He released her hand almost as quickly as he'd grasped it.

"Thank you," she said, at a loss of what else to say to this new side of him.

He leaned forward and spoke in a low voice. "I regret that we do not have much time together before I have to return to my estate. But I have duties to attend to, and I feel that if I remain, I will stand in the way of your progress."

Ellen stared at him. Whatever could he mean? "You're not staying in London for the Season?"

He gave her a half smile. "I had no reason to before, so I have already made arrangements. Besides, it will be difficult to watch the men vie over you when I myself can never—"

"Lord Kenworth," a woman's voice cut in. "I'd like to introduce you to my daughters."

He straightened immediately and stepped away from Ellen.

The interruption couldn't have been worse timing.

Ellen painted on a polite smile as Mrs. Livingstone introduced her two giggling daughters and heavily implied that Lord Kenworth would do well to ask them to dance.

But Lord Kenworth cut the conversation short by saying he unfortunately had a matter of urgent business to attend to.

Mrs. Livingstone's mouth fairly dropped open as he strode away. "Well, well, what was that all about?" she said in a rather loud voice. "He looked as if he were being pursued by a pack of hellhounds."

"What's happened?" Aunt Prudence asked, joining the group.

Mrs. Livingstone promptly filled her in, and soon she moved off in a huff with her daughters.

Aunt Prudence sidled up to Ellen and linked arms.

"What in the world did the marquess speak to you about during two dance sets? Everyone is talking about his interest in you." Her eyes twinkled as she studied Ellen. "You are a pretty young lady, but I had no idea you'd draw this much attention."

"I am not entirely sure why he singled me out in the first place," Ellen said, although she did know.

Aunt Prudence smiled. "I can tell you one thing. You have definitely caught that man's eye, along with many others in the room. You'll have a proposal before the month is out!"

Ellen tried to smile at her aunt, but her heart wasn't in it. Another gentleman was approaching, one whom she'd met at a musicale earlier in the week.

"I wouldn't doubt that you receive a half-dozen bouquets from the hothouse tomorrow along with invitations for an afternoon ride," Aunt Prudence said, squeezing Ellen's arm.

Ellen was asked to dance for the remainder of the sets, yet she never caught sight of Lord Kenworth again. His brother smiled at her in passing once, but they didn't speak either.

By the time Ellen and her aunt left, Ellen didn't know if she'd ever feel her feet again. The slippers she'd worn were beautiful and elegant, but they pinched at every move.

"Oh my goodness," her aunt said, as they relaxed into the carriage seats on the drive back to her townhouse. "Tonight was a great success. I cannot wait to see what tomorrow will bring. Just think, you caught the eye of a marquess. That alone will bring you a lot of attention and interest."

Ellen had been trying to make sense of Lord Kenworth's parting words to her, but the night had been a whirlwind of music, dancing, and conversation. All she wanted to do was crawl into her bed and get some sleep.

"Who is that?" her aunt's voice cut into Ellen's throbbing headache.

Their carriage had slowed as they approached their townhouse, but there was another carriage parked in front, and the ground-level windows blazed with light.

The groomsman helped out her aunt first, then handed Ellen down. They both hurried up the stairs to be met by the butler in the foyer.

"You have a visitor," the butler said, looking from Aunt Prudence to Ellen.

Aunt Prudence gripped Ellen's arm, and together they walked into the parlor, where a woman was waiting. Ellen didn't recognize her, but it was clear by the way that Aunt Prudence stiffened that she did.

"Lady Alice Kenworth," Aunt Prudence said.

Ellen did a double take. Was this a relative of Lord Kenworth? Then it became clear to her . . . this woman had the same eyes and cheekbones. She was his mother.

Lady Kenworth was openly studying Ellen as well. "I'd like to have a word with your niece."

Aunt Prudence looked at Ellen, curiosity and protectiveness in her gaze.

"All right," Ellen said, mostly to assure Aunt Prudence that she could leave. Ellen's heart was pounding, but she had no choice but to find out what Lady Kenworth wanted to speak with her about.

Once the door shut behind Aunt Prudence, Ellen took a moment to compose herself before turning to Lady Kenworth. The woman wore a deep-blue dress that was of the latest fashion, and it was clear that no cost had been spared in her wardrobe.

"Would you like refreshment?" Ellen asked, her voice sounding strangely breathless.

"No, thank you," Lady Kenworth said, her voice as sharp as her gaze.

"Perhaps you'd like to sit by the fire where it's warmer," Ellen said.

Lady Kenworth only seemed to straighten. "I am not here for a social call, Miss Humphreys. I am aware that it's very late and that you've had quite an eventful evening. It is for this reason that I have decided to come and speak to you directly and without delay."

Ellen could only nod. The woman had turned down every gesture of hospitality.

"You made a spectacle of my family tonight," Lady Kenworth said, bright spots of pink appearing on her cheeks. "Not only did you dance with both of my sons, but you danced with my eldest twice."

The barbed words that Lady Kenworth was throwing at Ellen made her feel like she was standing in the middle of a fierce windstorm. She wasn't sure how she should reply, and she wished that Aunt Prudence had insisted on remaining in the room. No doubt she was listening at the door, but that wasn't the same thing.

The woman raised one of her gloved hands and pointed at Ellen. "You, young lady, are to stay away from *both* of my sons. I don't know what sort of vixen you are, but you aren't even remotely in their social circle, so don't pretend that you are."

Blood rushed through Ellen's face, and she was sure her cheeks were bright red.

Lady Kenworth lifted her chin and turned away from Ellen.

The woman was going to leave now? After saying so many cruel things without a consequence?

Before Lady Kenworth could open the door, Ellen said, "You would rather that I give your sons the cut direct if one of them asks me to dance again?"

Lady Kenworth turned her head slightly. "There won't be a next time. I'll make sure of it." She tugged the door open. The foyer was empty as she strode through it and out the front door.

Where had everyone gone?

Ellen couldn't believe what a virtual stranger had just said to her. She sank into the closest chair.

"Whatever was that woman about?" Aunt Prudence said, coming into the room.

Ellen's eyes burned with tears, and she couldn't speak for a moment. Then it all came out. She told Aunt Prudence about meeting Lord Kenworth in the meadow. How they'd danced. How she'd kissed him. How she was filled with anxiety over possibly meeting him again. How she was so surprised that he'd asked her to dance. Twice.

"Oh, my dear," Aunt Prudence said, pulling Ellen against her ample bosom and patting her on the back. "You've gone and fallen in love with a marquess. No wonder your heart is breaking. But if he is worthy of you, then he will come, you will see. Any man who is his own man won't be swayed by a mother such as Lady Kenworth. If he is, then you don't want his kind for a husband anyway."

Ellen let herself become enveloped by her aunt's soothing words. She let herself believe in them. She let herself hope.

But the next day, Lord Kenworth did not call on her. He didn't send flowers or a note. Ellen had received plenty of those, but none were from Lord Kenworth or his brother.

Ellen pleaded a headache when her aunt told her that she had a visitor—one of the young men she'd danced with the night before but had hardly paid attention to his name or his conversation.

On the second day, there was still no word from Lord Kenworth.

The third day, it rained all day, and Ellen spent her time gazing out of the window wondering if a bit of weather would keep away an ardent suitor. The answer was yes.

On the fourth day, Aunt Prudence talked Ellen into accepting a ride through Hyde Park from one of her gentleman callers. But the entire time, Ellen thought of Lord Kenworth, his brother, and his mother, and how she'd probably never see any of them again. True to Lady Kenworth's insinuation, the invitations to events had sharply dropped off. It seemed that Ellen herself had been given the cut direct.

On the fifth day, Ellen convinced her aunt that it was time for her to return to the country. There, she would find a way to mend her broken heart.

Fourteen

"WHAT DO YOU mean there was no one in residence?" Quinn asked his brother Robert as they sat before the cheery fire in the library of his country estate. It was good to be back home, but it hadn't dimmed any of his thoughts about Miss Humphreys.

"I stopped by the townhouse like you suggested, but the butler said the lady of the house had gone on a holiday." Robert stretched his legs and took a sip of the brandy Quinn had offered him.

Three weeks had passed since the night at Grosvenor Square where Quinn had danced with Miss Humphreys and practically laid out his feelings before her. He couldn't remain in London for even a day longer after such an incident. He'd had to leave his mother's household and clear his head of her constant suggestions and advice.

He'd charged Robert with paying Miss Humphreys a visit to explain his absence and to make sure all was well with her. He also wanted word on whether she was being pursued by another gentleman. Had Miss Humphreys returned to her home in the country early? What a disappointment that must have been for her.

He'd hoped his own time away from London would give him the perspective he needed about Miss Humphreys. All he knew was that he hoped she wouldn't accept an offer of marriage from another man. The rest . . . the rest he knew he had to make up his mind on.

"I suppose I should have visited earlier, but so many other things interfered," Robert continued as he swirled the brandy in his glass.

"What do you mean, *earlier*?" Quinn asked. "Did you not pay a call the day after the Anderson ball?"

"Ah, no." Robert scrubbed a hand through his hair. "It was . . . actually, only yesterday that I stopped over."

Quinn shot to his feet. "*Yesterday*? You waited *three* blasted weeks?"

Robert's eyes rounded, and he raised his hand as if warding off a possible blow. "I told you. Things were complicated. You left me to watch over Mother, and it was all that I could do to appease her and work out some purchase deals on my own pair of stallions."

Quinn clenched his hands into fists and paced to his credenza. How many times had he thought to write Robert in order to inquire after Miss Humphreys . . . How many times had he stopped himself, determined to be patient? What a fool he'd been.

He turned to face his brother. "Has there been any word about her whereabouts?"

"As I told you, I inquired after only her aunt," Robert said, setting his glass on the side table by his chair. "I didn't want to give the servants something to gossip about."

"Of course." Quinn exhaled. "That's that, I suppose. She must think me the most terrible cad."

Robert tilted his head. "What, exactly, did you tell her at the Anderson ball? Did you reach an understanding?"

"No," Quinn said immediately. "There was no official understanding."

"Official, or unofficial, I think you owe me an explanation," Robert said, rising to his feet and helping himself to the decanter of brandy. "And then I'll tell you what I know."

Quinn stared at his brother. "I should call you out!"

Robert laughed. "For what? For dangling a bit of gossip?" He sobered when he saw that Quinn was not amused. "All right. Sit down, and I'll tell you. I can't talk when you're hovering over me and glowering."

Quinn strode back to the chair opposite of his brother and sat down. Folding his arms, he said, "Well?"

"Well . . ." Robert started. "It's the most extraordinary thing, really. I ran into the younger Mr. Humphreys, quite by chance, I assure you. None of that stalking bit I had engaged in before—"

"Continue," Quinn cut in.

"Yes, well, Mr. Humphreys—Gerald is his name— mentioned that he and his father were leaving soon for a visit to his family's estate in Harpshire," Robert said.

The man was speaking so slow that Quinn thought he might strangle his brother just to get him to speak faster.

"So, I asked after his family," Robert continued, "and he mentioned that his sister had been in London—which of course we already knew—and that there'd been some sort of to-do, so she made a quick departure back home."

Quinn leaned forward, staring down this brother. "A *to-do*? *What* to-do?"

Robert frowned. "I didn't ask."

When Quinn shot to his feet again, Robert added, "I didn't feel it was polite to beg for details."

Quinn tugged at his cravat and paced back toward his credenza.

"Look at it this way," Robert said, his voice falsely cheerful. "Miss Humphreys is back in the country, and you know just where to find her."

Quinn whirled to face his brother, ready to spit out his next angry thoughts, but then he paused. He *did* know where she lived—at least the general location. How many estates could there be in such a small town?

He couldn't help but wonder what she was doing. Was she furious with him? Disappointed? Would she even see him if he called on her at her home? Had the *to-do* been a result of their shared evening at the Anderson ball? Or something else he wasn't aware of?

It was only a few hours' ride from here. Wait. What *was* he thinking?

A chuckle sounded from Robert's direction. "You don't need *my* blessing. Although you still need to take on the task of convincing Mother that Miss Humphreys is up to the role of becoming the next Lady Kenworth."

Robert seemed to think Quinn was going to ride straight to Harpshire and propose this afternoon. Quinn scoffed. "Mother doesn't even know about Miss Humphreys. Besides, I'm not sure Miss Humphreys will have me, considering the way I've neglected her."

"You don't know, then?" Robert asked, setting down his glass.

"Know what?" Quinn said, not liking the knot that was growing in his stomach.

Robert let his head fall back against the chair and closed his eyes as he released a groan. "About Mother's visit to Miss Humphreys's residence in London."

Quinn went very still. "What visit?"

Robert opened an eye. "That night . . . after the Anderson ball at Grosvenor Square . . . Mother went to speak with Miss

Humphreys personally. Mother told me about it the next day at supper, but you weren't there of course. You were in such a hurry to get back to this place." Robert waved a limp hand. "I suppose that's why I truly delayed visiting and inquiring after her—I feared I'd be thrown out on my ear by Miss Humphreys's formidable aunt."

Quinn crossed the room until he was standing before Robert. "*What* did Mother say?"

"I'm sure I received only a very biased interpretation," Robert began.

Quinn gripped his brother's shoulder, hard enough that a bruise would likely be the result.

And then Robert spilled the entire conversation that had been relayed to him by their mother. The more Quinn heard, the more furious he became. Not only furious but embarrassed about his mother's behavior. Then the guilt swirled through him. Guilt for *his* actions. For leaving Robert to pay a visit Quinn should have made himself.

Guilt for knowing that the *to-do* had been caused by his mother, which was a direct result of his own actions. What must Miss Humphreys think of him? When Robert finished relaying all the details he remembered, Quinn was already pulling out parchment and trimming a quill.

"Since you neglected to tell me this vital information in a timely manner, I need you to take this letter to Mother directly." Quinn wrote the opening salutation to the letter that would shock his mother.

"Directly?" Robert straightened in his chair. "Do you mean leave tomorrow morning?"

"This afternoon," Quinn said. "Another day cannot be spent without Miss Humphreys knowing the truth. You will take this letter and explain to Mother that I intend to propose to Miss Humphreys if her father will give me his blessing."

"*Me? I* must explain?" Robert said, his mouth falling open.

Quinn looked up from the parchment. "I will inform her myself of the result of my proposal, but for now, I am extending this letter as a courtesy."

Robert's brows shot up. "You're really going to do it, aren't you?"

Quinn used the wax from a nearby candle to seal the letter. When he again met Robert's gaze, his brother was grinning.

Quinn rose to his feet and placed the letter into Robert's waiting hands. Nothing more needed to be said between the brothers. Quinn couldn't waste another moment.

By the time his horse was saddled and Quinn had urged the beast into a gallop, he estimated he'd arrive at the Humphreys estate a couple of hours before nightfall. He hoped that Miss Humphreys would be in residence and not visiting some other place with her aunt. He also hoped that her father would be at the estate and would take kindly to Quinn's offer. He hoped that Robert's journey to London would be swift and that his mother wouldn't cut herself off from Quinn. That she'd accept Miss Humphreys into her good graces. And most of all, he hoped to find forgiveness from a young woman whom he'd sorely neglected.

Fifteen

ELLEN HADN'T DANCED since the night of the Anderson ball. And she had no desire to. Still, she visited her meadow, though she no longer called it Little London. She wanted to forget London. She wanted to forget that fateful night at Grosvenor Square that led to the humiliating visit from Lady Kenworth.

Even through all the travails with her own mother and their secluded life in the country, Ellen had never felt so thoroughly decimated as that night. Not even the arrival of her father and brother to their country home had done its usual job of cheering her up. Yes, she was pleased to see them, but all she wanted was to be alone.

She'd found comfort only in confiding in Aunt Prudence, but life had to go on for all of them. Ellen couldn't spend week after week wallowing in her own mire of pity. So, she walked. She visited the meadow. And she walked some more.

This afternoon she'd spent at the meadow, haphazardly reading a book of poetry that hadn't been able to sufficiently distract her from thoughts and regrets over Lord Kenworth. Now it was nearly time to return home and dress for supper. The gold-orange streaks across the western sky told her of the approaching hour. Since her father, brother, and aunt were all in residence, they were having formal suppers together each evening. And in order to avoid even more fussing from her aunt, Ellen had forced herself to keep up her end of the conversation and eat as much food as she could—though Aunt Prudence still complained Ellen ate like a bird.

Speaking of birds, a group of birds stirred from the tree above her and flew away together. Ellen watched them for a moment, then returned to the sad book of poetry. She hadn't made much progress today, but she'd try again tomorrow, and the next day. For as long as it took until she could forget Lord Kenworth and London, and oh, so many things.

She closed the book and rose to her feet, then brushed off her skirts to get rid of any dirt or twigs that might have collected on them from the rock she'd been sitting upon. It was then she felt something shift in the air. She didn't know what to make of it, but her heart started to beat faster for no reason. Then the hairs rose on her arms as she realized she'd heard footsteps coming toward her through the foliage.

Ellen whirled about. Through the trees, she could see that someone was coming. A tall someone. A man. Her brother, perhaps? He knew where her meadow was. Her father? Less likely.

But the man who stepped into the clearing was neither her father nor her brother.

Her mind raced and fought to comprehend whether she was imagining Lord Kenworth return.

His gaze swept over her as if he were trying to determine whether she was real or an image. But he was in *her* meadow. Of course *she* was real.

"May I speak with you?" he said, his voice low, hesitant.

Hearing his voice again sent a rush of goose pimples across her skin. Ellen took a step back. She wasn't afraid of him. She didn't think he would accost her in any way. But she didn't want to face him when her emotions were teetering just at the sight of him.

"What are you doing here?" she finally managed to say, although her voice was a poor rendition of her usual voice.

"I've come to apologize."

Ellen stared at him. His dark hair was disheveled, much as the first time she'd met him. He wore a traveling cloak and boots, yet no gloves. Had he been riding or walking? And . . . he'd come to apologize. His eyes seemed to be pleading with her.

"You came all this way?" she asked, incredulous. "To Harpshire?"

"I thought you deserved an apology in person," Lord Kenworth said.

He took another step closer. This time she didn't move. He stood in the light of the fading sun now, and his dark hair took on a bronze sheen.

"That was very thoughtful of you," she said, hating the stiffness of her tone but knowing it was the only way she could stop the threatening tears. Heavens, she had never thought to see this man again. After no word for weeks and weeks, she had assumed that his mother had well convinced him how unsuitable she really was. Yet, here he stood. *It's only an apology. He is a gentleman, after all.* "You truly didn't need to come all this way—I mean, you must have other matters to attend to besides . . . this."

Lord Kenworth shook his head. "This is the most important thing I could attend to, and even so, I feel an apology is inadequate for the way I left London the very next morning following the ball and didn't know about how my mother treated you. I do not know how to reconcile my regret and my mother's cruelty. I can only hope you can find forgiveness in your heart. Her actions were unknown to me until today, actually, or I would have come much sooner." He took a breath. "I do not know if I can ever forgive myself for not knowing. As far as my mother is concerned, there is no accounting for her actions, and I have yet to confront her. I decided to come here first—to speak to *you*—and beg for your forgiveness."

Goodness. When this man wanted to apologize, he turned into a veritable talking saint.

"Ellen," he continued in a soft voice. "I hope it wasn't too presumptuous of me, but I've spoken to your father."

Her mind spun with confusion. First, he'd called her *Ellen.* Second, now he'd brought her father into the fiasco of his mother's set-down?

"Your father is agreeable to a match between us," Lord Kenworth continued. "All that is left now is your decision."

"My—my *decision*?" Ellen echoed. Her father was agreeable to a match between she and Lord Kenworth? That meant he'd asked for her hand in marriage . . . Slowly, she exhaled. Then, she inhaled. She was still able to breathe, apparently.

Lord Kenworth took another step toward her as the breeze pushed its way around them, tugging at her dress and threading through his hair. The sky seemed a gold-orange frame about his broad shoulders, but she could only stare into his eyes as their depths so intently captured hers.

Another step, and he knelt on one knee before her. "Miss Ellen Humphreys, my greatest desire is for you to be my wife."

Her thoughts scattered as she looked down at him. "What about . . . What about your mother?"

His gaze didn't falter; he didn't flinch. "I love my mother and will always make sure she is taken care of, but it's *you* I want to spend the rest of my life with."

Tears stung her eyes, and there was nothing she could do to hold them back. "Truly?" she whispered.

"Truly." He grasped her hand and drew it to his lips.

Then he kissed the back of her bare hand, and the touch of his lips against her skin sent warm sensations skittering along her arm. The warmth continued to spread throughout her body until she felt she might float.

Her father had given permission, and Lord Kenworth was not to be swayed by his mother's opinions. He was still waiting for her answer, his gaze steady on her. She swallowed against the growing lump in her throat as tears spilled onto her cheeks. "Yes," she said, and her voice caught on a half giggle, half sob. "I will marry you, Lord Kenworth."

He was on his feet in an instant, pulling her into his arms. He laughed and pressed a kiss against her hair. Ellen wrapped her arms about his neck, her heart pounding like mad as he tightened his hold on her. Then he pressed another kiss on her neck. His mouth was warm and soft, and her entire body hummed with sensation.

He drew away, but only enough so that he could look at her. Cradling her face with his hands, he said, "Call me Quinn, dear Ellen."

"Quinn," she breathed.

"I like that," he whispered.

"Call me Ellen," she whispered back.

He smiled as his gaze seemed to soak her in. "I like that," he echoed. His fingers brushed along her jaw, and then he leaned down and kissed her.

Even though this was officially their second kiss, Ellen felt as if this kiss had every sensation of their first kiss, except now she knew he desired her as much as she desired him. He kissed her slowly, possessively, and wholeheartedly. Would kissing him always be like this? She could only hope. And with that thought, she pulled him even closer, because it was finally starting to dawn on her that this man would be her husband . . .

She had to ask one question, though. "When did you

know?" she asked in between kisses. "When did you know you wanted to marry me?"

He lifted his head and gazed at her for a moment. "I think I started falling in love with you when I saw you dancing here by yourself, humming a random tune. But I knew I wanted to marry you when I watched you dancing with my brother."

Ellen smiled. "Perhaps that was your brother's reason to ask me to dance."

Quinn's mouth lifted into a smirk. "I wouldn't be surprised." He ran his hands down her arms, then around her back to settle at her waist. He proceeded to kiss her neck, and the warm shivers started all over again.

But Ellen had started to think about what would happen when they returned to her home. When they announced to her family their engagement. Her father had agreed, and surely her aunt would be delighted. She couldn't imagine her brother having any opposition . . . but what about her mother?

"Quinn," she said, the name sounding quite new on her tongue. "You may want to meet my mother before you agree to marrying me."

Quinn leaned his forehead against hers. "Your father told me about her . . . condition. I think that our mothers will become great friends once they meet. They suffer many of the same maladies, and they will have much to discuss."

"Do you really think they'll be friends?" Ellen asked. It was quite a thing to consider. "We are country folk. That alone will be hard for your mother to overcome."

"Mmm," Quinn said. "Let's talk about our mothers later. Right now, I want to kiss the woman I've fallen in love with."

Ellen laughed, but it was cut short when Quinn made good on his promise.

Epilogue

One Year Later

"I AM PERFECTLY able to get out of bed on my own," Ellen said as her husband drew back the covers. Yes, she was seven months into her pregnancy, her ankles were swollen, and she felt new aches every day, but she wasn't an infant herself.

Quinn leaned over and kissed her forehead. "You stubborn woman. I've taken the entire week off so that I might care for your every need while our mothers are visiting."

"That is exactly why you shouldn't be here, fussing over me," she said. "Our mothers will see that you're completely smitten with your overlarge pregnant wife. I am sure that neither of our fathers ever did half the things for their wives as you do for me."

"I don't care about other husbands," Quinn said, placing both hands on the bed on either side of her so that he was hovering mere inches above her. "I care about you, and you're not overlarge. You're the most beautiful woman I've ever seen."

Ellen reached up and traced his cheek. He hadn't even

288

been shaved yet or attended to his own morning ritual. "You are a good man."

Quinn lifted an eyebrow.

"You are the finest husband and the most handsome man *I've* ever seen," she added.

"That's better." Then he leaned down and kissed her.

Ellen looped her arms about his neck, enjoying the only private time they'd have all day. Their mothers had planned to visit at the same time so that one couldn't upstage the other. It had been like that since their marriage nine months ago. Quinn had been right. Once the shock of a marquess marrying a country gentlewoman had been replaced by other gossip among the *ton*, his mother had warmed up to Ellen. It might also have had something to do with the fact that Ellen had become pregnant soon after the wedding and Quinn was about to possibly provide a male heir.

The mothers spent their visits comparing their ailments and various treatments. Ellen's mother still wouldn't travel to London, but she seemed to enjoy visiting the Kenworth country estate.

They would both be breaking their fast about now, and if Ellen didn't appear soon, then one of them would be sending a servant to check in on her. But for now, her husband was kissing her, and she was kissing him back.

The kissing turned quite a bit more passionate than Ellen had planned on, and when Quinn didn't seem to be in the frame of mind to stop anytime soon, Ellen drew back. "Quinn, dear, we must join our mothers before they sound the alarm."

He sighed, his expression disappointed, which secretly delighted Ellen. "You're right."

And just when she thought he was going to move away from the bed and allow her to climb out of it, he scooped her into his arms. Ellen squealed and immediately tried to cover her mouth even as she continued to protest.

Quinn chuckled and carried her to the vanity bench, where he set her down.

The woman looking back at her in the mirror had changed over the months. No longer was she a lonely young woman, but she was a well-loved wife and soon-to-be mother.

"How is this?" Quinn asked, running a comb through Ellen's long hair.

"Lovely," she said, smiling at him in the mirror. "You should call Miss Nebeker, though, to come help me." The first thing that Ellen had done as a new marchioness was hire Miss Nebeker. "You also need to shave."

"You don't think my mother will approve?"

"*Your* mother would be horrified, and *my* mother would probably try to fire your valet."

Quinn laughed. "Your point has been made. I will return shortly to escort you down the stairs, Lady Kenworth."

Ellen took the comb from her husband and started to brush it through her own hair as she waited for him to send in Miss Nebeker.

When she was finally dressed and presentable, she found Quinn waiting in the corridor, making good on his promise to escort her. He'd been freshly shaved, and his cravat was well in place. He took her hand and pressed a kiss on it, then they walked down the stairs of the Kenworth Manor together.

Women's voices rang out from the dining room, and Ellen was grateful the tones were cheerful. She entered the room with Quinn, and both mothers immediately turned to look at them.

"Well, there you are at last. We thought you were indisposed," her mother said, her eyes bright and assessing as she scanned Ellen's form.

It was too much to expect her mother to greet her any other way. There would be no kiss, no embrace. Ellen appreciated that her mother had come to visit at all and seemed to have a conspiratorial friend in Quinn's mother.

"You look ready to deliver at any moment," the dowager said.

So, Ellen wasn't about to get any pleasant greetings.

Quinn squeezed her hand before he let go and moved to the sideboard. In that hand squeeze, she'd felt all the love and adoration that she could ever need, and she was grateful for it.

"Have a seat, wife, and I will make you a plate."

Ellen heard the silent gasps from both mothers as if they'd been audible. Both women had likely never had their own husbands serve them in such a way. But Quinn took immense pleasure in doing the small things for Ellen, many of which she could still do herself. Instead of arguing with her husband that she was perfectly capable of filling her plate from the sideboard, she sat down as directed and turned a smile toward the mothers.

"I trust that both of your journeys were pleasant and you found your rooms to your satisfaction," Ellen said. They'd arrived last night after Ellen had retired for the evening. So Quinn had seen to their comforts and told Ellen that she could welcome their guests in the morning.

"This estate is in better repair than I expected," her mother spoke first. "I thought the room would have a draft, but it was quite warm. Perhaps a bit too warm."

Ah, there was the complaint. Ellen merely smiled and took up her fork as Quinn set her plate before her. He knew her well and had filled the plate with her usual favorites. This made her want to lean over and kiss him, but the critical eyes of their mothers, in addition to the bulk of her swollen belly, stopped her.

"We could have the fire extinguished earlier in the evening if you'd like, Mother Humphreys," Quinn said in a perfectly conciliatory tone.

He really was quite the excellent marquess.

"Oh, that won't do at all," her mother said, waving a hand toward the window. "If it rains today, then I don't want the damp creeping in. If there's anything I can't abide, it's the damp."

"Well, then, we will watch for the rain," Quinn said, glancing at Ellen and giving her a wink before he turned back to face the mothers.

Quinn had opened up an entire Pandora's box by mentioning the weather.

His own mother took up the topic. "Those low clouds look quite threatening if you ask me. I'd advise everyone to stay indoors." Her gaze landed on Ellen. "Especially you, since we can't have you catching a cold while you are carrying a child."

Ellen didn't dare bring up her continued penchant for walking the countryside. Many times, Quinn accompanied her, but she often went out on her own. It was a way to get to know the tenants of the estate and have a bit of reflection time to herself. A bit of rain had never stopped her, and Quinn knew it.

She felt his hand squeeze her knee beneath the table, and she had to cover up a smile. Together, they would somehow survive the coming week with both of their mothers in residence.

The conversation at the morning table moved from concerns about the weather, to which names Quinn had been thinking of for his son—Ellen didn't dare correct anyone that they didn't yet know the gender of their child—and finally to local village gossip that the dowager seemed to have plenty of knowledge about and Ellen's mother was very interested in hearing.

When the patter of rain started on the windows, Ellen's mother straightened in her chair and said, "What did I tell you? Rain!"

Quinn's mother shook her head. "Let us move to the library and order a fire. We will be set to read and embroider all day."

Quinn joined the women in the library, and after another hour of conversation centering around herbs and poultices and their remedies for the aches and pains experienced by both women, he said, "I must take my wife to her rooms where she can rest for a short time before the lunch hour."

Ellen had never been so grateful for Quinn in her life; well, at least today. It seemed she frequently found many things to be grateful for. Once in their private chambers, Quinn said, "I never thought I'd come up with a good excuse to take a break. But then I thought of my pregnant wife and how you've made it a habit of taking a nap each day. You are always the perfect excuse."

Ellen laughed. "Now what will you do? They are in your library, and it looks like they're there to stay."

Quinn glanced toward the windows, where it was quite obvious that the rain wasn't going to let up any time soon. An afternoon ride would have to wait for another day.

He stepped close to her. "I will read poetry to you until you fall asleep."

Ellen sighed, hiding another smile. "How about you read me your diary?"

Early in their marriage, she'd discovered he kept a faithful diary. It took her another two months to convince him to let her read it. She became especially captivated by his diary entries during the time they were first getting to know each other.

Quinn raised his eyebrows as his hand settled at her waist. "You want me to read about the events of last week?"

"No," she said, placing her hands on his chest. "You know the parts I want you to read."

He grinned. "If you insist."

"I insist."

So Ellen leaned against her husband as they settled on the wide bed and listened to the timbre of his voice as he read to her about the day they met. She smiled as the memories swirled about her as he read his own memories. After a while, she no longer focused on the familiar words but on how it felt to listen to him while one arm was around her.

She felt herself growing more and more tired, and she yawned. "What will you write about today?"

He closed the diary, then laced their fingers together, not moving from his position.

"I will write about how I woke up next to the most beautiful woman I'd ever seen," Quinn said.

Ellen scoffed. "Will you note how swollen my ankles are and how pudgy my hands?"

He lifted her fingers to his lips. "I will only be truthful and say that your elegant hands are soft, and when I hold them, I feel complete."

Ellen lifted her head. "You are such a seducer."

He promptly kissed her on the lips.

"You prove my point." She rested her head against his shoulder again as he continued to speak in a low voice about what else he'd write in his diary.

Ellen closed her eyes, reveling in this cocoon of peace and love with her husband. Moving into Quinn's home had meant she'd had to leave her little meadow. But she'd found so much more with this man.

Ellen hovered between the worlds of wakefulness and dreaming as she realized she couldn't have come up with a better dream if she had written it down. Her husband adored her, and she adored him. Whatever might happen with their mothers' opinions, or however many children she had with Quinn, they would live their lives together, in their own little meadow of happiness.

Heather B. Moore is a *USA Today* bestselling author. She writes historical thrillers under the pen name H.B. Moore; her latest are *The Killing Curse* and *Poetic Justice*. Under the name Heather B. Moore, she writes romance and women's fiction; her latest include *Love is Come* and *Delilah's Desserts*. Under pen name Jane Redd, she writes the young adult speculative Solstice series, including her latest release *Mistress Grim*. Heather is represented by Jane Dystel of Dystel, Goderich & Bourret.

Heather's email list: hbmoore.com/contact
Website: HBMoore.com
Facebook: Fans of H. B. Moore
Blog: MyWritersLair.blogspot.com
Twitter: HeatherBMoore
Instagram: AuthorHBMoore